The Painted Lady

The Painted Lady

EDWARD MARSTON

First published in Great Britain in 2007 by
Allison & Busby Limited
13 Charlotte Mews
London W1T 4EJ
www.allisonandbusby.com

Copyright © 2007 by EDWARD MARSTON

The moral right of the author has been asserted.

A catalogue record for this book is available from
the British Library.

10 9 8 7 6 5 4 3 2 1

ISBN 0 7490 8162 7
978-0-7490-8162-1

Printed and bound in Wales by
Creative Print and Design, Ebbw Vale

EDWARD MARSTON was born and brought up in south Wales. A full-time writer for over thirty years, he has worked in radio, film, television and the theatre, and is a former Chairman of the Crime Writers' Association. Prolific and highly successful, he is equally at home writing children's books or literary criticism, plays or biographies, and the settings for his crime novels range from the world of professional golf to the compilation of the Domesday Survey. *The Painted Lady* is the sixth book in the Redmayne series.

Find out more about Edward Marston by visiting his website at: *www.edwardmarston.com*.

Also by Edward Marston

The Inspector Robert Colbeck series
The Railway Detective
The Excursion Train
The Railway Viaduct

The Redmayne Mysteries
The King's Evil
The Amorous Nightingale
The Repentant Rake
The Frost Fair
The Parliament House

The Nicholas Bracewell series
The Queen's Head
The Merry Devils
The Trip to Jerusalem
The Nine Giants
The Mad Courtesan
The Silent Woman
The Roaring Boy

The Laughing Hangman
The Fair Maid of Bohemia
The Wanton Angel
The Devil's Apprentice
The Bawdy Basket
The Vagabond Clown
The Counterfeit Crank
The Malevolent Comedy
The Princess of Denmark

The Domesday Books
The Wolves of Savernake
The Ravens of Blackwater
The Dragons of Archenfield
The Lions of the North
The Serpents of Harbledown
The Stallions of Woodstock
The Hawks of Delamere
The Wildcats of Exeter
The Foxes of Warwick
The Owls of Gloucester
The Elephants of Norwich

Chapter One

'A plague on it!' cried Henry Redmayne, smacking the arm of the sofa with a petulant hand. 'This is the worst news I ever heard in my entire life. It's left me prostrate with grief.'

'I feel betrayed,' said Elkannah Prout, morosely.

'We've *all* been betrayed, Elkannah. Every red-blooded man in London has been betrayed. Not to put too fine a point on it, our whole sex has been betrayed. And the sorriest victims of this betrayal are here in this room – you, me and poor Jocelyn.'

Henry indicated Jocelyn Kidbrooke, a portly man in his thirties who sat in a complete daze, still trying to absorb the grim intelligence. Kidbrooke's podgy face was a study in dejection. Had his own wife been violently snatched from him, he could not have looked more melancholy. Prout, by contrast, thin, angular and still passably handsome, was seething with rage, barely able to contain himself as he perched on the edge of his chair. He kept bunching his fists pugnaciously and swearing under his breath.

Drawn together by disaster, the three of them were in the drawing room of Henry's house in Bedford Street. Though they passed themselves off as gentlemen, they were confirmed rakes, pursuing lives of ceaseless pleasure in the capital city of dissipation. Prout was the oldest of them, a well-dressed bird of prey on the verge of forty. Henry Redmayne was younger but his wayward existence had robbed him of his good looks and given him in return a pale, drawn, pinched countenance that was deeply etched by years of corruption. All three friends were fashionably dressed but it was Henry who wore the most ostentatious apparel and had the most flamboyant periwig.

'I would never have believed it of her,' he declared.

'Nor I,' said Prout. 'It's shameful.'

'It's nothing short of indecent, Elkannah. When a woman guards her maidenhood like the Crown Jewels, then she should, in all honesty, only yield it up to someone who truly deserves it. In short,' said Henry, slapping his knee before rising to his feet, 'to one of us. Damn it all – we've *earned* it.'

'We spent time and money on the jilting baggage.'

'I offered her my undying love.'

'So did I, Henry – and so did Jocelyn.'

He gestured towards Kidbrooke but the latter was too absorbed in his thoughts to hear a single word that was being said. The others might talk of a shared feeling of betrayal. All that concerned Jocelyn Kidbrooke was his own misery. He did not hear the distant ring of the doorbell and he did not even look up when a servant showed a visitor into the room. Beaming happily, Sir Willard Grail made straight for Henry and shook his hand warmly.

'Henry, my darling-sin, how is't with you?'

'Very ill,' replied the other.

'Such sadness among friends?' He looked at the other two men. 'What ails you? Why these long faces? Why this dreadful whiff of despair in my nostrils? Have I come to a house or a hospital?'

'I can see that you have not yet heard, Sir Willard,' said Prout.

'Heard what?'

'The hideous truth about Araminta Jewell.'

'Dear God!' exclaimed Sir Willard, bringing both hands up to his throat. 'Do not tell me that the dear creature is dead.'

'It's worse than that.'

'*Worse?*'

'The little traitor is married,' said Henry.

Sir Willard Grail was dumbfounded. He was an affable man in his late twenties with an almost permanent smile on his lips. Tall, fair, lean and immaculately dressed, he cut an imposing figure. He did not look so imposing now. Reeling from the impact of the news, he seemed to shrink in size and lose all vitality. The characteristic smile was replaced by a grimace.

'Araminta is *married*?' he croaked.

'In secret,' said Henry. 'Behind our backs.'

'Married to whom? What sorcerer has bewitched her and stolen her away from us? Name the villain.'

'My tongue will turn black when I do so.'

'Why – who is the fellow?'

'Sir Martin Culthorpe.'

'Culthorpe?' Sir Willard spat out the name like a foul poison that he had inadvertently tasted. 'That angel of delight has sacrificed her virginity to Sir Martin Culthorpe? It's unspeakable.'

'But nevertheless true,' admitted Prout. 'It's an insult to all of us. Culthorpe is a sanctimonious nonentity.'

'Araminta does not think so,' said Henry, ruefully.

'What conceivable attraction can Culthorpe have for her?'

'Extreme wealth and a title.'

'I, too, have money,' said Prout, thrusting out his chest.

'But no title.'

'I have a title,' argued Sir Willard.

'Yet you lack the affluence to go with it,' noted Henry. 'And without wishing to be overly pedantic, I have to point out that you, Sir Willard – like Jocelyn here – are already married. Elkannah and I were the only bachelors in the hunt.'

'Apart from Culthorpe, that is.'

'A vile thief who stole the richest jewel in Christendom.' Henry flopped into a chair and stared vacantly at a painting of rampant satyrs in pursuit of a trio of naked nymphs. 'It's an ignominy that must not be borne, gentlemen. We are victims of a heinous crime.'

With a nod of agreement, Sir Willard lowered himself on to a chair. All four of them brooded in silence. Araminta Jewell was, by common consent, the most beautiful young woman in London and the fact that she kept her many suitors at arm's length only added to her allure. She was everything that the four men sought in a mistress and they had been so beguiled by her charms that they formed a Society for the Capture of Araminta's Maidenhood. The person fortunate enough to win his way into her bed was also destined to collect the large reward to which they had all generously contributed.

A disturbing thought made Henry sit up with a start.

'Hell and damnation!' he howled. 'Does this mean that we have to forfeit the contents of our fund to Sir Martin Culthorpe?'

'Never!' said Prout, defiantly.

'He achieved what four of us signally failed to do.'

'All that I lacked was time, Henry. Give me another month and she would have wilted under the pressure of my blandishments.'

'I looked to have seduced her within a fortnight,' said Henry.

'Away with these fond imaginings!' said Sir Willard, testily. 'You do but cry over spilt milk and that's ever a foolish exercise. As for Culthorpe, he'll not get a penny from us because he was not party to the wager, and I'll not pay any man to bed his wife.'

'Had I wed Araminta,' said Henry, 'you'd have had to pay me.'

'There was no mention of marriage in the articles we drew up.'

'Nor was it excluded, Sir Willard. I was always impelled more by love than by lust. For her sake,' he went on, dramatically, 'I'd have endured all the restrictions of holy matrimony."

Sir Willard smiled urbanely. 'Choose the right wife and there *are* no restrictions,' he observed.

'The matter is settled, then,' said Prout. 'Culthorpe gets no reward from us and the Society is hereby disbanded. My vote is for raiding the purse and spending it in a night of uninhibited abandon.'

'A capital notion, Elkannah.'

'But one too hastily conceived.' Henry was thoughtful. 'Why disband our Society when it can simply be re-christened? Why squander the money when it can be won afresh?'

'How?' asked Sir Willard.

'How else but by seeking our revenge? The milk may be spilt but it's still sweet enough for us to lick. Since we cannot secure the lady's maidenhood, we can at least cuckold the rogue who did.'

'Two horns on the head of Sir Martin Culthorpe.'

'With the man who puts them there taking the prize.'

'I like the idea,' said Prout with enthusiasm.

'I love it,' said Sir Willard. 'What about you, Jocelyn?'

All three of them turned to Jocelyn Kidbrooke, still seated and still deep in thought. Eyes blazing, he gnashed his teeth audibly.

'Did you hear my suggestion?' prompted Henry. 'The chase is still on and the winner takes all. What's your view of Culthorpe?'

Kidbrooke looked up. 'Something must be done about him.'

'That's why the Society must have a new objective.'

'There can be only one objective with regard to Sir Martin Culthorpe,' said Kidbrooke with quiet intensity. 'Araminta is in need of salvation. We must get rid of her husband.'

'How soon will you be ready to start?' asked Sir Martin Culthorpe.

'As soon as the lady is ready for me,' said Villemot. 'I hear so much about your wife's beauty that I long to meet her.'

'I want you to immortalise that beauty on canvas, Monsieur.'

'Then you come to the right man.'

Jean-Paul Villemot struck a pose, chin held up and arms spread out with a dancer's grace. He was a swarthy man in his

late thirties with a neat black moustache and beard giving
definition to a gaunt face. His command of English was good
but it was filtered through a strong French accent. Like Van
Dyke and Lely, he was a portrait painter who had built up such
a reputation in England that he was constantly in demand there.
They were in his studio, a large, low-ceilinged, untidy room
filled with half-finished paintings, discarded sketches and the
pungent smell of artist's materials. A black cat nestled in a chair.
An easel stood near the window to catch the light.

'Araminta will come here tomorrow,' said Sir Martin.

'How long have you been married?'

'Three weeks.'

'Three weeks?' echoed Villemot. 'And you are ready to let a
young wife out of your sight? I see you are no Frenchman.'

Sir Martin straightened his back. 'I'm a true-born
Englishman,' he attested, 'and proud to be so. That means I
have the most profound respect for the fairer sex.'

'So do I, *mon ami*. I love, honour and respect the ladies.'

The Frenchman's raised eyebrow went unseen by his visitor.
Sir Martin Culthorpe was clearly not a man for innuendo and he
was patently lacking any sense of humour. His face was pleasantly
ugly, his expression one of beetle-browed seriousness. Now in his
forties, he was upright, well-built and of medium height. While
the artist wore colourful attire in the French fashion, his client
chose only the most sober garments. Sir Martin was a rich
landowner, known for his piety and his charitable inclinations.
During the rebuilding of London in the wake of the Great Fire,
more than one church rising from the ashes was doing so with the
help of Sir Martin Culthorpe, who saw it as his Christian duty to
restore the spiritual fabric of the capital.

'Now,' said Villemot, rubbing his hands together, 'we come to
the very important point.'

'Have no fears on that score, Monsieur. I'm a wealthy man. I
know that you are expensive but I want only the best. I have
heard your terms and accept them willingly.'

'I do not talk of money, Sir Martin.'

'Oh?'

'I talk only of clothing. I think, maybe, that you would prefer that your wife, she is painted in a dress.'

'Of course,' said Sir Martin, stiffly. 'Isn't that always the case?'

'No, no,' replied the artist with a broad smile. 'Some husbands, they like to see their wives or lovers *deshabille*. Look, I show you.' Moving to his easel, he drew back the cloth that covered the portrait on which he was working. '*Voila!*'

Sir Martin gasped in horror. Pretending to be a Greek goddess was the nude figure of a gorgeous young woman, carrying a quiver of arrows that hid nothing of her ample curves. What stunned him was that Sir Martin believed he recognised the face as belonging to Lady Hester Lingoe and he recalled, with dismay, that she had always shown a keen interest in the Classical world. It had never occurred to him that she might take it to such lengths. Ashamed of what he had just seen, he turned away in disgust. Jean-Paul Villemot quickly drew the cloth over the painting.

'It is not to your taste, I think,' he remarked.

'It most certainly is not,' said Sir Martin, righteously. 'I came in search of a portrait – not of an obscenity like that.'

The Frenchman shrugged. 'What I am asked, I paint.'

'Then I'll ask for something very different, Monsieur.'

'We come back to the lady's wardrobe, then.'

'My wife has already chosen what to wear.'

'But she may not have chosen well,' said Villemot, wagging a finger. 'Lady Culthorpe only sees what is in the looking-glass. Jean-Paul Villemot, he has the eyes of the artist.'

'What do you mean?'

'I will pick out the colour to enhance your wife's beauty and the fashion to display her at her best. Let her bring three or four dresses and try them on for me.'

'That's far too unseemly,' protested Sir Martin. 'My wife is no doll to be dressed and undressed at another man's pleasure. If you must give advice about what Araminta should wear, you will have to visit our home and explore her wardrobe.'

'*Tres bien*! I will come this very afternoon.'

'We'll be ready for you, Monsieur.'

'And the portrait, it is of your wife only?'

'Who else?'

'Many husbands, they like to celebrate their marriage with a painting of themselves and their bride. This is not for you?'

'No,' said Sir Martin, firmly. 'My face does not belong inside a gilt frame. It's too unsightly. I would only spoil the picture.'

'As you wish.'

'That brings us to the question of your fee, Monsieur Villemot. I know that you do not ask for money until the portrait is finished but I insist on paying in advance.'

'Thank you,' said the artist, taking the fee from him, 'though it was not necessary. I never want the money before I start. The only thing I want from my clients is that they keep to one simple rule.'

'Rule?'

'When someone sits for me, he or she must be alone.'

'But I was hoping to accompany my wife.'

'Then you need to find another artist to paint her portrait,' said Villemot, folding his arms with a flash of temperament. 'While I work, I do not allow anyone to look over the shoulder. It holds me back. I must have – what do you call it? – the freedom of expression.'

'Araminta is very shy,' argued Sir Martin. 'She needs me there. I swear that I'll keep out of your way.'

'You will keep out of my studio or I am not for you.'

'This is an unfair condition to lay upon me.'

Villemot was adamant. 'I do not break the rule for anyone.'

There was a silent battle of wills. As the client, Sir Martin had expected to be there during the early sittings but that was evidently not the case. He was worried. He did not relish the thought of leaving his young wife alone with the Frenchman. Glancing at the easel, he was reminded that Villemot had painted his last subject as a nude and that the lady in question had disported herself naked on the very couch on which Sir Martin was sitting. That made him very uneasy. Another fact had to be considered. Apart from his natural prejudice against foreigners, Sir Martin felt certain that Villemot would be a Roman Catholic and he feared that Araminta might somehow be tainted if the man had uncontrolled access to her.

He was in a quandary. Eager for his wife to be painted by the leading artist of the day, he yet wanted to supervise their contact. The problem was that, while he was ready to place complete trust in Villemot's artistic abilities, he did not have equal confidence in his moral standards. In appearance and manner, he was altogether too effusive and unconstrained for Sir Martin's liking. If he let his wife alone with the man, she would be subjected to his practised charm. The anxious husband searched for a compromise.

'Let me stay in the next room,' he suggested.

'*Impossible*!' exclaimed Villemot. 'I sleep in that room and I allow no strangers in there. Until my new house, it is built, I rent only three rooms. In any one of them, Sir Martin, you would be in the way.' He clapped his visitor on the shoulder. 'I know what you think – that I am alone with Lady Culthorpe – but is not true.'

'No?'

Emile, he is always with me.'

'Emile?'

'*Mon valet.*' He raised his voice. 'Emile!'

The door opened at once and a figure scurried into the room. Short, slim, excessively well-groomed, Emile was a dapper individual in his forties with an air of studied deference. He wore a white shirt, a long, black waistcoat and black breeches. His shoes gleamed. When he was introduced to the visitor, he gave a bow. Sir Martin was immediately reassured. With the valet at hand, his wife would never be wholly alone with the artist.

'You see?' asked Villemot. 'If Lady Culthorpe, she wishes for the rest or for something to drink, she has only to call for Emile.'

'*Mon plaisir*,' said Emile with another bow. Villemot clicked his fingers to dismiss him. '*Excusez-moi*, Sir Martin.'

The valet withdrew as speedily as he had come. Sir Martin's fears were allayed. He recalled something that Villemot had said earlier.

'You are having a house built in London, you say?'

'Yes,' replied Villemot. 'My life, it is here now. When I have a proper place to live, my wife, she will join me from Paris.'

Sir Martin was relieved. 'You are married, then?'

'Oh, yes. But I could not ask my wife to share three rooms in someone else's house. She would never accept that. Monique deserves a place of our own. That is why I want the house to be built *tout de suite*.'

'Who is the architect?'

'A very clever man – Christopher Redmayne.'

Christopher Redmayne examined the model with great care, looking at it from every angle. Jonathan Bale, the man who had made it, watched him nervously, desperate for approval and fearful of rebuke. Bale was a big, solid man in his late thirties with the kind of facial features that only a loving wife could find appealing. When working as a parish constable, he knew exactly what to do. As the maker of a scale model, however, he was in uncharted territory.

Christopher let out a sigh of admiration. 'It's good, Jonathan.'

'Thank you, Mr Redmayne.'

'In fact, it's very good.'

'I did my best.'

'It far exceeds my own mean abilities,' confessed the

architect. 'I can see a building in my mind's eye, and I can draw it to perfection, but I'm all fingers and thumbs when it comes to making a model. You have a real talent.'

'I was a shipwright for many years,' said Bale, nostalgically. 'You never lose the knack of working with wood.'

'Building a galleon is very different from creating a model of a new house, yet you adapted your skills with ease.' He reached for his purse. 'Let me pay you.'

'No, no, Mr Redmayne – not a penny.'

'A labourer is worthy of his hire.'

'It was a joy to work on.'

'Designing the house was also a joy,' said Christopher, 'but I expect Monsieur Villemot to pay me for it. Come now,' he went on, extracting a handful of coins from his purse. 'Let's have no more of this nonsense. Take what you've rightly earned.'

'Thank you, sir,' said Bale, holding out a reluctant palm.

Christopher paid him the agreed amount and added some extra money by way of a bonus. Bale had done exactly what had been asked of him in half the time allowed. The constable looked at the coins.

'You've given me too much.'

'It will help to pay for all the midnight oil you burned.'

'Sarah will chide me for taking more than I deserve.'

'Your wife has far too much common sense to do that. There are scant rewards from being a parish constable,' said Christopher, 'and only someone as public-spirited as you would take on the work. When you're employed by me, you'll get a decent wage.'

'Thank you,' said Bale, touched. 'You're very generous.'

'Strictly speaking, it's Jean-Paul Villemot's generosity so you should be grateful to him. Every penny I've given you comes from my client.' He pointed to the model. 'He'll be overjoyed with this.'

'Good.'

They were in Christopher's house in Fetter Lane, a place that

was so much larger and better furnished than Bale's humbler
abode that he always felt vaguely uncomfortable there. Holding
his hat in both hands, he stood beside the table as the architect
subjected the model to an even closer scrutiny. Tall, lithe and
dashing, Christopher had long reddish hair that curled at the
ends. Even in repose, he seemed animated. He and Bale were
unlikely companions, divided by religion, social standing and
every other measurement against which they could be set. Yet
they had been drawn together over the years and each had come
to value the friendship highly.

Christopher had first met the dour constable when the client
for whom he had designed a house had been murdered. Since
the crime had taken place in Bale's own ward of Baynard's
Castle, he dedicated himself to solving it with the aid of the
architect. In the course of their partnership, a mutual respect
had developed and it had slowly increased with the passage of
time. It was gratifying to both of them that they could at last
work together on something that was quite unrelated to crime.

'What do you think of the house?' enquired Christopher.

'Too grand for the likes of me, Mr Redmayne.'

'More suitable for Paris than for London?'

'Yes,' said Bale, wrinkling his nose, 'it is a bit Frenchified.'

'A man is entitled to reside in a house that reminds him of his
native country,' said Christopher. 'And there are aspects of
French architecture that I find very endearing. When I was
studying my trade, I learned a lot on the other side of the
English Channel.'

'I prefer a plain house with none of this decoration.'

'Engage me as your architect and I'll design it for you.'

Bale smiled. 'I'm happy with the house I've got, sir.'

'And with the wife and children you share it with, Jonathan.'

'I'd not change them for the world.'

Christopher felt a pang of envy. Whenever Bale returned to
his home in Addle Hill, his family were invariably there to
welcome him. Though he shared it with two servants,

Christopher's house always seemed rather empty by comparison, even more so since Susan Cheever had returned to Northampton for a while with her father. Shorn of his beloved, Christopher felt desperately lonely and could only keep sadness at bay by throwing himself into his work. He longed for the day when he and Susan could share a home and have children of their own. Until then, he reflected, the only family he had in London was his brother, Henry, whose sybaritic existence appalled him and whose proximity was often an embarrassment.

It was uncanny. Even as he popped into Christopher's mind, his brother came calling. The bell rang insistently, Jacob, the ancient servant, went to open the front door, and, seconds later, a grinning Henry Redmayne was shown into the room.

'Christopher!' he said, doffing his hat and embracing his brother affectionately. 'How good to see you looking so well.'

'I wish that I could say the same of you,' said Christopher.

'My doctor tells me I'm in the best of health.'

'Then you must change your doctor. Your eyes are bloodshot, your cheeks are sallow and you look as if you've not slept for a week.' He indicated his other visitor. 'You know Jonathan, of course.'

'Oh!' said Henry, seeing Bale for the first time and frowning with candid dislike. 'Yes, I've met your tame Puritan once too often.'

'Learn from his example and lead a cleaner life.'

'I'd die of boredom!'

'There's nothing boring about my life, Mr Redmayne,' said Bale, staunchly. 'It's full of interest. Unlike some, I do an honest job.'

'Why, so do I,' retorted Henry, stung by the insinuation, 'so you can take that note of criticism out of your voice. I work at the Navy Office and serve my country accordingly. I venture to suggest that I contribute more to the safety of the nation than someone who merely arrests a few drunkards and stops an occasional tavern brawl.'

'You forget something, Henry,' said his brother. 'There was a time when you and Jonathan were colleagues. You might victual the ships but he helped to build them, and that's a much more difficult proposition. See here,' he continued, standing back to reveal the model on the table behind him, 'this is an example of his work. Jonathan is still a master carpenter.'

Henry was impressed. '*You* made this, Bale?'

'At your brother's instruction,' said the other.

'Then I congratulate you. That house is fit to stand in any street in Paris. If I'm not mistaken,' he said, excitedly, 'what you have brought to life is the London residence commissioned by none other than that greasy Frenchman, Jean-Paul Villemot.' He leaned over the model to inspect it. 'Is that not so?'

'I believe it is, Mr Redmayne.'

'Then this is a happy coincidence because it's the very matter I came to discuss with Christopher.' He turned to bestow a meaningful smile on the constable. 'Good day to you, Bale.'

'And to you, sir.'

After a round of farewells, Bale took his leave, even though he was pressed by Christopher to stay. When he had seen his friend out, the architect came back into his study. Henry had crouched down so that he could peer through the front door of the model.

'You had no right to put Jonathan to flight like that,' said Christopher, sharply. 'He was here as my guest.'

'That gloomy face of his makes me shiver.'

'He's a friend of mine.'

Henry stood up to face him. 'Since when has a friend taken precedence over your own flesh and blood?' he said, irritably. 'I'm your brother, Christopher.'

'I have regretted the fact many times.'

'Do not jest with me.'

'I speak in earnest, Henry, as you well know.'

'Put my past mistakes aside,' said the other. 'I'm aware of my faults and I've done everything in my power to address them.

What you see before you is a new, reformed, reclaimed, utterly responsible Henry Redmayne.' He spread his arms. 'What think you of him?'

'That he looks horribly like the same old reprobate.'

'The change is within me, Christopher. It's not yet visible to the naked eye. But it will be, it will be. I have renounced sin.'

'You'll tell me next that the Thames has renounced water.'

Henry laughed. 'You are right to be cynical,' he conceded. 'I have wandered too readily from the straight and narrow until now. I own it and I condemn it. Henceforth, I'll mend my ways.'

'How many times have I heard you say that?'

'This time, I mean it, Christopher.'

His brother was sceptical. 'To what do we owe this miraculous transformation?' he asked, wearily.

'To the only thing that matters in this world – to love, a love so deep and all-embracing that it's brought me to my senses. I've met her at last. I've seen the woman I wish to marry, the divine creature I intend to worship for the rest of my days. And you, my dear brother,' he added, waving a hand at the model, 'are in a position to help me win her love. Who commissioned this house?'

'You guessed aright – Jean-Paul Villemot, the artist.'

'So you will be in constant discussion with him.'

'Naturally,' said Christopher. 'I intend to take this model across to him tomorrow morning.'

Henry quivered all over. 'Then *she* will be there.'

'Who?'

'The lady I adore, my wife-to-be.'

'What on earth are you talking about?'

'Destiny.'

'Ah,' said Christopher with growing suspicion. 'I've heard you talk of destiny before and it always brings disaster in its wake.'

'Not this time,' insisted Henry. 'All I need is a little assistance from my brother and my destiny will be fulfilled. Play Cupid for me, I beg you. Bear letters to the lady and contrive a moment when I may speak to her alone.' He tapped the miniature house. 'Distract the artist with one model and leave the other one – namely her – to me. Chance has contrived more than I could have dared hope. You are my bridge to Paradise. Help me now and you will one day welcome Araminta as your dear sister-in-law.'

'Araminta?'

'Araminta Jewell. Villemot is engaged to paint her portrait.'

'I do not know the lady.'

'Then you have never looked upon perfection.'

'Indeed, I have,' said Christopher, thinking of Susan Cheever.

'Araminta is a Jewell by name, and a jewel by nature. I'm consumed with passion for her. She must be mine.'

'Then find someone else to be your pander for I'll not take on the office. My only business with Monsieur Villemot concerns the new house he asked me to design.'

'Could you not oblige your brother in the process?'

'No, Henry, I could not. Let's hear no more of Araminta Jewell.'

'Culthorpe,' corrected the other.

'What?'

'She was tricked into marriage by Sir Martin Culthorpe.'

Christopher was aghast. 'You want me to ease you into the bedchamber of someone else's wife?' he demanded. 'Even by your low standards, that's a revolting suggestion. How could you even ask such a thing of me?'

'Her marriage was a grotesque error.'

'If it took her out of your reach, I'd say that it was a tactical triumph. What can you be thinking about, Henry? Do you really mean to pin your hopes of happiness on such a patent impossibility?'

'*Amor vincit omnia*,' declaimed Henry, groping for the only Latin tag he could remember. 'Love conquers all. Araminta wants me, needs me and yearns for me. The fact that she is at present encumbered with a husband is but a disagreeable irrelevance. She's mine, Christopher,' he asserted, a hand to his heart, 'and I call upon you, as a brother, to smooth the path of true love.'

'The lady and her husband have already found it.'

'You refuse my request?'

'It would be ignoble of me even to consider it,' said Christopher with vehemence. 'She is protected by the bonds of holy matrimony. You meddle with those at your peril.'

Henry crossed to the door. 'Then I'll do so alone,' he said, huffily. 'Since you have failed me, I'll achieve my ends without your help. Come what may, I'm determined to have her – and a dozen husbands will not stand in my way.'

Sweeping out with a theatrical flourish, he slammed the door.

Christopher groaned. There was trouble ahead.

Chapter Two

Traffic was heavy in the Strand that morning but the carriage rumbled along at a steady speed. Inside the vehicle, Sir Martin Culthorpe was too busy giving instructions to his wife to notice the endless series of coaches, carts, barrows, riders and pedestrians that went past. Lady Culthorpe sat beside her husband and listened patiently.

'Be polite but not too forward,' he told her.

'No, husband.'

'Do not, on any account, discuss any domestic matters.'

'It would never cross my mind to do so.'

'Touch on nothing of a personal nature.'

'You have my word.'

'Above all else, Araminta,' he stressed, 'guard against Monsieur Villemot's charm. He is a ladies' man with all the faults of the breed.'

'You do him wrong,' she said, earnestly. 'He talks of nobody but his wife and he does so with great tenderness.'

'In the company of a Frenchman, a young woman can never be wholly secure.' She bit back a giggle. 'I'm serious, Araminta.'

'I know you are.'

'As your husband, it behoves me to think of such things.'

'You've dwelt on nothing else these past few days and your fears have proved groundless. Monsieur Villemot has shown me the utmost respect. Emile, his valet, has been kind and attentive to me. I have also got to know Clemence.'

'Clemence?'

'The cat,' she said. 'She is adorable. When I sit in that studio,' said Araminta, 'I feel that I am among friends.'

She squeezed his hand and looked lovingly up at him. The new Lady Culthorpe was short and shapely with the kind of arresting beauty that would turn anyone's head. She wore a blue dress whose delicate hue matched her eyes. Exposing her shoulders, it was back-laced and had puffed elbow sleeves slashed to reveal a darker material beneath. The looped skirt was tied back by bows at the rear to show the lining. Decorated with neat embroidery, the petticoat was also prominently displayed. Her high-heeled shoes were of blue satin with a bow at the instep.

Jean-Paul Villemot had selected the clothing to complement her features and her complexion. Her oval face had an unforced loveliness and was surmounted by silken fair hair puffed above the ears and held away from her cheeks by wires. Since she was almost half his age, she looked more like Sir Martin's daughter than his wife. But there was no doubting her devotion to him. For his part, he took the most inordinate pride in being with her, glancing at her time and again as if not quite believing that she had actually married him.

'You must learn to trust me,' she said.

'I do so implicitly, my dear.'

'Beauty is as much a curse as a blessing. It is pleasing to look at in a mirror but it does, alas, attract all sorts of unwanted admirers. Dealing with them requires tact and firmness, Martin.' She pulled a face. 'Against my wishes, I have perforce had a lot of practice in fending off amorous gentleman.'

'I thank God that I was not one of them.'

'You would never be listed among such unprincipled rascals and nor,' she added, 'would Monsieur Villemot. Where others tempted me with momentary pleasures, you offered your heart, your hand and all that you possessed. Rash impulse has no appeal for me. I chose the sweetness and commitment that can only come from true love.'

'Thank you, Araminta!'

'Having made that election, I'll never go astray from it.'

Sir Martin smiled fondly. 'I am rightly censored,' he said. 'Why should I try to lay all this advice upon you when you are well able to take care of yourself? The truth is that I hate to have you out of my sight for a single minute.'

'Then let me find the way to be constantly in view.'

'I do not follow.'

'The portrait,' she explained with a laugh. 'When that is done, you can gaze upon me every hour of the day. In releasing me for the sittings, you are ensuring that I will always be there with you.'

'I need to see you in person as well as in paint.'

'You shall see both.' The carriage turned a corner and rattled along a winding street before slowing to a halt. 'Here we are at last.'

'One more thing…'

'I'll not hear it,' she said, putting a hand to his lips. 'I'm yours and yours alone. The only reason I agree to spend time alone with another man is so that I can forever be in my husband's company.'

'So be it.'

Sir Martin was content. Using an index finger to lift her chin, he kissed her softly on the mouth. All of his anxieties had been stilled. He could leave her in a room full of French artists and be certain that her virtue would be untarnished. He reproached himself in silence for raising imaginary fears. When the door was opened for Araminta and she alighted from the carriage, he let her go without a tremor.

Jean-Paul Villemot was so delighted that he clapped his hands.

'They have begun work already?' he said. '*Merveilleux!*'

'I've just come from the site,' said Christopher Redmayne. 'They have started to dig the foundations.'

'And the builder?'

'Samuel Littlejohn – a man I've worked with many times before, Monsieur. He employs skilled men and knows how to get the best out of them. It's a pleasant change for him to work on a house in the French style.'

'Designed by a genius of his profession.'

'I merely followed where you led, Monsieur.'

'Every idea you give me, it is very good.'

Christopher was grateful for the compliment but felt that it was undeserved. He had not so much designed the house as copied it from a set of prints that his client had brought from France, incorporating features from a number of them, into a unified whole. What had needed skill was the problem of adjusting the dimensions of the various elements to the available land. Since the site was not large, the house would have a narrower façade than he would have liked but he compensated for the lack of width by introducing additional height. Occupying a position between houses with Dutch gables, the Villemot residence would certainly stand out.

'I love the wooden model you show me,' said the artist.

'Good. An immense amount of work went into it.'

'I cannot wait to show it to my wife, Monique.'

'The model or the house?'

'Both, *mon ami*!'

'Sam Littlejohn will not keep you waiting,' Christopher promised him. 'He builds fast and he builds well. Now that spring is here, he can count on better weather. He does not dally.'

'Then he is the man after my own heart. Some artists, they take an age before they even begin a painting. Not me. At a first sitting,' said Villemot, with a gesture towards the easel near the window, 'I draw all the sketches I need. At the second, I am putting paint on the canvas. My rivals, they say that I rush things.'

'They are simply jealous of you.'

'None of my clients complain.'

'I'm not surprised,' said Christopher, looking around the studio. 'I've seen some of your portraits and they are exceptional.'

'Does that mean you wish me to paint you, Christopher?'

'No, no! I'm not a suitable subject.' He smiled as an image of Susan Cheever came into his mind. 'But I may know someone who is.'

The Frenchman winked at him. 'A lady?'

'A very special lady.'

There was a tap on the door and it opened to admit Emile, who escorted Araminta Culthorpe into the studio. Taken aback by her poise and beauty, Christopher blinked in astonishment. The whole room seem to fill with her fragrance. After dismissing Emile with a nod, Villemot moved forward to greet her.

'And here is another very special lady,' he said, bestowing a kiss on the back of her hand. 'Delighted to see you again, Lady Culthorpe.'

'Thank you, Monsieur Villemot.'

The artist stood back to introduce her to Christopher. When she heard his surname, the smile froze on her lips and she became wary.

'You are not related to Henry Redmayne, I hope,' she said.

'My brother,' confessed Christopher.

'I see no resemblance at all between you.'

'I think you'll find none, Lady Culthorpe. We do not look alike, think alike, or act alike. Henry and I have chosen very different paths through life. While he works at the Navy Office, I toil away as an architect.'

'Christopher has designed the house for me,' explained Villemot.

'Oh,' said Araminta with interest.

'I showed you the model yesterday.'

'It was very striking. Did you build it, Mr Redmayne?'

'No, Lady Culthorpe,' he replied. 'I drew up the plan but someone else did the carpentry. Actually, it was his first venture.'

'Then you must retain his services. I've never seen anything so intricately done. It was like a magnificent doll's house.'

'Wait until it's built. Then you'll see it in its full glory.'

'I look forward to doing so, Mr Redmayne.'

While she had been speaking, Araminta had been appraising him and she was clearly impressed by what she saw. She decided that it was unjust to take a dislike to him because he bore a surname that she had come to detest. For his part, Christopher was both stirred and alarmed. He could see only too well why Henry had come under her spell. Lady Culthorpe was a remarkable young lady.

But she was quite unlike any of the women that his brother had pursued in the past and that disturbed him. There was something almost ethereal about her, an other-worldly quality, compounded of beauty, innocence and shining integrity. Instead of furthering his brother's lecherous designs, Christopher vowed to do everything in his power to shield her from him.

He became conscious that he was holding the two of them up.

'I do apologise,' he said, eyes never leaving her. 'I am obviously in the way so I will bid you both farewell.'

'Wait!' said Villemot, intercepting him before he could leave. 'You have not told me how Lady Culthorpe comes to know your brother.' He looked from one to the other. 'Well?'

Christopher was discreet. 'That's immaterial,' he said. 'Henry belongs to Lady Culthorpe's past and is best left there.'

'I couldn't agree more,' she said.

'Goodbye, Lady Culthorpe.'

'Goodbye.'

He gave her a polite bow before letting himself out of the room.

'I think, maybe, there is an interesting story here,' said

Villemot with a conspiratorial smile. 'About you and Christopher's brother.'

Araminta would not be drawn. 'You heard what Mr Redmayne told you,' she said, briskly. 'It belongs in my past.'

'Of course.'

'So I'd be grateful if you did not raise the subject again.'

'My lips, they are sealed.' His exaggerated pout made her laugh and she relaxed. 'Is there any drink Emile can bring for you before we start, Lady Culthorpe?'

'No, thank you.'

'Sitting in one position, it is thirsty work.'

'I'll be fine, Monsieur Villemot.'

'Then let us begin.'

He conducted her across to the couch, waited for her to sit then arranged her skirts so that its folds fell in the correct way. Going across to his easel, he removed the cloth that covered the painting and checked the position that Araminta had been in earlier. Villemot came back to her to make a few adjustments, turning her head slightly to the left and asking her to hold her hands in her lap. Clemence, the black cat, watched it all from the comfort of her chair. It took some time before the artist was completely satisfied with the angle at which Araminta was sitting. Losing interest, Clemence yawned lazily and went back to sleep.

'How much longer must I do this?' asked Araminta, taking care to hold her position.

'You are tired already?'

'No, Monsieur Villemot.'

He was hurt. 'You do not like it here?'

'I like it very much.'

'Then where is the problem?'

She gave a slight shrug. 'I suppose the truth is that I'm not used to being looked at so intently.'

'But you were *born* to be looked at, Lady Culthorpe,' he said with an admiring smile. 'Such beauty should not be hidden away. It should be seen and enjoyed. Jean-Paul Villemot, he is the artist who will capture that beauty for all time.'

'You flatter me, sir.'

'No man could do that.'

There was a glint in his eye that she had not seen before and a note of esteem in his voice that bordered on veneration. It was the first time that he had ever expressed his affection for her so openly and it unsettled her. Araminta was worried what he might be thinking as he gazed at her for hours on end.

'You did not answer my question, Monsieur,' she said.

'What question?'

'How many more sittings will there be?'

'One,' he said, picking up his palette and starting to mix the oil paint. 'Two, at most.'

'Is that all?'

'Yes, Lady Culthorpe. I have been working on your head and shoulders and, for that, I need you here in person. No other woman could have such a lovely face, such skin, such hair, such a neck. Is like painting a Venus.' Arminta's discomfort increased. 'When I work on the dress, someone else can wear it for me.'

'Someone else?'

'Why should you have to sit there when someone can do it in your place? I have a couple of models to call on or I could even use that pretty maid of yours.'

'Eleanor?'

'She is the same height and shape as you – the same age, too. I think you would like to lend the dress to someone you know.'

'I'd certainly not allow a stranger to wear it.'

'What about the pretty Eleanor, then?'

She pondered. 'It's a possibility,' she said at length.

'Then let her be your double.'

Araminta was not at all sure that she liked the idea. Eleanor was familiar with her mistress's wardrobe and had handled its contents of it many times, but she was still only a maid. She lacked the bearing to wear such an exquisite dress. Araminta had another reason to feel disquiet. Visiting her London home, Villemot had only met Eleanor for a fleeting moment yet he had noticed how young, petite and shapely she was. Her elfin prettiness had not escaped him either. The readiness with which he suggested using her as a model for Araminta showed that he had taken an interest in her. Eleanor was a capable and self-possessed young woman, but she would be more susceptible to the artist's flattery than her mistress was.

While he painted, Villemot liked to hold a conversation, believing that it helped his sitters feel more at ease, rescuing them from having to hold a pose in silence for lengthy periods. To dispel her faint uneasiness, Araminta initiated the discussion, moving it to what she considered to be the safe topic of Villemot's married life.

'Has your wife ever been to England before?' she asked.

'No,' he replied, 'not yet.'

'What will she think of London?'

'Monique will love it. The English, they are friendly. I first came here to paint a portrait of Lady Bellstock and her husband was kind enough to help me meet many people.' He applied the first paint to the canvas. 'Do you know Lord Bellstock?'

'My husband does,' she said. 'In fact, when Sir Martin first decided that he wanted a portrait painted of me, he asked Lord Bellstock for advice about a suitable artist. He recommended you.'

'Then I owe him my thanks.'

'He was obviously pleased with what you did for him.'

'I like to give my clients exactly what they want,' he said, easily. 'You must make sure that I do so for you, Lady Culthorpe. At least, with you, I do not have to cheat on the canvas.'

'Cheat?'

'I can paint you exactly as you are – not a blemish in sight.

With Lady Bellstock, it was different. Her husband, he wanted me to make her younger and thinner than she was. The portrait was a disguise.'

'Well, I don't wish you to disguise me, Monsieur Villemot.'

'That would be – we have the same word in French – sacrilege.'

The glint returned to his eye and it troubled her once again.

'What is Paris like?' she said, trying to find a neutral subject.

'Very beautiful?'

'More beautiful than London?'

'Oh, yes,' he replied, proudly. 'It does not smell any sweeter and it is just as noisy with all those people, but Paris, it was not destroyed by a fire like London. When I first come here, the city was still in ruins. It looked so ugly. Slowly, it is getting better.'

'Will it ever rival Paris?'

He shrugged expressively. 'I am French. To me, no city in the world will ever be as good as Paris.' He beamed at her. 'I'll take you there one day. Would you like that, Lady Culthorpe?'

The directness of his question shocked her and she was lost for words as she considered its implications. A faint blush came to her cheeks. Noticing it at once, he gave her an emollient smile.

'With your husband, of course,' he added.

'I'm still not sure if I should have taken the money,' said Bale, guiltily.

'Then I'd have taken it for you,' said his wife.

'All I did was to help a friend, Sarah.'

'There was more to it than that.'

'No, there wasn't.'

'Mr Redmayne employed you, Jonathan. He told you at the very beginning that he'd pay you for your work.'

'But that's the strange thing,' said Bale, scratching head. 'It did not really feel like work.'

'Well, it felt like work to me, I know that. You laboured for hours every evening. We hardly saw anything of you.'

'Mr Redmayne wanted it finished as soon as possible.'

'And you did exactly what he asked of you,' she pointed out, 'so you ought be rewarded for your pains.'

'What pains?'

Sarah was forthright. 'You may not have felt any, but I did. So did the children. We *missed* you, Jonathan. It's not enough for you to spend the whole day walking the streets in all weathers. When you get back home, you have to find something else to keep you away from us. I want to see my husband,' she said, giving him an affectionate dig in the ribs. 'The children want to see their father.'

'I read to them every night.'

'Yes – then you went straight back to that model.'

They were in the kitchen of their house in Addle Hill and Sarah Bale was tiring of her husband's inability to accept the wage that he had earned. She was a stout woman of medium height with an energy that never seemed to flag and a love of her husband that was never found wanting. However, it did not mean that she was blind to Bale's faults or slow to remind him of them. Above all else, she was a supremely practical woman and she knew how crucial the extra money was to the family. She gave him an impulsive hug.

'It's good to have you back again, Jonathan,' she said.

'You were the one who told me to accept Mr Redmayne's offer,' he remembered, 'so it's unfair to blame me for what happened.'

'I'm not blaming you.'

'I was so pleased to be asked, Sarah.'

'So you should be. It was an honour.'

'Mr Redmayne has done us so many favours in the past.'

'And you've done favours for him. Don't forget that.'

'I wasn't sure if I could do it at first,' he admitted, 'but, as soon as I picked up my tools, I felt as if I was back in the shipyard again. There's something about the smell and feel of wood.'

'Yes,' she said. 'It keeps you away from your family.'

It was only mild criticism. Sarah was very fond of Christopher Redmayne and always delighted to see him. When he had last called at the house, she expected him to ask her husband to help him solve another crime. Instead, it was Bale's skill as a carpenter that was in demand. She was thrilled by the thought that a rising young architect should entrust such an important task to her husband, and, during his moments of self-doubt, had urged him on.

'Mr Redmayne obviously liked what you did for him,' she said.

'He seemed very happy with my work.

'What were his exact words?'

'I can't remember.'

'You must do, Jonathan. Tell me what he said.'

'He didn't have time to say very much at all,' recalled Bale. 'His brother arrived and I felt that I was in the way.'

Sarah scowled. 'Is that the infamous Henry Redmayne?'

'Yes, my love – it is.'

'How can such a fine gentleman as Mr Christopher Redmayne have such a disgraceful brother?'

'It's a mystery to me, Sarah. I've never met two siblings so unlike each other. Their father is the Dean of Gloucester Cathedral, as you know. A true Christian gentleman. He must be so proud of one son and so disappointed in the other.'

'What exactly is Henry Redmayne like?' she pressed.

Bale took a deep breath. 'I will tell you…'

Henry Redmayne was the first member of the Society to arrive at Locket's, the celebrated ordinary near Charing Cross, where excellent meals were served at fixed prices and regular hours. Frequented by the gentry, Locket's was a babble of excited voices as Henry took his seat at the table. Sir Willard Grail soon joined him, sweeping off his hat before giving his friend a cordial greeting. Sitting beside Henry, he imparted his news.

'Some devilish intelligence has come to my ears, Henry.'

'Of what nature?'

'It seems that we may have a competitor.'

'What do you mean, Sir Willard?'

'Araminta – I simply refuse to call her Lady Culthorpe – our own, dear, matchless Araminta is having her portrait painted.'

'Really?' said Henry, concealing the fact that he already knew. 'What artist has been given the privilege of gazing upon her until he swoons with her beauty?'

'That confounded Frenchman – Jean-Paul Villemot.'

'This news is worrying.'

'So it should be,' said Sir Willard. 'He has the advantage over us. While we can only approach her by letter or by sending her gifts, he is left alone with her in his studio. It's monstrously unfair. In such a situation, Villemot may achieve what the four of us seek.'

'Surely not,' said Henry, confidently. 'Culthorpe would not entrust his young wife to the man if he had the slightest doubt about him and Villemot has to beware of scandal. He would not dare to lay a finger upon Araminta.'

'Yet women account him irresistibly handsome.'

'Frenchwomen, perhaps – the English have more taste.'

'That is not the case, Henry. More than one English rose has praised Villemot in my presence – Lady Hester Lingoe, for instance. She said that sitting for him was one of the most exhilarating experiences of her life.'

'Everything is a most exhilarating experience to Lady Hester,' said Henry, tartly. 'Her emotions have the consistency of gunpowder. Apply the smallest amount of heat and she explodes into exaggeration. I remember her telling me once that reading Catullus in the original Latin had uplifted her soul to a new eminence. What nonsense! Besides, he went on, 'we are not comparing like with like here, Sir Willard. The gorgeous

Araminta is a species of saint. No woman with Lady Hester's history could ever aspire to canonisation.'

'I still have qualms about Villemot.'

'Set them aside.'

'I'll not be bested by a foreigner.'

'No,' said Henry, boldly, 'you'll be bested by me, Sir Willard.'

Before the other man could reply, the waiter came up to their table and they ordered a bottle of wine. No sooner had the waiter gone than Elkannah Prout took his place, exchanging greetings with his friends before taking the empty chair at the table. The newcomer's eyes were darting. His wig was so full and luxuriant that he looked like a ferret peering through a bush.

'I bear tidings,' he announced.

'We have already heard them, Elkannah,' said Sir Willard.

'I think not.'

'Henry has just been apprised of the information. Araminta's portrait is being painted by that creeping Frenchmen, Villemot.'

'Is that the sum of your intelligence?' asked Prout.

'Yes.'

'Then you know only half the news.'

'There's more to add?'

'Much more – though I suspect that Henry already knows it.'

'Not I,' said Henry, feigning ignorance.

'Your brother must surely have told you.'

'Christopher and I rarely speak, Elkannah.'

'That's not true,' said Prout. 'You are always trying to borrow money off him to settle your gambling debts. Something as important as this would hardly go unmentioned.'

'Something as important as what?' asked Sir Willard. 'I am still in the dark here. Pray, shed some light, one of you.'

'Jean-Paul Villemot is having a house built in London.'

'He's rich enough to afford it.'

'He's also astute enough to choose a talented architect. The fellow goes by the name of Christopher Redmayne.'

Sir Willard goggled. 'Henry's brother?' he said, understanding the situation at once. 'But that means he will have an excuse to call on Villemot at any time. He could devise a way to meet Araminta.'

'It would never cross his mind,' said Henry.

'It would cross *your* mind.'

'That's a gross slander, Sir Willard. I abide by the rules of the Society. The four of us fight on equal terms. I would never stoop to subterfuge in any way,' he lied, bristling with righteous indignation. 'I had no knowledge of the fact that Christopher had been engaged by the artist and would never use him to further my ends. Were I to attempt such a thing, he would reject the notion outright. My brother is no puritan but neither does he take any delight in the chase. The mere whisper of what our Society was about would discountenance Christopher. He believes in love and marriage.'

'So do I,' said Sir Willard, 'when occasion serves. But I still fear that you may have stolen a march on us, Henry. If your brother calls on Villemot while that Jewell among women is there, he will be able to bring back gossip about her that only you will hear.'

'Christopher is not given to passing on gossip.'

'I agree,' said Prout. 'I've met him. Henry's brother is a decent, honest, conscientious young man and, unless I am mistaken, he has another glaring defect – he is a devout Christian.'

'That's true, Elkannah. Our father is forever holding Christopher up as an example to me. My brother leads a good life while I prefer to lead an adventurous one.'

'If you want someone to worry about, Sir Willard, it is not him. The real danger comes from within the Society.'

Sir Willard was puzzled. 'How can that be?'

'The person to watch is Jocelyn.'

'Why – what has he been up to?'

'Telling the truth,' said Prout, 'and it unnerved me. When we heard that Araminta had been married, all of us were shaken to the core but we three have at least accepted the situation and determined to make the best of it. Jocelyn will not accept it.'

'He must,' said Henry.

'Facts are facts,' added Sir Willard. 'Araminta will not divorce her husband for our benefit.'

'More's the pity!'

'Jocelyn wants to effect his own divorce,' said Prout. 'We spent last night together and I saw him in his cups. I've never known him so roused and belligerent.'

'What did he tell you?'

'That he'll not let anyone stand between him and Araminta. He's set his heart on winning her love. Jocelyn told me that his mind is made up. If he cannot enjoy her favours by fair means, he'll not scruple to resort to foul ones. His meaning was clear,' warned Prout. 'To achieve his ambition, he's even prepared to murder Sir Martin Culthorpe.'

When she was finally released from the long morning session in the studio, Araminta Culthorpe was grateful. She was not merely spared the discomfort of sitting in the same position for an hour at a time, she was liberated from the searching gaze of Jean-Paul Villemot. The artist did not upset her again with any suggestive remarks but she no longer felt completely safe in his presence. Their relationship had subtly changed and Araminta needed to get away in order to examine the changes from a distance. As the carriage bore her back home to Westminster, she reflected on what had happened and speculated on what might come at a future meeting.

The problem confronting her was simple. Should she or should she not confide in her husband? And if so, what exactly should she tell him? Araminta could hardly say that she felt threatened in the artist's company because that was not true. In essence, all that had happened was that he had made some inappropriate comments. Other ladies would no doubt have accepted them as compliments but, as a young woman newly married, she had been somehow unable to do so. She had felt vulnerable. Jean-Paul Villemot, in her opinion, had overstepped the bounds of propriety.

What she had to calculate, she decided, was her husband's reaction. If she told him that she had been offended by the artist's behaviour, he would cancel the portrait at once and engage someone else to paint it, and Araminta did not believe that anyone in London could rival Villemot. If, on the other hand, she made only a minor complaint, Sir Martin would feel obliged to challenge the artist and that, too, could result in the abandonment of the project.

However she presented it to him, Sir Martin would be hurt and she wanted to spare him any pain. For that reason, she resolved to sort out the matter herself without involving him in any way. After all, Araminta consoled herself, there would be no more sittings to endure. Unless he called her back, she and Villemot might never be alone in the same room again.

Having reached her decision, she felt much better. Her only concern now was to change out of the dress she had worn at the studio, ideal for the painting but not entirely suitable for a warm day in May. It was something she was more likely to wear to a formal event than put on at home for the day. When the carriage delivered her to her front door, she rang the doorbell. It never occurred to her that she was being watched by someone who stood on the opposite side of the road, partly concealed behind a tree.

Let into the house, Araminta went straight upstairs to change with her maid on her heels. Eleanor Ryle was pleased to see her mistress return. A bright, open-faced, inquisitive young woman with a mop of brown hair, Eleanor helped her out of her dress.

'Monsieur Villemot chose well,' she said, stroking the material. 'This has always been my favourite.'

'Then you may get a chance to wear it, Eleanor.'

'Me, m'lady?'

'Monsieur Villemot does not need to keep me sitting there

for hours while he paints the dress,' said Araminta. 'Someone else can wear it in my stead and he suggested you.'

'But he doesn't even know that I exist.'

'Yes, he does. He noticed you when he called here.'

Eleanor giggled. 'Really?'

'He thought that the dress would fit you perfectly.'

'Oh, I could never wear it as you do, m'lady. It becomes you. On me, it would not look the same at all.'

'I wonder,' said Araminta, weighing her up. 'Let me see. Hold it against you, Eleanor.'

'Yes, m'lady.'

Taking a step back, the maid held the dress up against her, grinning happily as she did so, as if a private dream was just being fulfilled. Eleanor was short enough and slim enough to wear it even though the dress was not the ideal colour for her. Araminta studied her for a full minute.

'I believe that it will do,' she said.

Eleanor was overjoyed. 'Then I am to *wear* it?' she cried.

'We'll see. I need to discuss the matter with my husband.'

'Of course.'

'Where is he, by the way?'

'Smoking a pipe in the garden,' replied Eleanor. 'He asked me to call him as soon as you returned.'

'Well, let me dress quickly,' said Araminta, crossing to the wardrobe. 'I don't want to keep him waiting.'

Sir Martin Culthorpe was a creature of habit. Twice a day, he always liked to smoke a pipe and the garden was the place in which he preferred to smoke it. Even on cold days, or when it was raining, he would venture outdoors and shelter in the arbour while he puffed away. Only heavy snow or a violent thunderstorm could confine his pipe to the house. It was not merely the pleasure of inhaling the tobacco that he savoured. Sir Martin was a contemplative man and a stroll in his garden was the perfect time to reflect on the issues that preoccupied him.

By comparison with the garden on his country estate, the one in Westminster was quite small but it was still large enough for him to promenade for five minutes or so without retracing his steps. Formal in design, it had endless trees and neat rows of bushes dividing it up and creating private corners where he could sit without being visible from the house. At the centre of the garden was a large pond with a fountain in the shape of Neptune, and there was a great deal of other statuary dotted here and there.

Pulling on his pipe, he strode along between an avenue of mulberry trees, wondering how his wife had fared at her latest sitting. Sir Martin still could not believe his good fortune in having married Araminta Jewell and he vowed to devote the rest of his life to her. What he did not realise, as he turned leisurely into a shaded grotto, was that his life was just about to come to an end.

Chapter Three

Christopher Redmayne liked to keep a close eye on any project in which he was involved. Even at the earliest stage, he visited a site regularly to watch work in progress. More illustrious architects would not have deigned to spend so much time amid the dirt and dust of construction, preferring to dispatch their assistants to take care of such matters, but Christopher worked alone and would not, in any case, have delegated such a task to another. He loved to see the foundations being laid and to watch a building rise slowly from the ground and take on the shape he had envisaged when bent over his preliminary drawings.

The important work of designing churches, livery halls and public buildings in the wake of the Great Fire went to more famous members of his profession, but Christopher had no objection to that. There was still plenty for him to do. The blaze had destroyed over thirteen thousand houses, wiping them from the face of the city and leaving only charred remains in their stead. Architects and builders were therefore in great demand so there was no shortage of work for able men. All over London, Christopher had made his small, personal contribution to the rebuilding of a great city that he loved.

'No disrespect to you, Mr Redmayne,' said Samuel Littlejohn as he washed down his food with a swig of beer, 'but, when my father was a builder, he never worked with architects. The client would tell him what he wanted, show him an example of it in a drawing then leave him to it. My father did the rest.'

'That's because he was a master builder, Sam,' said Christopher with a smile, 'part of a tradition that went back for centuries. It was a big mistake to let people like me take over some aspects of his work.'

Littlejohn chortled. 'We've learned to respect you, sir.'

'That's all we ask.'

Having inspected the site that morning, Christopher was dining at a nearby tavern with Littlejohn, a man whose bulk belied his name. He was a brawny man of middle years with a capacity for hard work and a jovial manner. His weather-beaten face and rubicund complexion gave him the appearance of a farmer but he was essentially an urban creature, having begun with, then inherited, the building firm that his father had started. Christopher was very fond of him though the partnership between them had got off to a difficult start because the client whose house they were building was murdered when only the cellars had been constructed. Their contract with him was promptly declared null and void.

There had been an additional problem for Christopher in that the builder's daughter, Margaret Littlejohn, had become infatuated with him and caused him considerable embarrassment by stalking him. He had deemed it sensible to work with other builders for a time. As soon as the girl had been safely married to someone else, however, Christopher resumed his work with Littlejohn and they proved to be an effective team. The builder was a rough and ready man whose table manners were less than refined, but who was nevertheless an amiable dinner companion. What Christopher liked about him was that he always spoke his mind. After chuckling over an incident that had occurred during the last house on which they had worked together, Littlejohn became solemn.

'We could have one problem,' he warned.

'I know what you're going to tell me,' said Christopher, trying to anticipate him. 'That façade is too elaborate. We'll need the very best stonemasons to work on it, Sam.'

'I'm not worried about the façade, sir.'

'Then it must be that staircase Monsieur Villemot insists upon having. I've never seen anything so grand outside a French chateau.'

'Let him have his staircase, Mr Redmayne. Let him have anything and everything he wants. If, that is,' he said, darkly, 'he'll occupy the house when it's built.'

'Why else would he commission it?'

'Because he needs more room.'

'Then where is the problem?'

'He's an artist.'

'So? Artists need somewhere to live just as much as anyone else. Architects, too, oddly enough. We all need a roof over our heads.'

'Mr Villemot is a *French* artist.'

'What difference does that make?'

'Only this, sir – he could be unreliable.'

'I don't see why.'

'I built a house for a Frenchman once before,' said Littlejohn, taking another sip of beer, 'and, before it was finished, he sailed back to France without a word. We never saw him again. He owed us a lot of money. We were left with a half-built house and no client. I'd hate to be in that position again.'

'Was the client an artist?'

'In a manner of speaking – he was a dancing master.'

'Well, I can assure you that Jean-Paul Villemot is not going to dance off to Paris. He prefers to work in London, where he's the toast of his profession. He won't let us down, Sam,' said Christopher, airily. 'He intends to stay and see the project through.'

'What about his fits?'

'I didn't know he was subject to them.'

'Not *those* kind of fits, sir,' said Littlejohn. 'I was talking about the other kind – the sort that all foreigners seem to have, but especially the French. They have these fits of temper, funny moods, silly ideas, sudden changes of mind. The dancing master was like that. He made our lives a misery with his fits. You never knew where you stood with him from day to day.'

'What you're saying is that he was capricious.'

The builder nodded. '*That's* the word I was trying to think of.'

'Well, you've no need to apply it to Monsieur Villemot.'

'I wish I could believe that, sir.'

'He seems to have a most equable temperament and he's promised not to interfere in our work in any way. He's far too busy, painting portraits of the rich and famous. Take heart, Sam,' said Christopher, 'nothing can possibly happen to stop this house being built and paid for in full. If it did,' he added with a carefree laugh, 'then *I'll* be the one having a fit.'

When she had changed her dress and her shoes, and had her hair brushed by her maid, Araminta Culthorpe took a last critical look in the bedroom mirror before deciding that she was ready.

'Shall I find Sir Martin?' volunteered Eleanor Ryle.

'No, thank you,' said Araminta. 'I'll find him myself.'

'Will you talk about the painting with him?'

'In a while, Eleanor.'

'I'd so like to wear that blue dress, Lady Culthorpe.'

'I know.'

'It would be wonderful to work as Mr Villemot's model.'

'We shall see.'

Leaving the maid with reason to hope, Araminta went out of the room and down the stairs. She walked across the hall and along a passageway that led to the garden. When she let herself out of the house, she could see no sign of her husband so she assumed that he was sitting on a bench in one of his favoured places. She went off to explore the garden, looking for the telltale sign of tobacco smoke rising over a hedge or curling up into the sky behind some statuary.

Araminta was so glad that she had elected to say nothing about her occasional moments of disquiet at the studio. Now that she was back in her lovely house, wearing a different dress and taking on the role of a doting wife once more, she could forget all about Jean-Paul Villemot. Memories of their exchanges could not reach her there. She felt safe and secure in a marriage that had changed her life for the better in every way. To most people, Sir Martin Culthorpe would have seemed an unlikely choice for someone who could have had the pick of society but she knew that she had accepted the right husband. He gave her love, protection and social standing. His greater age did not deter her in the least because it brought with it wisdom and experience. Sharing his religious conviction and having the same charitable disposition, she looked forward to helping him in his work and developing a true partnership with him. Meanwhile, Araminta needed to find her husband and take him in to dinner.

'Martin!' she called. 'Where are you?'

When there was no reply, she walked as far as the fountain at the very heart of the garden then raised her voice above the noise of the falling water.

'Martin – I'm back!'

Still, there was no response. Araminta followed the main path between the avenue of maple trees, looking to left and right as she did so in case he had turned down one of the side paths. There was no trace of him. Quickening her step, she walked on until she reached the end of the little avenue. She went around the angle of the rhododendrons and into the secret grotto beyond. Araminta let out a sigh of relief. Her search was finally over.

Apparently asleep, Sir Martin Culthorpe was seated on a bench with the sun slanting across his face. He looked somehow older but that did not worry his wife. Feeling an upsurge of love, she ran across to him, intending to wake him up by kissing him on the forehead, but she felt something hard beneath her foot. She looked down to see that it was his clay pipe, broken in two and lying on the path.

Araminta was suddenly apprehensive. Now that she looked at him more closely, she could see that her husband was sitting in a most unnatural position. She felt alarmed. Wanting to reach out to him, she was somehow held back from doing so. Instead, in trepidation, she took an involuntary step backwards. Mouth dry and heart pounding, she stared at him with growing anxiety.

'Are you unwell, Martin?' she whispered.

As if in response to her question, he suddenly pitched forward and landed headfirst on the path. It was only then that she saw the huge bloodstain from the wound in his back.

Christopher Redmayne had promised to call at the studio that afternoon to discuss with Jean-Paul Villemot the schedule of payments during the building of the new house, and to retrieve the model made by Jonathan Bale. As his horse trotted along the road, he smiled at the memory of his encounter with Samuel Littlejohn. The builder clearly had a jaundiced view of foreigners, suspecting them of being universally difficult, volatile and unpredictable. That had not been Christopher's experience. He had designed houses for a Frenchman, a Dutchman, two Germans and a Swede. None of them had given him the slightest trouble. The only clients of his who had been obstinate and argumentative were native-born Englishmen. Chief among them, he was forced to admit, was Sir Julius Cheever, Member of Parliament and father of the woman he loved. It was a sobering thought.

Jean-Paul Villemot had so far been the perfect employer, recognising, in Christopher, a fellow-artist and trusting his instincts. Whatever advice the architect gave had been readily accepted. Once the general principles of the design had been agreed upon, Christopher had been allowed a free hand.

Littlejohn might fear the tantrums of an excitable foreigner but Christopher did not share his unease. He firmly believed that there would be no problems of that nature ahead.

Arriving at the house, he dismounted, tethered his horse and rang the bell. The door was soon opened by a maid who showed him upstairs to the suite of rooms rented by Villemot. In response to his knock, it was Emile who invited him into the studio, explaining that his master was out but that he would soon return.

'*Voulez-vous l'attendre?*' he asked.

'*Oui,*' replied Christopher.

'*Asseyez-vous, s'il vous plait.*'

'*Merci, Emile.*'

When Christopher sat down, the Frenchman excused himself and left the room. Evidently, he was much more than a valet. Emile was also Villemot's cook, butler, book keeper, companion and general assistant, performing all his functions with quiet efficiency. His English was not yet as fluent as that of his master but Christopher guessed that it would be in due course. Emile struck him as the kind of man who could do anything to which he addressed his mind.

Glancing around, Christopher decided to take a closer look at the studio. When he got to his feet, however, he realised that he was not alone. Clemence was regarding him with a degree of suspicion through one open eye. Like the valet, the black cat exuded a deep sense of loyalty to her master. When Villemot left the studio, Clemence remained on guard. Christopher did not know what test he was being subjected to but he seemed to pass it because the cat eventually closed her eye, curled up and went back to sleep.

Christopher felt at home. The studio had the same amiable clutter as his study in Fetter Lane and the same accumulation of recent projects, either abandoned or awaiting completion. What drew his attention was the easel on which the portrait of Lady Araminta Culthorpe was resting. It was covered by a piece of cloth and he could not resist lifting it up so that he could take a peep at the painting. What he saw astounded him.

Aware of Villemot's reputation for speed, Christopher could not believe the artist had done so much in such a short period of time. The background still needed to be sketched in, and the dress required a lot more work on it, but the head and shoulders of his subject were almost finished. The verisimilitude was amazing. Villemot had not merely caught her beauty and her serenity, he had brought out Araminta's character in the portrait. She looked exactly like the quiet, serious, thoughtful, intelligent young woman that Christopher had met in that very studio. On the canvas before him was an image of pure contentment and he was duly moved.

It pained him to recall that his brother posed a threat to her, and he knew that Henry was not discouraged by the fact that she was now married. Some of his other conquests had had husbands. Henry regarded holy matrimony as nothing more than a further hurdle to be cleared before he seized his prize. Looking at Araminta's face and reminded of her rare qualities, Christopher promised himself that he would do everything in his power to keep his brother away from her. Nothing would be permitted to spoil her radiant happiness.

Unable to take his eyes off her, he stood there for several minutes in admiration of her unequivocal loveliness and of the artist's skill in capturing it. It was only when he heard the front door open below that he came to his senses. Pulling the cloth back over the portrait, Christopher resumed his seat. Feet pounded audibly up the stairs then the door was flung open and Jean-Paul Villemot burst in. When he saw the visitor, he came to a halt and pointed an accusatory finger at him.

'What are you doing here?' he demanded.

'We arranged to meet, Monsieur Villemot,' said Christopher, rising to his feet. 'If it's inconvenient, I can come again another time.'

The artist glared at him. He seemed to be angry, confused and upset. Christopher noticed that the sleeve of his coat was torn. Turning to the door of the adjoining room, Villemot barked a name.

'Emile!'

The valet materialised at his elbow. '*Oui, Monsieur*?'

Villemot was brusque. 'I've told you before, Emile,' he chided. 'When we have the guest, you must always talk in English. You understand, no?'

'Yes, sir,' said Emile, apologetically.

'Did I say I would meet Mr Redmayne this afternoon?'

'You did.'

Breathing heavily through his nose, Villemot stood there for a few seconds as if only half-believing his valet. At length, he took off his hat and tossed it carelessly on to the chair where Clemence was fast asleep. With a squeal of protest, the cat awoke, leapt from the chair, shedding the hat as she did so, and fled to a corner of the room. Emile went across to comfort her by stroking her fur.

'Leave her alone,' snapped Villemot. 'Away!'

It was an abrupt dismissal but Emile seemed accustomed to it. Without hesitation, he went off into the next room and closed the door behind him. Villemot made an effort to be hospitable.

'I am sorry,' he said. 'I forget.'

'No apology is needed,' Christopher assured him.

'We were going to talk about the payment?'

'Only if you wish to do so, Monsieur Villemot,' said the other. 'I have the feeling that this is not the ideal time for you.'

'Why not?'

'You seem distressed.'

'No, no, that is not true. There is nothing wrong with me.'

Christopher had already made an alternative diagnosis. The artist was flushed and perspiration was trickling down his face. He was unsteady on his feet yet, judging by sound of his voice, had not been drinking. Christopher had never seen his client in such a state before. Villemot resented his scrutiny.

'What are you looking at?' he asked, truculently.

'I wondered if you were altogether well, Monsieur.'

'I am as well as any man, Mr Redmayne.'

'Well, I'm bound to say that you do not look it.'

'How I look is nothing to do with you,' said Villemot, pushing past him to walk to the other end of the room. 'You are not the doctor. I do not ask for your opinion.'

'Then I withdraw it at once,' said Christopher, raising both hands in a calming gesture. 'I did not intend to annoy you. I simply came here to talk business.'

'You came for money, Mr Redmyane.'

'That's why you invited me.'

'You English are all the same. Money must always come first. You think of nothing else.'

'On the contrary, Monsieur Villemot,' said Christopher, eager to correct a misapprehension. 'I'm always more interested in a project itself than in any payment. It's the initial design that preoccupies me and I provided that without asking for a penny from you. It was your idea to include a schedule of payments in the contract.'

'It was yours,' insisted the artist.

'I beg to differ.'

'You have chased me for money from the start.'

'All that I've received to date is the small advance that you gave me and most of that went to Jonathan Bale for building that model. The person who now needs money is Mr Littlejohn because he has to buy building materials and pay wages to his men. I don't think that's unreasonable.'

'No,' said Villemot, thinking it through. 'It is not.'

'Then we need to put the details in writing.'

The Frenchman bridled. 'Why – don't you trust me?'

'Of course.'

'It's because I am the foreigner. You think I will not pay. You believe that we are not like you but we always honour our debts.' He became more agitated. 'It is an insult for you to come here like this and ask for money when we already have the contract.' He walked across to confront Christopher. 'Do you know who I am?'

'Yes, Monsieur.'

'Do you now *what* I am?'

'Everyone knows that.'

'I am the best portrait painter in the whole country,' said the artist, tapping his chest with pride. 'I am rich enough to buy ten houses and still have money left over, so you do not need to have the worries about Jean-Paul Villemot. He is a man of his word. I hoped that you knew that,' he continued, his voice rising in fury. 'I cannot work with someone who does not respect me.'

The tirade continued for a couple of minutes and Christopher was unable to say a word. He stood in silence as Villemot lost his temper and delivered a series of stinging and undeserved rebukes. At the peak of his attack, he stopped, looked around in dismay, realised what he had been saying and produced a smile of appeasement.

'Christopher,' he said, embracing him. 'Do not listen to me. I do not know what I am talking about.' He kissed the architect on both cheeks. 'We are still the good friends – no?'

'Yes,' said Christopher without conviction. 'We are still friends.'

'Thank you, *mon ami*.'

'But I suggest that we postpone this discussion.'

'We will talk about it now. You must hear me.'

But the voice he heard in his ear was not that of Jean-Paul Villemot. It belonged to Samuel Littlejohn and it gave him a timely reminder. The French artist could be a problem, after all.

It took time for her to accept the truth. As she stared down at the motionless figure of her husband, Araminta kept expecting him to stir, to regain consciousness, to display visible signs of life. But he did not. He lay in a heap at her feet, exhibiting the bloodstained coat as an explanation of what had happened. Sir Martin Culthorpe had been stabbed in the back and there was an ugly slit in the material where the dagger had gone in. It held a hideous fascination for her. Araminta could not turn her head away from it.

Then, finally, when every last shred of hope had been wrung from her, when she could no longer deceive herself, when the fervent prayers she had been sending up to heaven met with no answering reassurance, she accepted that her husband had been murdered. The moment she did that, she sought oblivion and went down in a faint. For some while, Araminta lay side by side with her husband, like marble statues of a married couple on a tomb, except that he was on his front while she rested on her back.

Several minutes passed. When her eyelids flickered open, she looked up to see the foliage of the grotto arching over her like a fretwork to shade her from the sun. She needed time to work out her bearings. Moving her hand, she touched another then drew it back in horror when she saw that she had just slipped her fingers into the palm of a dead man. Overcome with grief and convulsed with fear, she dragged herself to her feet and staggered back down the garden towards the house.

Araminta opened her mouth to scream for help but no words came out. Instead, she blundered on until she reached the door, opened it wide and stumbled through it. She met Eleanor Ryle in the hall. The maid was frightened at the state her mistress was in. Araminta's hair was dishevelled, her dress was scuffed and there was a trickle of blood from her temple where it had struck the ground. Eleanor reached forward to grab her before Araminta collapsed.

''What's the matter?' she cried.

'It's my husband,' gasped Araminta. 'He's been attacked.'

The alarm was raised and the butler took command. After ordering a servant to help the maid take the distraught wife upstairs, he rushed into the garden to search for his master.

When he saw that Sir Martin had been stabbed to death, he sent one servant to fetch a surgeon and another to bring a constable. He also called the rest of the domestic staff together to break the appalling news to them.

Araminta, meanwhile, was lying on her bed, sobbing quietly and dabbing at her tears with a lace handkerchief. She gave her maid a halting account of what she had seen. Eleanor sat beside her, grieving over the loss of Sir Martin while trying to offer succour to his widow. The maid was utterly bewildered.

'Who could have done such a thing?' she said.

'I've lost him, Eleanor. I've lost my dear husband forever.'

'How could anyone get into the garden?'

'I don't know.'

'Did you see anyone else there?'

'No.'

'Was the garden gate open?'

'I didn't look, Eleanor.'

'This is terrible,' said the other, vainly trying to discern all the implications of the crime. 'You were so happy together and married for such a short time. It's *cruel*, m'lady. That's what it is – it's downright cruel.'

'He didn't deserve this,' said Araminta breathily, chest heaving as she spoke. 'My husband was a kind, gentle, considerate man. He never did anyone any harm – yet *this* happens.'

'It's so unfair.'

They heard voices from the garden. Araminta sat up in bed.

'What's going on?' she asked.

Eleanor went to the window to look out. 'There are some men walking down the garden,' she said. 'One of them is a constable.'

'Will he take the body away? Don't let him do that.'

'He won't do anything you don't want, m'lady.'

'I need to see him again before…'

'Maybe that's not such a good idea,' said the maid, coming

back to her and taking her hand. 'You've already seen more than you can bear. You should not have to look at him again.'

'I don't want him taken.'

'Sir Martin can hardly stay in the garden.'

'I'm not ready for him to go yet.'

Eleanor nodded sympathetically. 'I'll tell them,' she said, moving to the door. On the way she passed the wardrobe and cast a wistful glance at it. 'Does this mean I won't get a chance to wear that blue dress, m'lady?'

'What?'

'I was thinking about that portrait of you.'

'Nothing is further from my mind, Eleanor.'

'You might want it finished,' suggested the other hopefully. 'In memory of Sir Martin, I mean.' She saw Araminta's pained reaction and repented. 'That was a silly idea. I'll go and speak to them.'

She left the room quickly. Alone at last, the young widow of Sir Martin Culthorpe was able to give full vent to her anguish. Pulling back her head, she emitted a long, loud, high-pitched cry of agony.

The news spread like wildfire. By evening, hundreds of people had somehow got hold of the information that Sir Martin had been killed in the quiet of his garden. Henry Redmayne was among them. He immediately spotted an opportunity for personal gain. When his horse had been saddled, he rode swiftly to Fetter Lane to call on his brother. Christopher was stunned by what he was told.

'Sir Martin is *dead*?'

'According to all reports,' said Henry.

'What of his wife?'

'She was unhurt – thank God!'

'But how is she? The poor woman must be heart-broken.'

'It seems that she actually found the body in the garden.'

'That's dreadful,' said Christopher, wondering how Araminta

could possibly cope with such an ordeal. 'It's something she'll never forget. It will prey on her mind forever.'

'She'll need comfort,' said Henry, composing his features into an expression that fell well short of true compassion. 'I mourn Sir Martin deeply. He was a good man.'

'I never heard you say a kind word about him.'

'In death, I appreciate his many virtues.'

'What use is that?'

'I grieve with his wife, Christopher,' said Henry. 'She's too young and fragile to be a widow. My heart goes out to her.'

'Your heart is always going out to one woman or another.'

'This one is different.'

'That could be your motto,' said Christopher harshly. 'Have it translated into Latin and set beneath a coat of arms. On second thoughts, let the motto be in French for that's more suited to blighted romance.'

'You mock me unjustly.'

'Then do not lay yourself open to mockery. You are ever your worst enemy, Henry. Father pointed out the cure. You should have married and settled down years ago.'

'I never listen to sermons from the old gentleman, whether delivered from the pulpit or from directly beside me. The simple fact is,' said Henry, soulfully, 'that I've never met a woman who could make me repent of my sins longer than a few short weeks. Until now, that is. Until I first set eyes on Araminta Jewell.'

'Her name is Lady Culthorpe.'

'But she lacks the husband who gave it to her.'

'You surely do not imagine you could take his place, do you?' said Christopher, shaken by the thought. 'Heavens above, man – Sir Martin's body is not yet cold and you are already trying to devise a way to get at his widow.'

'I love her, Christopher.'

'Well, I can assure you that your love is not requited. When I was introduced to the lady myself, she baulked at the very name of Redmayne because of the way you'd hounded her. You are the last person in the world to whom she would turn.'

'At the moment, perhaps,' Henry agreed, 'but time heals all wounds. Araminta will come to see me in a new light. With your help, I will gradually get closer to my angel.'

Christopher was acerbic. 'Count on no assistance from me,' he said, looking his brother in the eye. 'I'd sooner see her carried off by a tribe of cannibals than fall into your clutches. The woman is suffering, Henry. Do you know what that means? Common decency alone should be enough to make you stay your hand.'

'I'll keep my distance from her yet nourish my hopes.'

'You *have* no hopes.'

'I do if you intercede on my behalf.'

'I'll oppose you every inch of the way, Henry.'

'But you've not heard my request yet.'

'I'll not listen to any request made across the dead body of Sir Martin Culthorpe,' said Christopher. 'When he was alive, he could defend his wife's honour. That duty falls to people like me now.'

'You sound more and more like Father every day. Hear me out,' said Henry, silencing his brother with a gesture. 'Araminta deserves a decent interval in which she can bury her husband and mourn his passing. I accept that and undertake to stay well clear from her.'

'That's the first civilised thing you've said.'

'Meanwhile, however, there remains the question of the portrait.'

'What of it?'

'Only that Villemot is known for the speed and excellence of his work. The chances are that her portrait has already taken on enough shape for her to be recognised.'

'It has,' conceded Christopher. 'I saw it this very afternoon.'

'And?'

'It's a truly astonishing likeness.'

'I knew it!' exclaimed Henry. 'Buy it for me.'

His brother gaped. '*Buy* it?'

'Yes, Christopher – make an offer. Araminta will have no need of it now and she will certainly not want it finished. I will buy it in its present state and give it pride of place in my bedchamber. Buy it for me,' he urged. 'Villemot would never sell it to me but he would part with it to a friend like you. Purchase it on my behalf.'

'That's a disgusting idea, Henry.'

'Do you not want to make me the happiest of men?'

'I prefer to save Lady Culthorpe from being ogled by my brother. How could you even think of such a thing?'

'It's an important first step in getting closer to Araminta.'

'Then I'll advise Monsieur Villemot to destroy the portrait. It must never be in your possession,' said Christopher, thinking of the powerful effect that it had had on him when he had peeped at it. 'By rights, the decision about its future lies with Lady Culthorpe. My feeling is that she may well want it burned.'

'I'll not see Araminta go up in flames,' wailed Henry. 'Let the portrait go to someone who will cherish it. Let me feast my eyes on her day after wonderful day.'

'No, Henry – that would only feed your lust. Apart from anything else, you have no money to buy such a painting. Even in its present form, it would be expensive. How would you raise the capital?'

'I was hoping that you might help me there, Christopher.'

'Me?'

'Never forget that it was I who introduced you to your first client and set you off on your glittering career.'

'I accept that and have repeatedly expressed my gratitude.'

'Do so in a more pecuniary way.'

'I've loaned you money time and again, Henry.'

'And I mean to repay it,' said the other, indignantly. 'You know that you can rely on your brother. One good night at the card table and I can discharge all my debts to you – including the money you lend me to buy that portrait.' Henry brightened.

'I'd be able to refund that when I win the wager.'

'What wager?'

'The one that I've made with three like-minded friends of mine.'

His brother was sickened. 'If they are like-minded, they must be seasoned voluptuaries in the mould of Henry Redmayne. That being the case,' he said with repugnance, 'this wager will doubtless pertain to the very person whom we've been discussing. True or false?'

'True, Christopher.'

'Then you are even more mired in corruption than I feared. Not content with harbouring designs on the lady's virtue, you place bets upon the outcome with your fellow rakehells.' Crossing to the door, he pulled it wide open. 'I'd like you to leave now, please.'

Henry was wounded. 'There'll be no loan?'

'Not a brass farthing.'

'What about the portrait?'

'To keep it away from you,' said Christopher with determination in his eyes, 'I'd be prepared to stand guard over it day and night with a loaded musket.'

'A regiment of soldiers would not be able to ensure its safety,' boasted Henry, taking up the challenge. 'I spurn you, Christopher Redmayne. Instead of a brother, I have a mealy mouthed parson.'

'I only seek to save you from your own wickedness.'

'Here endeth the lesson!' taunted Henry.

'You would do well to mark it.'

'I prefer to enjoy my time on this earth.'

'Yes,' said Christopher, sadly. 'I've seen the trail of victims you leave behind you after you've enjoyed them and I'm resolved that Lady Culthorpe will not be the next one.'

Henry was outraged. 'Araminta is not my victim!' he roared. 'She is my salvation. Until I can make her mine, I'll have that portrait of her on my wall. Mark *this* lesson, if you will,' he

THE PAINTED LADY   67

continued, arm aloft. 'The portrait belongs to me. It's destined to hang in my house and woe betide anyone who tries to stop me from getting it.'

Storming out, he left the air charged with his passion.

Word of the crime provoked a varied response among members of the Society. When three of them met at a tavern that evening, it was only Elkannah Prout who showed any real compassion.

'The wager must be cancelled,' he said. 'It's unsporting – like hunting an animal that is already badly wounded.'

'I concur,' said Sir Willard Grail. 'She needs time a long time to recover – months, at the very least.'

'I think we should call off the chase altogether.'

'Oh, I don't agree with that, Elkannah.'

'We should forget all about our wager.'

'You were the one who advocated the creation of the Society for the Capture of Araminta's Maidenhood. You cannot back out now.'

'Her maidenhood has been surrendered, Sir Willard.'

'A mere detail.'

'And so has our *raison d'etre*.' Prout was decisive. 'The game is not worth the candle,' he said. 'We had the excitement of pursuing the lady hotfoot but we must now let her go free. I'm sure that Jocelyn agrees with me.'

Jocelyn Kidbrooke had made no contribution to the debate thus far but he had not missed a single word of it. Toying with his wine glass, he gave his opinion.

'I do not agree with either of you,' he said, bluntly.

'You must take one side or the other,' argued Prout.

'No, Elkannah. You call for the whole project to be abandoned. Have we come so far and invested so much to back out now? That would be madness and I'll not hear of it.'

'Then you must take my part,' said Sir Willard.

'Hold off our assault for months on end? That's ludicrous.'

'It's seemly, Jocelyn.'

'And that's precisely what I have against it,' said Kidbrooke, slapping the table with a flabby hand for emphasis. 'Since when have we espoused seemliness and respectability? They are the sworn enemies of real pleasure. You may have been converted to propriety, Sir Willard, but I have not – nor, I dare venture, has Henry. He and I will think alike. The race is still on.'

Prout blenched. 'You'd allow Araminta *no* period of grace?'

'A week is more than adequate. That will give her time to bury her husband and embrace the notion of widowhood.'

'She needs to mourn, Jocelyn.'

'What she needs is solace,' Kidbrooke declared, 'and I intend to offer it to her. If the two of you prefer to stand aside out of a false sense of sympathy, you leave the field clear for Henry and me.'

'So be it,' said Prout. 'I resign from the Society. I'll happily forfeit my stake in the enterprise.'

'Well, I'll not do so,' said Sir Willard, forcefully. 'I've put in too much money to quit the contest now. Jocelyn is right. What place has morality in the deflowering of a virgin? We do but follow the natural impulse of our sex.'

'Araminta is no longer what she was when I devised the Society and you would do well to bear it in mind, Sir Willard. A virgin cannot be deflowered twice. Sir Martin Culthorpe has already performed the office that we all aspired to.'

'We do not know that,' said Kidbrooke.

'Of course, we do. They were married for weeks.'

'Some wives have been married for years before they discovered the delights of the flesh. Some husbands simply do not know what they are about in the bedchamber. Culthorpe may be one of them.'

'Who could possibly resist Araminta?' asked Prout.

'A husband who respected her too much,' said Kidbrooke. 'A man who led a celibate and God-fearing life for over forty years before he even thought about marriage – in short, Sir Martin Culthorpe. I doubt if they even shared a bed on their wedding night and, if they did, it was surely occupied by two virgins. That's what irks me most,' he added through gritted teeth. 'Culthorpe had that jewel of womanhood in his grasp yet he had no idea what to do with her.'

'Jocelyn makes a telling point,' said Sir Willard, his interest renewed. 'Araminta may still be untouched.'

'I'm certain of it. She still has that wondrous bloom on her.'

'You've *seen* her?'

'Only from a distance.'

'When?'

'Recently.'

'Where?'

'That's my business,' said Kidbrooke, evasively. 'The point is this. One of us may still be able to fulfil the original aim of the Society. Now that good fortune has removed her odious husband, Araminta is there for the taking, gentlemen.'

'Not by me,' said Prout.

'What about you, Sir Willard?'

'All my senses have been revived,' said the other with a wolfish grin. 'So beautiful yet still a maid? No husband left to safeguard her? The lure is irresistible. I'm with you, Jocelyn. I begin to drool already. Araminta is fair game.'

Jean-Paul Villemot had worked on the portrait until fading light made him stop. He had never been so inspired by any woman who had sat for him before. Araminta Culthorpe was a positive gift to an artist. He set up candles around his easel so that she remained in view as the paint slowly dried. Long into the evening, he kept returning to look at her, relishing her beauty afresh on each occasion as if seeing it for the first time. As he watched, he drank wine and it made him increasingly maudlin. When he had emptied one bottle, he opened another. He went back to the portrait again and lifted his glass in honour to Lady Culthorpe before taking another sip of wine.

Villemot set the glass aside. Taking hold of the painting with both hands, he brought it gently towards him until it was only inches from his face. His face was aglow, his eyes moist.

'*Ma cherie*!' he sighed.

Chapter Four

Jonathan Bale looked after his parish with an almost paternal care. Whenever a serious crime was committed on what he saw as his territory, he took it as a personal affront and bent all his energies to solving it. He hated to see Baynard's Castle Ward soiled in any way but even he could not keep pace with the petty theft, drunkenness, domestic violence, prostitution, fraud and tavern brawls that were regular events there. Bale was fettered by mathematics. There were too many villains and too few constables.

While one pickpocket was being arrested, others were plying their trade nearby. If he felt obliged to part one angry husband and wife, Bale knew that other married couples would be having similar squabbles behind closed doors. He could not be everywhere at the same time but he liked to think that his presence had some impact. The local inhabitants admired and respected him. Because he had won their trust, they were much more likely to report incidents to Bale than to any other constable. Some of the others who patrolled the streets were too old, too wayward or too inept to be of much use to anyone. They lacked Bale's fierce civic pride and commitment. None of them – Tom Warburton, especially – had his stamina.

'I'm thirsty, Jonathan,' he said.

'You always are at this time of the day, Tom.'

'I think I'll step into the Blue Dolphin.'

'Off you go,' said Bale, tolerantly. 'You know where to find me.'

'I won't tarry.'

Warburton hurried across the road to the tavern with his dog bounding along beside him. He was a tall, stringy, humourless man in his forties with a tendency to try to beat confessions out of supposed malefactors. In an affray, Warburton was a good man to have at one's side but he was far too reckless at times and Bale had often had to restrain him, reminding him that they were appointed to quell violence and not to initiate it. Bale did not mind being left alone. It gave him the opportunity to meet up with an old friend.

Following his established route, he went round the next corner and strode briskly along the street until he came to a large gap between two tall new houses. Under the supervision of their employer, workmen were busy digging on the plot of land.

'Good morning, Mr Littlejohn,' greeted the constable.

'Mr Bale!' rejoined the builder, turning to see him. 'I was hoping that I might bump into you now that I'm back in your ward.'

Bale sized him up. 'You've put on weight.'

'Blame my wife for that. She feeds me too well.'

'You are keeping busy, I hope.'

'Busier than ever, my friend.'

The two men had been brought together when Christopher Redmayne had designed his first house. Since it was being built in Baynard's Castle Ward, the constable noticed it when out on his rounds but he paid it no attention. It was simply one more house, rising out of the ashes. Dozens of others were being constructed in every street. The situation soon changed. When the murder had occurred on the site of the new house, Bale was drawn into the investigation and had therefore met Samuel Littlejohn. They had got on well together and their paths had crossed a few times since then.

'I hear that we are partners,' said Littlejohn, genially.

'Partners?'

'According to Mr Redmayne, you built a model for this house.'

'I tried to,' said Bale, unassumingly.

'I'm told it was very good. If the architect and the client approved of it, it must have been. Mr Redmayne promised to show it to me when he gets it back from Mr Villemot.'

'I hope you like it, Mr Littlejohn.'

The builder grinned. 'If I do, I might be offering you a job as a carpenter. Have you never thought of taking up your old trade?'

'Never – I'm happy watching over the streets here.'

'You'd earn a tidy wage from me.'

'But I'd have to give up being a constable.'

'Do you like the work that much?'

Bale shrugged. 'It suits me, Mr Littlejohn.'

'Then I'll not try to entice you away.' He glanced around. 'Things seem to be quite peaceful in this part of the city.'

'Wait till this evening when the taverns start to fill up.'

'Do you have a lot of trouble?'

'Anyone who works near the river has trouble,' explained Bale. 'This part of the district is safe enough but there are some tough characters along Thames Street. Sailors, fishermen and those who work in the docks seem to need a good fight at least once a week. What's even worse,' he added, scornfully, 'is that they also need the company of loose women.'

Littlejohn was broad-minded. 'We might feel the same urges if we'd been away at sea for months on end.'

'Speak for yourself, sir.'

'I'm not condoning it, Mr Bale, just trying to understand it.'

'It's against the law and a sin before God.'

'When enough drink is taken,' said the builder, 'people seem to forget all about God. My men certainly do. Because they work hard, they expect to drink hard. Try to preach a sermon at them when they've downed their beer and you'd hear language that would burn your ears off.'

Bale seized his cue. 'Drinking, whoring, fighting, cursing – it's all one, Mr Littlejohn,' he said, sternly. 'It's part of the penalty we pay for having a dissolute King who revels in every vice of the city, and courtiers who fornicate openly and try to drag everyone down to their own bestial level.'

'Things are not as bad as that.'

'I see it happening every day. Corruption starts at the top and trickles down. In the last ten years, London has become a sink of iniquity. It was never like this under the Lord Protector.'

'You may be right,' said Littlejohn, tactfully suppressing his monarchist sympathies in the interests of friendship. 'I leave crime and corruption to you, Mr Bale. All that I can do is to help rebuild this city to its former glory.' His cheeks glowed with pride. 'They say that Paris is more beautiful, Madrid more ornate, and Venice finer than both. But, to me, London is better than all three and always will be.'

'I'd say the same, Mr Littlejohn. For all its faults, there's no place on earth like this city. Well,' said Bale, looking at the plot beside them, 'that's why so many foreigners come to live here.'

'Jean-Paul Villemot among them.'

'Have you met the gentleman?'

'Not yet.'

'Mr Redmayne has nothing but good to say of him.'

'Then I'm content. Mr Redmayne is a good judge of character.' He gave a hearty laugh. 'He must be if he chose the both of us.'

'Oh, I did very little,' said Bale.

'You built the house in miniature and won the client over. That's half the battle in this trade. All we have to do is to turn your wooden model into a splendid brick house that will make Mr Villemot glad he decided to move from Paris to London.'

* * *

Christopher Redmayne was working in his study when he had an unexpected visitor. It was his servant, Jacob, still spry in spite of his advanced age, who gave his master the warning.

'The French gentleman is coming to see you, sir.'

Christopher was surprised. 'Monsieur Villemot?'

'Yes, Mr Redmayne.'

'Are you, sure, Jacob?'

'I saw him through the window,' said the old man, 'so I sent the lad out to take care of his horse.'

When he had first moved into the house in Fetter Lane, Christopher had only employed one servant, responsible for everything in the house. Now that he had made his mark in his profession, the architect had taken on a youth to do the more menial tasks. It spared Jacob a lot of work and gave him someone he could instruct, cajole and generally order about.

'You'd better show Monsieur Villemot in,' said Christopher.

'I will, sir.'

Jacob went out to invite the Frenchman into the house, guiding him to the study before fading out of sight. Christopher offered his hand to his visitor but Villemot wanted a more demonstrative greeting. Embracing the other as if he had just discovered a long-lost friend, he kissed him on both cheeks. He was extravagantly contrite.

'Have you forgiven me, Christopher?' he asked.

'For what?'

'The way I behave to you yesterday.'

'There's nothing to forgive,' said Christopher.

'I was in the bad mood and I spoke with anger.'

'That's not true at all.'

'It is,' said Villemot. 'I raise my voice. I am ashamed.'

'The whole matter is best forgotten,' said Christopher with a smile of pardon. 'I certainly won't let it come between us. We all have bad moods from time to time.'

'I am better now, Christopher. It will not happen again.'

'Thank you.'

'But that is not the only reason I come here today,' said the other, his face darkening. 'You have heard the awful news?'

'Yes, my brother told me.'

'How did he know?'

'Henry has a way of finding out these things,' said Christopher.

'I was only told yesterday evening,' said Villemot. 'It made me so sad. I liked Sir Martin. He was a good man – and a very lucky one to be married to Araminta – to Lady Culthorpe.' He hunched his shoulders in despair. 'It is the tragedy, Christopher.'

'I know. I feel so sorry for his wife.'

'Who could do such a thing?'

'I hope that we soon find out. But I'd hate you to think that this is what usually happens in London, because it does not. Most of us are perfectly safe in our own homes,' said Christopher, 'especially in the part of Westminster where Sir Martin lived. Aristocrats and politicians inhabit that area. There's comparatively little crime.'

'This is more than a crime,' said Villemot. 'It is the calamity.'

'I agree.'

'That's why I need your advice.'

'Advice?'

'About what to do, Christopher,' he explained. 'I do not know the rules in this country. I know what I *want* to do but it may not be the right thing. I would like to go to the house to tell Lady Culthorpe that I have the great sympathy.'

'That might not be wise,' cautioned Christopher.

'I want her to know that she can call on me for any help.'

'Lots of people will feel the same, Monsieur Villemot, but I don't think that Lady Culthorpe would want anyone to intrude on her grief. She's probably still dazed by what's happened. It would be a kindness to leave her alone until she has recovered from the shock.'

'But there is the portrait to think about.'

'It won't even enter her mind, I fear. You may have to accept the inevitable. The portrait will never be completed.'

'Yes, it will,' asserted Villemot with a flash of spirit. 'I will finish it as a matter of honour.'

'Lady Culthorpe will certainly not be able to sit for you again.'

'Her husband paid me handsomely for the painting of his wife. Jean-Paul Villemot, he does not let the customer down.'

'But the commission has been revoked by his death.'

'I do not agree.'

'You can hardly complete the portrait without Lady Culthorpe's permission,' said Christopher, worriedly. 'In the circumstances, she may want it destroyed.'

'Never!' cried Villemot. 'I'll not allow it.'

'Strictly speaking, the portrait belongs to her.'

'It belongs to me, as the artist, until I am ready to hand it over. If Lady Culthorpe, she no longer wants it, I will give her back the money that her husband paid me.'

'I don't think that would be necessary.'

'It is necessary for *me*, Christopher,' insisted the other. 'I have the conscience. I could not keep the fee I did not earn.'

'But you *have* earned it. If you complete the portrait, you'll have done exactly what Sir Martin asked of you.'

'I do not see it that way.'

'Ultimately,' said Christopher, 'the decision lies with Lady Culthorpe and she won't be in a position to make it for a long while. I hope that the portrait will be kept safe in the meantime.'

'I would guard it with my life – so would Emile.'

'We don't want it to fall into the wrong hands.'

'The wrong hands?'

'Yes,' said Christopher with his brother in mind. 'Lady Culthorpe is a very beautiful woman. If it were known that a famous artist had painted her portrait, there might be any number of her admirers who would like to acquire it.' He remembered Henry's plea for a loan. 'They might even try to buy it from you.'

'It is not for sale.'

'What if you were offered a large amount of money?'

'I would throw it back in the face of the man who holds it out to me,' snapped Villemot. 'No money on earth could buy that portrait from me. Araminta – Lady Culthorpe – will be treasured.'

'I'm relieved to hear you say it.'

'Why is that, Christopher?'

'Lady Culthorpe may not want it herself,' said the architect, 'but she would be very distressed if it went astray. Beauty like that will not have gone unnoticed. She will have had many suitors and was only able to shake them off by getting married. Now that Sir Martin is no longer able to shield her,' he went on, 'there may be some who are unscrupulous enough to try to take advantage of her.'

'I'll not allow it!' howled the artist. 'I'll protect Araminta.'

'You'd help her best by protecting that portrait of her.'

Villemot snatched his dagger from its sheath. 'I'd kill the man who tried to take it from me!' he threatened, brandishing the weapon. 'I'd cut him into shreds.'

There was a long, uncomfortable, embarrassed silence. Villemot was shamefaced at his outburst and Christopher was startled by his visitor's explosive rage. The dagger glinted in the light from the window. Before the Frenchman could put it back in its sheath, there was a thunderous knocking at the front door.

'See who that is, please, Jacob!' called Christopher.

'I'm on my way, sir,' replied the servant from the passageway.

'Thank you.' He looked at the dagger. 'I suggest that you put that away, Monsieur Villemot.'

'Yes, yes, of course,' said the other, sheathing the weapon. 'I did not mean to pull it out like that, Christopher.'

But the architect was not listening to him. His attention was diverted by the sound of raised voices at the front door. Shortly afterwards, Jacob put his head into the room and licked his lips nervously before speaking.

'There are two officers at the door, sir,' he said.

'What do they want?' asked Christopher.

'They say that they have a warrant for the arrest of...' Jacob looked with dismay at Villemot.

Christopher was mystified. 'On what possible grounds?'

'The murder of Sir Martin Culthorpe.'

'But that is ludicrous!'

'I did not kill him!' said Villemot, trembling.

'Shall I show them in, Mr Redmayne?' asked the servant.

'No, Jacob. I want to see this so-called warrant for myself.'

Gesturing for Villemot to stay where he was, Christopher went out of the room and marched purposefully down the passageway to the front door. Two burly men in uniform stood on the threshold.

'My name is Christopher Redmayne, gentleman,' he said, 'and I own this house. May I help you?'

'Yes, sir,' said the older of the two men, gruffly. 'We are given to believe that Jean-Paul Villemot might be here.'

'He called on me to discuss business.'

'So his valet told us.'

'What's this nonsense about a warrant of arrest?'

The man was offended. 'It's not nonsense, Mr Redmayne,' he said, pulling a scroll from his pocket and unrolling it for Christopher to see. 'Read it for yourself. He's being arrested for stabbing Sir Martin Culthorpe to death yesterday afternoon.'

'That's preposterous! Monsieur Villemot is no killer.'

'Let the court decide that, sir.'

'Sir Martin was employing him. Why on earth should he murder a client who had paid him a large fee? It does not make sense.'

'The only thing that makes sense to us is a name on a warrant. We'll have to ask you to stand aside so that we can take the gentleman into custody.'

'Where will he be held?'

'That's for the magistrate to determine.'

'There's been a grotesque mistake here,' protested Christopher.

'Mr Villemot is the person who made it,' said the man, grimly. 'Now, will you invite us in or do we have to force an entry?'

Christopher stepped back. 'No force will be needed,' he said. 'You can come in.' The officers walked quickly past him. 'It's the last door on the right.'

'Thank you, sir.'

The two men went along the passageway and into the study. Christopher was about to follow them when the older man rounded on him angrily.

'Is this some kind of jest, sir?'

'What do you mean?'

'There's nobody here.'

'There must be,' said Christopher, easing him aside so that he could go into the study. 'This is where I left him.'

Jean-Paul Villemot was not in the study now. Since there was only one door, his method of departure was clear. He had lifted the window and fled. Christopher's stomach heaved. He felt compromised. The older of the two officers nudged his companion.

'After him, Peter,' he ordered. 'Search the garden.'

Peter did not stand on ceremony. Cocking a leg over the windowsill, he pulled the other behind him and trotted down the garden, looking in all directions for the fugitive. Until that moment, Christopher could not believe that Villemot had had anything to do with Sir Martin Culthorpe's death, but his sudden flight was hardly the action of an innocent man. And Christopher was well aware that the Frenchman possessed a dagger.

'You'll have to come with us,' said the officer, taking him roughly by the arm. 'I'm placing you under arrest.'

Christopher was scandalised. 'But I've done nothing wrong!'

'You helped a wanted man to get away from us.'

'That's ridiculous.'

'Yes, you did,' said the man, tightening his grip. 'You kept us

THE PAINTED LADY   81

talking at the door so that he'd have time to climb out of that
window. That's what I'd call aiding and abetting an escape.'

'But I didn't know that he was *going* to escape.'

'Tell that to the magistrate, sir.'

'I know my rights,' yelled Christopher. 'Let go of me.'

'Not until we have you safely locked up, Mr Redmayne. You
obstructed two officers in the execution of their duty.'

'That's an absurd accusation!'

'Yes, you did,' said the man, officiously, 'and the law does not
take kindly to that. You may have saved your friend for a little
while but it will cost you a spell in prison.'

Christopher reeled as if from a blow. He was a criminal.

Henry Redmayne was as good as his word. Having set his heart
on acquiring the portrait of Araminta Culthorpe by whatever
means necessary, he first went to see where it was kept. The
rooms that Villemot rented were in a house in Covent Garden
within easy walking distance of Henry's own home in Bedford
Street. He sauntered past the house on the other side of the
street and gave it only a cursory glance. When he paused at the
corner, however, he turned to take a closer look at the dwelling,
noting that there was an alleyway that led to the rear. He was
still trying to assess the easiest way of getting into the house
when he felt a tap on his shoulder. He spun round to look into
the fleshy face of Jocelyn Kidbrooke.

'What are you doing here, Jocelyn?' he asked.

'I happened to be passing,' said Kidbrooke, blandly.

'You live over a mile away. You'd not come to Covent Garden
without a particular reason.'

'I have one. I came to see you, Henry.'

'Then why not call at my house?'

'Because I knew that you'd come here sooner or later,' said
Kidbrooke. 'You found out where Villemot has his studio
because you know that there's a portrait of Araminta inside.'

'You misjudge me.'

'I know you too well to do that. You want that portrait. I waited to see how long it would be before you came in search of it. If you're thinking of trying to purchase it, save your breath.'

'Why?' Henry was alarmed. 'You've not bought it already?'

'I made a generous offer for it.'

'Damn you, Jocelyn!'

'This is a contest – each man for himself.'

'Does that mean you *have* the painting?'

'Alas, no,' admitted Kidbrooke, sorrowfully. 'My offer was refused. I didn't speak to Villemot himself – he was out at the time. His valet assured me, however, that his master would not part with the portrait of Araminta for a king's ransom.'

'What did you say to that?'

'I thanked the fellow politely and withdrew.'

'But you did gain access to the house?'

'That's my business.'

'It's mine as well,' said Henry, irritably, 'so do not hold out on me. Where are his rooms – upstairs or downstairs? And which one is his studio? That's what I'd really like to know.'

Kidbrooke was smug. 'Then you'll have to find out for yourself.'

'I thought that we were friends.'

'Not when there's a lady in the case.'

'We must all compete on equal terms, Jocelyn.'

'That's rich, coming from you,' said the other with a derisive laugh. 'I've never met anyone so ready to gain an advantage over his rivals. You'd stop at nothing, Henry. I'll wager that you've already asked your brother to secure that portrait for you by trading on his friendship with the artist.'

'That's a vile accusation,' said Henry, counterfeiting righteous anger. 'Christopher has no part in this venture and I would never even think of involving him.'

'In other words, he rebuffed your entreaty.'

'There *was* no entreaty.'

'You sneaked off to see him without telling us.'

'I've not seen my brother for weeks,' lied Henry, tossing his head and making his periwig flap. 'As for sneaking off, Jocelyn, you are the one who did that. You agreed to dine with us at Locket's yesterday but you never turned up.'

'I had business elsewhere,' said Kidbrooke.

'Yes – you were pursuing Araminta, I dare swear, while the rest if us were eating our meal.'

'My wife requested me to dine with her.'

'Since when have you ever listened to your wife?'

'We had things to discuss.'

'The only wife in whom you have any interest is the one who was married to Sir Martin Culthorpe,' said Henry. 'I think you went spying on her again through that telescope that you bought.'

Kidbrooke shifted his feet uneasily. 'Arrant nonsense!'

'Then where were you?'

'At home with my wife.'

'I'm surprised that you remember where your house is,' said Henry with heavy sarcasm. 'You spend so little time there that you probably wouldn't recognise your wife if she stood only inches away from you. Can you even recall her name?'

'Cease this railing!'

'No? I thought not. Araminta has eclipsed her completely.'

'That's enough!' shouted Kidbrooke.

He looked as if he was about to strike Henry but the blow never came. Instead, both men were diverted by the sound of someone ringing a bell and pounding on a door. They looked down the street to see two officers, standing outside the house where Jean-Paul Villemot lived and worked. Henry's eyebrows arched inquisitively.

'What's going on here, I wonder?' he said.

Christopher Redmayne had never been so overjoyed to see his friend. Hauled before a magistrate, he had then been summarily locked in Newgate, kept in a noisome cell with a group of desperate prisoners and denied any right of appeal. It was only because he was able to bribe one of the turnkeys that his message was duly delivered. A couple of hours later, to his intense relief, he peered through the bars and saw Jonathan Bale being conducted down the stairs by the prison sergeant. Christopher could not believe his good fortune when the cell door was unlocked so that he could step through it. With the jeers of the other prisoners ringing in his ears, he walked away with Bale.

'What happened?' asked Christopher.

'I spoke to the magistrate,' replied Bale, 'and told him that it had all been a misunderstanding. I vouched for you, Mr Redmayne. Since the magistrate knows me well, he agreed to release you, pending further investigation.'

'There's nothing to investigate, Jonathan. I'm innocent.'

'I know that, sir. I spoke to Jacob.'

Christopher was taken aback. 'You went to my house?'

'Yes, sir,' said the other. 'I needed to hear all the facts.'

'Well, I can't tell you how grateful I am to you. I knew what a cesspool Newgate was because I visited my brother when he was held here, but I was on the right side of the bars then. When you're locked up with those bickering ragamuffins,' said Christopher, shuddering at the memory of what he had endured, 'it's like being in the seventh circle of hell. I don't know which was worse, the stench, the noise or the random violence.'

'Let's get you out of here where we can talk properly.'

Christopher had to go through the formalities of being signed out by the prison sergeant then taken through a series of doors. When he was finally allowed to leave the prison altogether, light rain was falling but it nevertheless seemed like a glorious spring day to him. Having lost it for two intolerable hours, he found that freedom was a heady experience. As they were standing near one of the main gates into the city, they were caught up in swirling traffic but Christopher didn't mind in the least. He had been liberated.

They slipped into one of the first taverns they came to and found a table in a quiet corner. Unlike Tom Warburton, Bale did not as a rule drink on duty, but he accepted the offer of a tankard of beer on this occasion. Christopher treated himself to a cup of Canary wine. Bale sampled the beer.

'Strong stuff,' he opined, 'but not as good as the beer that my wife makes. Sarah has a real gift as a brewer.'

'I know, I've tasted her beer.' Christopher sipped his wine. 'That tastes like nectar,' he said. 'All they served in prison was black, brackish water. It made me feel sick just to look at it.'

'Let's make sure that you don't have to go into Newgate again, sir, nor into any other gaol.'

'How do we do that, Jonathan?'

'The first thing we have to do is to find Mr Villemot,' said Bale. 'It was him that got you into this trouble. If you were to be involved in catching him, it would stand you in good stead with the magistrate.'

'There must be officers already out looking for him.'

'But they don't know him, sir – you do. You'll have a much better idea of where he's gone to ground.'

'I'm not sure about that,' confessed Christopher. 'Besides, I'm not at all convinced that Monsieur Villemot had anything to do with the murder. What could he possibly hope to gain by killing Sir Martin Culthorpe?'

'That's not the way to look at it, Mr Redmayne.'

'Why not?'

'Innocent or guilty,' said Bale, solemnly, 'the gentleman avoided arrest by taking to his heels. That's a crime in itself and he'll have to answer for it. The longer he's on the loose, the worse it is for him.'

'I suppose so.'

'The only place where the truth will come out is in court.'

Christopher was rueful. 'I beg leave to doubt that,' he said. 'Nobody showed much interest in the truth when I was arrested. The magistrate had the nerve to call me deceitful.'

'Be that as it may, sir, Mr Villemot must be found.'

'Oh, I agree, Jonathan. We need this whole matter sorted out as quickly as possible or a lot of people are going to be hurt.'

Bale frowned. 'A lot of people?'

'Yes,' said Christopher, 'and you're one of them. Do you want to spend all that time making a model of house that will never be built? I certainly don't want to design one that stays on a piece of paper. If Monsieur Villemot is convicted, we all stand to lose – you, me and Sam Littlejohn, not to mention all his men.' Christopher shook his head in dismay. 'Because it was in the French style, Sam was really looking forward to building this house.'

'I know, sir. I spoke to him this morning.'

'Did you meet him on the site?'

'Yes,' said Bale, 'he was very pleased to have got this contract. It will be a terrible shock if he suddenly loses it.'

'Then let's try to ensure that never happens.

'It's bound to, if Mr Villemot is guilty of the murder.'

'I still believe he's innocent,' said Christopher, loyally.

'Then why did he run away from the officers?'

'I've been thinking about that, Jonathan. We have to remember that he's French and, as such, viewed with suspicion by people who are unable to see beyond their own prejudices. If I were in a foreign country,' he reasoned, 'and were accused of a crime I did not commit, I fancy that my first instinct would be to do exactly what Monsieur Villemot has done. That's not to excuse it, mark you,' he emphasised. 'What he did was wrong and he must be held to account for it. Our job is to help him clear his name.'

'Only if he is innocent,' warned Bale.

'Quite so.'

'Where do we start looking, Mr Redmayne?'

'At the obvious place,' said Christopher. 'His lodgings.'

* * *

Elkannah Prout stared at him in utter disbelief. He was bemused.

'Are you *serious*, Henry?'

'Deadly serious.'

'You saw this happen with your own eyes?'

'I can call on a second witness,' said Henry Redmayne, 'for Jocelyn was standing beside me. Two officers banged on the door of the house then went inside. When they came out again, I asked them what was afoot and they told me they were hunting Villemot.'

'Do they really think he was the killer?'

'Yes, Elkannah.'

'But he'd have no reason to murder Sir Martin.'

'He'd have the best reason in the world,' said Henry. 'He's infatuated with Araminta.'

'He's only known her for a few days,' argued Prout.

'I only saw her for a few minutes before I was ensnared, and the same goes for the rest of us. We all saw her from afar. Think how it must have been for someone who was allowed to look upon her at close range for long periods of time. The most telling thing of all, Elkannah, is that Villemot is a Frenchman.'

'So?'

'He comes from a nation of uncontrollable lechers.'

Prout blinked. 'You think this crime was driven by lust, then?'

'The only way he could possess her is by getting rid of her husband,' said Henry. 'That's another aspect of the French. They are prone to impetuous action.'

They were in a coffee house in Holborn, oblivious to the stream of chatter all around them. Henry was still amazed by what he had learned, eager to accept Villemot's guilt because it served his purpose. If the artist were arrested, he would not be able to mount guard over the portrait of Araminta. The holy grail of art was suddenly within Henry's reach. Elkannah Prout seemed less ready to believe in the artist's guilt. He sipped his coffee thoughtfully.

'No,' he decided, putting down his cup, 'it would be madness. Who could possibly expect to endear himself to a woman by killing her husband? That's sheer lunacy.'

'Villemot expected to get away with it. In time, he must have hoped, Araminta would turn to him for comfort and wed him.'

'But the fellow is already married.'

'So is Jocelyn,' said Henry, 'but that hasn't stopped him from having wild thoughts about a future with Araminta. The same goes for Sir Willard. It was less than two years ago that we attended his wedding yet he already behaves as if the ceremony never took place.'

'My only interest at the moment is in Villemot.'

'So is mine, Elkannah.'

'How could he imagine that he would escape detection?'

'The French are a peculiar breed.'

'Even they do not think they can murder at will, Henry.'

'A warrant is out for his arrest, that's all I know. Unless there was strong evidence against him, he would not be being pursued with such vigour. The law does not often make mistakes.'

Prout smiled. 'I wonder that *you* should say that.'

'Why?'

'Because you were once wrongfully arrested and imprisoned.'

'Do not remind me,' said Henry with a shiver. 'There's no more harmless creature on this planet than me, yet I was accused of foul murder. But for my brother, I'd have been hanged for the crime.'

'I was just thinking about your brother.'

'What put Christopher into your mind?'

'Has he not designed a new house for the artist?'

'Indeed, he has,' said Henry, snapping his fingers. 'I'd forgotten that. It was a lucrative commission. Poor Christopher! When his client is convicted, my brother will lose a large amount of money.'

* * *

'You must be able to tell us *something*,' said Christopher, urgently. 'We're trying to help your master, Emile, but we can't do that unless we can find him.'

The valet looked beleaguered. 'I know nothing.'

'What did you tell the two officers?'

'It's a crime to hold back information,' warned Bale. 'It may be different in your country but, in England, you have to tell the truth to any law officers. Do you understand?

'I'm sure that he does, Jonathan. Don't frighten him with veiled threats or we won't get a single word out of him.'

They were in Villemot's studio and the visitors were attempting to question Emile. It was proving difficult and not only because his grasp of English was uncertain. The valet was frightened. For the second time that morning, two officers had come to the house to demand to know the whereabouts of his master. In their wake, two more people wanted to interrogate him. Clemence was equally scared. Sensing danger, she stood on the chair with her back arched and her fur bristling. She took particular exception to Bale and hissed every time that the constable looked in her direction.

Christopher had seen the studio before but it was a revelation to his companion. Its combination of striking art and spectacular disarray was almost overwhelming for Bale, and he did not like the atmosphere of the place. The sense of excess repelled him. Nor did the little French valet reassure him. Neat, smart and wholesome he might be, but there was something about Emile that worried Bale. What puzzled him was that he could not work out what it was.

'Let's try again,' said Christopher, patiently. 'Do you believe that your master has committed this crime, Emile?'

'*Non!*' The answer was decisive.

'Has he ever been in trouble before?'

'*Non!*' replied Emile, hurt by the suggestion.

'So why did they want to arrest him?' The valet looked blank.

'We won't leave until you tell us,' said Christopher. 'What did those officers say when they first called?'

'They look for Monsieur Villemot,' said Emile.

'But why? They must have had cause to do so.'

'A warrant would not be issued without evidence,' said Bale. 'Did they tell you what that evidence was, sir?'

Emile shook his head. Clemence gave her loudest hiss yet.

'Where did Monsieur Villemot go?' asked Christopher. 'When I called to see him yesterday afternoon, he was not here. Where was he, Emile?'

'He went out for the ride,' said the other.

'Where?'

'I do not know.'

'How long was he gone?'

'A long time, Monsieur Redmayne.'

'An hour – two, perhaps?'

'Two, I think.'

'So he was away from this house when the crime took place?' After a pause, Emile gave an affirmative nod. 'I saw him when he came back,' Christopher continued, 'and he was very disturbed. He was perspiring and he looked ill. Also, the sleeve of his coat was torn.'

'I mended that,' said the valet, promptly.

'Did *you* think he was in a strange mood?'

'I work for Monsieur Villemot. His moods are not strange to me.'

'Is he often in that state?'

'There's only one reason that would have brought those officers here,' said Bale, 'and that was evidence from a witness. Sir Martin Culthorpe lived in Westminster, Emile. Was your master seen in the vicinity of his house yesterday?'

The valet bit his lip. 'Yes,' he conceded.

'Do you know why he went there?'

'No.'

'How many years have you worked for him?'

'Three.'

'Then you must have got to know him very well in that time. If you work so closely together, he'd trust and confide in you.' Bale took a step closer to him. 'What did he tell you yesterday afternoon when he got back?'

'Nothing.'

'What did he do?'

Emile glanced at the easel. 'He worked on the portrait.'

'The one of Lady Culthorpe?'

'Yes. He painted until it got too dark.'

'That does not sound like the behaviour of a man who had just killed someone,' said Christopher, trying to win Emile's confidence. 'He would have been much more likely to disappear. Instead, he came back here to get on with his work. Is that correct?'

'It is, Monsieur Redmayne.'

'When your master spoke to me earlier, he told me that he first heard about Sir Martin's death yesterday evening.'

'Is true,' said Emile. 'A servant came from the house. He tell us Lady Culthorpe will not be here again.'

'How did Monsieur Villemot react?'

'He was upset.'

'I'm sure he was. Listen, Emile,' said Christopher, gently, 'we are very anxious to help your master. Can you give us any idea where he might be?'

'*Non.*'

'Does he have friends in London?'

'Yes – many friends.'

'Anyone in particular?' There was a long pause before Emile shook his head. 'I think there and you do Monsieur Villemot no favours by keeping the name from us. Where would he go, Emile? Who could he rely on to hide him?'

Emile backed away slightly, wrestling with his conscience. He was in a quandary. Wanting to protect his master, he knew that fleeing the law might look like a confirmation of guilt. Unless his name was cleared, Jean-Paul Villemot would be hunted all over London. If anyone should find him, it was preferable that it was a friend like Christopher Redmayne and not two officers, annoyed at the way that he had eluded them in Fetter Lane. Emile bit his lip again.

'I do not know where he is,' he said with unmistakable honesty.

'But you might have some idea?'

'I could be wrong, Monsieur Redmayne.'

'You know your master better than anyone,' said Christopher.

'There was a lady,' admitted Emile. 'She was his friend.'

Bale was suspicious. 'What sort of friend?'

'He was painting her portrait.'

'Who was she and where does she live?'

'Don't press him, Jonathan,' advised Christopher. 'Let him tell us in his own good time.'

'Her name was Lady Hester Lingoe,' said Emile.

'I fancy I've heard my brother mention her.' Bale shot him a knowing glance. 'Believe it or not, some of Henry's friends are quite respectable. Let's not rush to judgement on this lady.' He turned to Emile. 'What can you tell us about her?'

'They were friends, this lady and my master.'

'Go on,' encouraged Christopher.

'Is all I know. The painting is still here.'

'Could we see it, please?'

'If you wish.'

'We do, Emile. Show us the portrait of Lady Hester Lingoe.'

The valet went across to a framed portrait that stood against the wall with a cloth over it. Picking it up, he had second thoughts and hesitated. The visitors waited in silence. Emile eventually decided that there was no point in hiding something that might lead them to his master. He pulled the cloth away to reveal the nude portrait of Lady Hester Lingoe, posing as Artemis, goddess of the hunt and the moon.

Christopher gaped in wonder but Bale was so shocked that he began to splutter, turning his head away from the painting in sheer embarrassment. It was Christopher who recovered first.

'I think that we had better visit the lady,' he said.

Chapter Five

Araminta was still in a daze. Twenty-four hours after the murder of her husband, she sat in the window of her bedchamber and gazed with mingled pain and curiosity at the garden where she had found his body. In spite of all the evidence to the contrary, she could not accept that he was gone. Araminta tried to keep up her spirits by pretending that he was simply unwell and that, once treated by his physician, he would recover and return to her. She clung with pitiful desperation to a false hope even though she knew that Sir Martin's body had been taken to the coroner for examination.

Since the moment of discovery in the grotto, she had not slept a wink. Araminta had insisted on keeping a vigil. Fatigue had rounded her shoulders and made her head droop. It had also put dark rings under her eyes but she refused to yield up to sleep. She told herself that she had to be ready to welcome her husband back home again. So preoccupied was she is staring through the window that she did not hear the door open, nor see her maid slip into the room. Eleanor Ryle was carrying a wooden tray bearing food and drink. Setting it down on the table beside the bed, she came across to her mistress.

'How do you feel now, m'lady?' she enquired, gently.

'I'll be fine when Sir Martin returns.'

'The cook has made you some breakfast.'

'I want nothing.'

'But you haven't eaten a morsel since yesterday morning.'

'I'm not hungry, Eleanor.'

'You must be.'

'Take the food away, please.'

'Why don't I leave it beside the bed?' said the other, coaxingly. 'You might want to have it in a little while.'

Eleanor knew that it was unlikely. It was the fourth tray of food she had brought into the bedchamber and, like the first three she feared that it would remain untouched. She understood why. For several hours after the murder, she had lost her own appetite but the pangs of hunger had eventually overcome her resistance. Eleanor knelt solicitously beside her mistress.

'You need some sleep, m'lady,' she said.

'I'm not tired.'

'You must be.'

'No, Eleanor.'

'At least, lie down on the bed,' the maid recommended. 'Then you can have a proper rest.'

'I don't want a rest.'

'You can't sit in that chair all the time. You're exhausted.'

'Just leave me be.'

'But I hate to see you in this state, m'lady.'

'There's nothing wrong with me.'

'You're punishing yourself in vain.'

'I have to wait for my husband. He'd expect it of me.'

'But he's not coming back,' said Eleanor, softly.

Araminta looked at her properly for the first time. She was fond of Eleanor. They had been together for years and she had come to place great trust in the maid. Eleanor was capable, obedient and loyal. She had devoted herself to the service of her mistress, sharing her woes and celebrating her moments of joy. When she had told them of her marriage to Sir Martin Culthorpe, some of Araminta's friends believed that she had made a gross mistake she would soon regret. Their reaction had disturbed her. It was Eleanor who had comforted her, assuring her that she had made the right decision and telling her that she had never seen her mistress so happy. It had brought Araminta and her maid even closer together.

'What did you say, Eleanor?'

'It's wrong to pretend that it never happened, m'lady.'

'I'm not pretending.'

'You are,' whispered the maid. 'Sir Martin is dead and you know it. He was murdered in the garden. You found his body.'

Araminta was befuddled. 'Did I?'

'Don't you remember? The doctor came to verify the cause of death, then he spoke to you. He said that you must rest. He offered to give you something to help you sleep but you refused to take it.'

'Is this true?'

'Yes, m'lady.'

'When did this all happen?'

'Yesterday afternoon.'

'My husband is dead?'

'They took his body away,' explained Eleanor. 'There's no point in sitting here like this because he will never come back.' Araminta was still not persuaded. 'There are lots of things to do, m'lady. There are so many people to be told – friends and relations. There are funeral arrangements to discuss. None of these things can be done if you just sit there in the window all the time.'

Araminta gave a pale smile, then, as if hearing of the murder for the first time, she suddenly burst into tears. Getting to her feet, Eleanor hugged her and let her cry her fill, rocking her to and fro like a mother with a child. At length, Araminta made an effort to control herself, pulling a handkerchief from her sleeve to wipe the rivulets from her cheeks. She looked up at the maid.

'Who killed him, Eleanor?'

'Don't worry yourself about that, m'lady.'

'I want to know. Tell me.'

'Nothing is certain as yet,' said the other. 'An officer called at the house earlier today and spoke to the butler.'

'What did he say?'

'It's perhaps best if you don't know. I don't want you upset any more. Let the law deal with the killer.'

'But who is he?' demanded Araminta. 'Give me his name.'

'What use will that be?'

'It will make me understand. It will help me to fit my mind to this horror. Who was the devil who took my husband away from me?'

'They are out searching for him, m'lady.'

'Tell me his name. I can see that you know it.'

'I only know what Mr Rushton – what the butler told me. A warrant has been issued for the arrest of the man they suspect.'

'*And*?' Araminta was impatient. 'Come on, girl – speak!'

'It's the French artist, m'lady.'

'Monsieur Villemot?'

'That's what I heard.'

Araminta was aghast. Someone she considered to be a friend had stabbed her husband to death. Bringing both hands up, she buried her face in her palms. Her body trembled, shook, then went into a series of convulsions as she tried to cope with the dire news. Enfolding her once more in her arms, Eleanor stroked her hair to soothe her.

'I told you that it was better if you didn't know, m'lady.'

As Jonathan Bale approached the house, he had grave reservations.

'We do not know if the gentleman is there,' he complained.

'I agree,' said Christopher, 'but, by the same token, we do not know that he is *not* there. In view of what Emile told us, we should at least look into the matter.'

'I think it will be a wasted journey, Mr Redmayne.'

'Have more faith, Jonathan. You heard what his valet told us. Monsieur Villemot became very friendly with Lady Lingoe.'

'Yes,' said Bale, disapprovingly. 'Having seen that portrait of her, I shudder to think what kind of friendship it was.'

Christopher laughed. 'This is no time for maiden modesty.'

'That painting was indecent.'

'It was unexpected, I'll admit that.'

'A woman, disporting herself like that – it was lewd.'

'Not at all,' said Christopher. 'It had great artistic merit. It was firmly in the Classical tradition.' He rolled his eyes. 'If you want to see lewdness and bad taste of the worst kind, you should look at some of the paintings in my brother's house.'

'I've seen them, sir. They are coarse and immoral.'

'That, alas, is why Henry bought them.'

By keeping up a good pace, they finally reached Piccadilly, a wide thoroughfare that took its name from a tailor who had made his fortune by selling picadils, a high, stiff collar much in vogue at Court earlier in the century. Open fields were still in view but more and more houses were being built in the area, and Christopher had designed one of them. Emile had given them the address and it did not take them long to find the Lingoe residence, an imposing abode of white stone with a Classical façade that the architect stopped to admire. He marvelled at its beauty.

It only served to unsettle Bale. He was never at ease in the presence of wealth and privilege, and the house symbolised both. Its sheer opulence revolted him. Understanding his reluctance to enter the building, Christopher had a solution to the problem.

'If he's there,' he predicted, 'he will not give himself up. My guess is that he will try to sneak away again.'

'Shall I cover the garden, sir?'

'Please do, Jonathan. Cut off his escape.'

'Only if he's inside,' said the constable, dubiously.

'There's one way to find out.'

After giving his friend plenty of time to walk to the rear of the house, Christopher rang the bell. The butler who opened the door was a tall, stately man in his forties with a searching gaze. It took him a second to establish that his visitor was a gentleman. Christopher's elegance, respectability and air of wholesomeness impressed him.

'Yes, sir?' he asked.

'I'd like to speak to Lady Hester Lingoe,' said the other.

'Is she expecting you, sir?'

'Not exactly.'

'Lady Lingoe is not in the habit of receiving chance visitors,' said the butler, 'especially while her husband is out of the country.'

'I have a feeling that she'll agree to see me. Tell her that it concerns a portrait that she recently had painted.'

'May I give her your name, sir?'

'Christopher Redmayne.'

The butler invited him in, closed the front door and disappeared down a corridor. Christopher had the opportunity to look around and he was intrigued. Marble predominated. Statues of classical heroes stood everywhere, all of them armed and most of them naked. It was like being back in Rome, a city that Christopher had once visited when deciding to follow architecture as a profession. The gilt-framed art also had a classical theme. He was still studying a dramatic painting of Leda and the Swan when he heard footsteps clacking down the corridor. He looked up to see Lady Hester Lingo sailing gracefully towards him.

She was a full-bodied woman of medium height with bright red hair dressed in broad plaits in the style of a Roman matron. Her long tunic with its wide flounce was fastened along the upper arm by some gold brooches. An outer garment of silk was wrapped around her like a shawl. Christopher was irresistibly reminded of an illustration he had once seen of a Roman priestess. Though she was nearing thirty, her face had a sculptural splendour and seemed to be totally unlined. When she got closer, however, he saw how artfully Lady Lingoe had used cosmetics to conceal any signs of aging. The lady in the painting at the studio was indeed a painted lady.

'Mr Redmayne?'

'Yes,' said Christopher.

'You must be Henry's younger brother.'

'Do you know Henry?'

'We are acquainted,' she said with a noncommittal smile. 'He mentioned to me that his sibling was a brilliant architect.'

'My brilliance has yet to be proven,' said Christopher, 'but I revel in my work. I am in awe of your house,' he went on, looking around the hall. 'It's taken my breath away. I am pleased that you favour the Ionic Order. The shaft is more slender in proportion than the Doric and the capitals more intricate. The cornice-mouldings are small masterpieces.'

'I'm glad that you approve, Mr Redmayne,' she said, 'but you did not come here to show your appreciation of my house. I believe that you came to talk about a portrait for which I sat.'

'Yes, Lady Lingoe.'

'Well?'

'It's rather a delicate subject,' said Christopher, feeling that the hall was too large, cold and echoing a place for a private conversation. 'Is there somewhere else we might go?'

She kept him waiting for an answer. 'Very well,' she replied after long cogitation. 'Follow me.'

Lady Lingoe opened a door and took him into the library, a sizeable room with shelves of books against two walls, topped by a series of marble busts of Greek and Roman poets. When he was waved to a chair, Christopher sat in the shadow of Catullus.

'What is this about a delicate subject?' she said.

'It concerns the artist, Monsieur Villemot. I believe that he befriended you while painting your portrait.'

'Do you have any objection to that?'

'None at all, Lady Lingoe.'

'Have you *seen* the portrait?'

'Briefly,' he said with evident discomfort.

She gave a brittle laugh. 'There's no need to be quite so coy, Mr Redmayne,' she said. 'As an architect, you must be accustomed to nude figures, if only carved in marble. Why feel ashamed – I certainly am not? The portrait is a present for my dear husband on his fiftieth birthday. Lord Lingoe is in Holland at the moment, attending to his ambassadorial duties. I wanted to surprise him with the gift.'

'I'm sure that he will be delighted with it.'

'We share a common passion for classical antiquity.'

'I gathered that, Lady Lingoe.'

She sat opposite him. 'I'm still waiting to hear what brought you to my door, Mr Redmayne.'

'The death of Sir Martin Culthorpe.'

'Really? I had no idea that he had passed away.'

'He was murdered, Lady Lingoe – stabbed in his garden.'

'Good heavens!' she exclaimed. 'When was this?'

'Yesterday.'

'Has the killer been apprehended?'

'Not yet.'

'These are dreadful tidings. I did not know Sir Martin well but I nevertheless grieve for him. Murdered in his garden – how frightful! That young wife of his must be in torment.'

'She is, Lady Lingoe.'

'I'm full of sympathy for her,' she said with unfeigned sincerity, 'though I fail to see what connection my portrait can have with the crime.'

'It's not *your* portrait that's relevant here,' said Christopher, 'but the one Monsieur Villemot was painting of Lady Culthorpe. For reasons I don't fully understand, he is suspected of committing the crime and a warrant has been issued for his arrest.'

'Jean-Paul, a killer?' she cried, incredulously. 'That's an absurd suggestion. I know the man and can vouch for his character.'

'So can I, Lady Lingoe. I've designed a house for him and it has meant our spending a lot of time together. Like you, I hold him in high esteem. I do not believe he's guilty. However,' added Christopher, 'he has, unfortunately, behaved like a guilty man.'

He told her about the attempted arrest of Villemot at his home and how, in the wake of the artist's escape, he had been imprisoned. Since he had still not been fully exonerated, Christopher wanted to dispel any doubts about his own innocence by persuading Villemot to give himself up so that he could confront the charge against him and clear his name. Lady Lingoe was very attentive.

'M. Villemot has a good friend in Christopher Redmayne.'

'He needs help. Our judicial system is foreign to him.'

'It's no wonder he fled from it,' she said, levelly. 'Fascinating as all this may be, however, I still do not see how *I* am involved.'

'It was Emile who suggested your name, Lady Lingoe.'

'The valet?'

'He was aware of the warm friendship between you and his master. If he would turn to anyone for assistance, Emile surmised, Monsieur Villemot would probably come here.'

'Well, he has not done so.'

'How would you respond if he did?'

'I find that question impertinent, Mr Redmayne,' she said, curtly, 'and I think less of you for asking it.'

'My apologies, Lady Lingoe – I only sought to warn you.'

'Of what?'

'The consequences.'

'I am not unaware of those, sir.'

'Harbouring a fugitive is a crime,' said Christopher, 'even though you may be – as I am – convinced of his innocence. All that I did was to talk to two officers for a short while and I was locked in a cell in Newgate.'

'That would never happen to someone like me,' she said with disdain. 'Not that the situation would arrive, I can assure you. Jean-Paul would simply never come here.'

'But he does know where you live.'

'Of course.'

'And he has probably been here before.'

'You are lapsing into impertinence again, Mr Redmayne.'

'Then I'll tender my apologies once more,' he said, getting up from his seat, 'and bid you farewell. Thank you for agreeing to see me.'

'I was grateful to hear the news.'

Christopher smiled disarmingly. 'I was grateful to have the opportunity to see inside this remarkable house,' he said. He looked over his shoulder at Catullus. 'You keep good company, Lady Lingoe.'

'I choose my friends with extreme care,' she said, pointedly.

'Monsieur Villemot is lucky to be one of them.'

'Goodbye, Mr Redmayne,' she said, rising to her feet. 'The butler will show you out. You'll have no need to call again.'

'None at all,' he agreed. 'Forgive this intrusion. I can see that it was a mistake to assume that he would come here. As a good friend, he would not dare to cause you such embarrassment. At least we are united on one thing, Lady Lingoe?'

She was icily cold. 'Are we?'

'Yes – we both have Monsieur Villemot's well-being at heart.'

Henry Redmayne was annoyed. Having brought what he believed was the latest news regarding the crime he was dismayed to hear that Sir Willard Grail had already heard it.

'From *whom*?' he demanded, peevishly.

'I have my sources,' said Sir Willard.

'Well, you might have had the grace to pass on the tidings to the rest of us. Villemot's guilt changes everything.'

'Does it?'

'Yes, Sir Willard, it does. It opens up the possibility of collusion. If Araminta was drawn into a romantic entanglement with the artist, it may be that she actually encouraged him to remove her husband so that they could in time be together.'

'Given her character, I think that highly unlikely.'

'Love has the power to corrupt a saint.'

'But it would not drive her to the point of condoning a vile murder, Henry. If she had developed an attachment – and it seems beyond the bounds of possibility to me – then she and the Frenchman could have had clandestine assignations to satisfy their lust. In plotting the death of Sir Martin,' he pointed out, 'they would be ensuring that they were pushed apart.'

Henry Redmayne had called at his friend's house and the two of them were now conversing in an arbour in the garden. It was a tranquil place with a feeling of privacy that was only disturbed by birdsong and the buzzing of insects. Sir Willard waved a hand.

'It was in such a place as this that Sir Martin was killed,' he said. 'One is entitled to feel secure in one's own garden. He must have been taken completely by surprise.'

'How did Villemot gain entry to the garden?'

'The gate was left unlocked, it transpires.'

'How did you know that?'

'I like to keep well-informed.'

'What other details are you hiding from us, Sir Willard?'

'That's for you to find out.'

'If it's true that the gate was unlocked,' said Henry, 'then my contention that Araminta was a confederate may still hold.'

'Only in your mind,' Sir Willard told him. 'I spoke to the doctor who attended her after the murder. She was overwhelmed with grief and Araminta is not given to dissembling.'

'You knew about the garden gate? You talked to the doctor? You seem to have done everything but arrest Villemot for the crime.'

'He is still at large, Henry.'

'But I daresay you know where he's hiding.'

'I could hazard a guess or two.'

'Go on.'

'I'm not so foolish as to tell you,' said Sir Willard, patting his friend's knee. 'If I can track down Villemot on my own account, it would endear me to Araminta. Only the capture of her husband's killer would soften her bereavement.'

'We need to declare a moratorium on our pursuit of her,' said Henry, piously. 'I would suggest a period of three months.'

'Elkannah urged that we call off the chase altogether.'

'That's far too precipitate.'

'He wants no more of the business.'

'Then he can withdraw of his own accord. That still leaves three of us in the hunt. Jocelyn will certainly not pull out.'

'He does not even believe in giving Araminta any time to mourn the loss of her husband,' said Sir Willard, 'and he has a point. As soon as the funeral is over, she is there for the taking.'

'Surely not!' Henry's finer feelings asserted themselves for once. 'By all the laws of decency, we must allow her a long respite.'

'You may do so, Henry – we will follow our own inclination.'

'Must it be left to the two bachelors – Elkannah and me – to teach the pair of you the basic courtesies?'

'Marriage blunts the appetite for such things. While you are being virtuous, Jocelyn and I will dedicate ourselves to vice, especially as he has offered a delicious enticement.'

'Enticement?'

'Araminta may still be in possession of her maidenhood,' said the other with a confiding smirk. 'By all external signs, Sir Martin reached middle age without once experiencing the joys of carnal knowledge. When he had not yet lost his own virginity, how could he, with any confidence, have claimed hers?'

'A moot point, to be sure.'

'Elkannah has already resigned from the Society he invented.'

'That was very high-minded of him.'

'What about you, Henry?' asked Sir Willard. 'Now that we may revert to our original intention and go in pursuit of

Araminta's maidenhood once again, will you stand aside in the name of morality?' He gave a teasing grin. 'Or will you join Jocelyn and me in the hunt?'

Henry wavered. His finer feelings began to crumble.

Nothing had happened to dispel Jonathan Bale's doubts. In his opinion, he had been waiting at the rear of the house far too long. He turned a lugubrious face on Christopher Redmayne.

'This is a waste of time, sir,' he said. 'I've been standing at this spot for over half an hour.'

'Tarry a little longer, Jonathan.'

'The man is not inside the house.'

'I believe that he is.'

'I thought that Lady Lingoe told you otherwise.'

'She could have been lying.'

'Why should she do that, Mr Redmayne?'

'I can think of only one reason,' said Christopher, 'and that is to help someone. She did not deny that she and Monsieur Villemot had become close friends.'

'Too close,' complained Bale, thinking of the nude portrait. 'A married man should not be allowed to see his wife in that state, yet she allowed a stranger to view her body.'

'That should tell you something about her, Jonathan.'

'It tells me that Lady Lingoe is shameless.'

'A kinder way of putting it is that she lacks the inhibitions that would keep most women from posing in such a way. She certainly has a more liberal cast of mind than I've encountered before among the aristocracy.'

'Liberal or brazen?'

Christopher laughed. 'I can see that you're unfamiliar with the tradition of nude painting,' he said. 'It has a long and honourable history.' Bale snorted. 'Yes – *honourable*. The greatest artists of the Renaissance showed what could be done with nude figures.'

'Then I'm glad I've never seen their paintings,' said Bale with frank displeasure, 'and I'm sorry to hear you praise them.'

'I praise artistic excellence wherever I find it. There were many examples of it inside the house.'

'I'm more worried about Lady Lingoe.'

'In what way?'

Bale shuffled his feet. 'Did you tell her you'd seen that painting of her at the studio?'

'Of course.'

'She must have been mortified.'

'Not for a second,' said Christopher. 'If anything, she seemed quite pleased. Lady Lingoe is not one to hide her light under a bushel.'

'It's not her light that needed to be kept hidden,' grunted Bale.

'I think that it's just as well that I spoke to her and not you.'

'I'd have been afraid to look her in the face.'

'But she *enjoys* being looked at, Jonathan.'

'Not by me,' said Bale. 'Neither of us would have got what we came for in that house, sir. It's clear to me that Mr Villemot is simply not there.'

'I have a sneaking suspicion that he is.'

'Why?'

'I felt I was being subtly deceived.'

'How much longer must we stay?'

'Until he comes out.'

'But why here?' said Bale. 'He could leave by the front door.'

'The stables are here at the rear, and I'm sure that Lady Lingoe would provide him with a horse. She might even advise him where to go. Be patient,' said Christopher. 'It's only a question of time.'

Jean-Paul Villemot was in a state of panic. Thinking that he was safe in the house, he had been alarmed to be tracked down so quickly. He and Lady Lingoe were in the library of her house.

'How did he know that I'd be here?' he asked.

'Your valet gave him this address.'

'Emile is an idiot!'

'He could not be sure that you'd be here,' said Lady Lingoe, 'and he must have known that, even if you had come running to me, I'd never give you away.'

'Thank you, Hester – I had nowhere else to go.'

She smiled. 'I was touched that you thought of me.'

'I think of you often.'

'Good.'

They gazed at each other for a few moments and he reached out to squeeze her hand. Lady Lingoe soon put affection aside in favour of practicality.

'It's not safe for you to stay here, Jean-Paul,' she said.

'Why not?'

'Others may come looking for you. Mr Redmayne was sent on his way but it will be more difficult for me to fend off any officers. You must get away as soon as possible – otherwise both of us will be in trouble.'

'I would not put you in the danger,' he said, considerately. 'You are my good friend, Hester.'

'And I'm happy to remain so.'

'Where will I go?'

'To our country house near St Albans,' she decided. 'They'll know nothing of this affair there. You can bear a letter to the steward. He'll look after you.'

'If I am to leave London, I will need the horse.'

'A servant is saddling one for you even as we speak.'

'*Merci beaucoup!* You think of everything, Hester.'

'That's what friends are for, Jean-Paul. You gave me your word that you did not kill Sir Martin Culthorpe and I accept it without question. That being the case,' she went on, sitting at a table so that she could write a letter. 'I'll do everything in my power to help you avoid arrest.'

'I am sorry that Christopher suffered because of me,' he said.

'Yes, he struck me as an admirable young man. An alert one,

too,' she recalled. 'That's why I tried to get rid of him before he had time to question me too closely.' She began to write. 'Ride to Lingoe Hall and you'll be perfectly safe. Nobody would look for you there.'

'What about you, Hester?'

She looked up at him. 'Oh, I'll be joining you before very long, Jean-Paul. It will be the fulfilment of a dream,' she confessed, touching his arm. 'I'll have you all to myself at last.'

'I'm sorry, Mr Redmayne,' said Bale, 'but I'm neglecting my duties in Baynard's Castle Ward. I can't stand around here all day.'

'It would be unfair to keep you any longer,' said Christopher. 'You've already done me a huge favour today by securing my release from Newgate. To ask anything else of you would be an imposition.'

'What about you, sir?'

'I'll linger for a short while.'

'It will be in vain.'

'You are probably right, Jonathan.'

They were still lurking at the rear of the house in Piccadilly. After a farewell handshake, Bale walked back in the direction of the city. Sad to see him go, Christopher was loath to abandon his post. After his conversation with Lady Lingoe, he felt certain that Villemot was in the house, sheltered by a friend who would surely report to him that Christopher was on his trail. The information would alarm the Frenchman and make him anxious to get away.

He could easily understand why the artist had been drawn to Lady Lingoe. She was a handsome woman and, though the portrait of her was nominally for her husband, she did not have the look of a wife who moped in his absence or prayed for his early return. The age gap between the couple was significant. Knowing that she was attractive to men, she had given Christopher the impression that she liked exerting that attraction, albeit with carefully chosen targets. Even at a casual meeting, the architect had felt her power. In the more intimate setting of an artist's studio, that power could be overwhelming. Resting against a tree, Christopher stood up when he heard the clatter of hooves from the other side of the wall. He rushed to stand beside the door that led to the garden and the stables. Unlocked from the other side, it swung open to allow Jean-Paul Villemot to bring a bay mare out into the street. Before the artist could mount, Christopher leapt out to stop him.

'Stay here, Monsieur Villemot,' he pleaded. 'Running away will only get you into more trouble.'

'Leave me alone, Christopher.'

'But I've come to help you.'

'I don't need your help.'

Villemot pushed him firmly in the chest and sent him reeling backwards. The artist was in the saddle immediately, kicking the mare into a canter. He did not get far. Jonathan Bale stepped out from behind a clump of bushes some thirty yards away and waved his hat wildly at the horse. Frightened by the obstruction, the animal came to a halt and reared. Villemot was hurled from the saddle and hit the ground with a thud.

Christopher ran up to join them, grabbing the reins to bring the horse under control. Bale, meanwhile, stood over the fallen figure.

'I thought you'd gone,' said Christopher.

Bale smiled. 'I had a feeling you might need some help, sir.'

Having been compelled to accept the truth of the situation, Araminta Culthorpe threw herself into a frenzy of activity. Instead of sitting in her bedchamber and staring out at the garden, she came downstairs to the drawing room to write a series of letters, make decisions and give orders to the servants. She even consented to eat some food at last. Delighted by the signs of improvement in her mistress, Eleanor Ryle was nevertheless worried that she might overtax herself.

'You must try to rest, m'lady,' she advised.

'There are too many things to do, Eleanor.'

'Let someone else do them for you.'

'That's out of the question,' said Araminta. 'Who else could write to Sir Martin's brothers but me? Who else could pass on the tidings to his sister in Kent? They deserve to hear from me in person. While he was alive, I tried to be a good wife to my husband. Now that he's dead, I'll not shirk my duty.'

'What about your own family, m'lady?'

'I've sent word. It should reach them by this evening.'

'They will want to comfort you.'

'That's why I ordered rooms to be prepared for them and food to be ordered. In a day or two, the house will be full. We must be ready for them, Eleanor.'

'If you take to your bed, everyone will understand.'

'My place is here, acting as mistress of the house.'

'At least, let me do *something*,' implored the maid. 'I want to take the burden off your shoulders, m'lady.'

'You do that simply by being here, Eleanor.'

Araminta got up from her chair to give her a hug of gratitude. She suddenly became aware of how tired she was. Her eyelids were heavy, her body aching and her legs unsteady. Making a conscious effort to shake off her fatigue, she reached for a sheet of paper on the table and handed it to Eleanor.

'Look at this,' she said. 'See if there's anything I've missed.'

'It's such a long list,' noted the maid, running her eye down the names and the items. 'You've been so busy these past few hours.'

'There's still a lot more to be done.'

'I don't think so, m'lady.'

'My brain is addled. I'm sure I've missed things out.'

'Only one thing, as far as I can see.'

'What's that?'

'The portrait.'

Araminta was perplexed. 'Portrait?'

'The one that Mr Villemot was painting of you.'

'Oh, *that* – I've tried to forget it, Eleanor. That portrait was the start of all our woes. If I hadn't become acquainted with Monsieur Villemot, none of this would have happened.'

'We don't know that for certain.'

'I do,' said Araminta, sadly. 'I feel it in my bones. When you first told me that Monsieur Villemot was the killer, I could not believe it. He would never do anything to cause me so much pain. But, as I wrote those letters,' she continued, 'I became more and more convinced that I was wrong. There were moments when I felt profoundly uneasy in his company. I was never sure what was going through his mind.' She swallowed hard. 'Now, alas, we know.'

'There is still the portrait to be considered.'

'He can never finish it if he is convicted of the murder.'

'Another artist might do so in his place, m'lady.'

'That's inconceivable,' said Araminta.

'Then you might want it in its present condition,' said Eleanor. 'I know that Sir Martin paid for it even though Mr Villemot told him he should wait for it to be finished first.'

Araminta was wistful. 'That was my husband's only fault. He was too trusting. He had such faith in Monsieur Villemot's skill that he insisted on giving him the money before the first sitting.'

'That means the portrait is your property.'

'Not any more.'

'Why not?'

'It's a symbol, Eleanor. Whenever I look at it, I'll remember the wonderful man who commissioned it, the loving husband who was snatched away from me before his time.'

'Sir Martin would want you to keep it.'

'The decision is out of his hands,' said Araminta with a sigh. 'As for me, I've no use for it. To tell you the truth, Eleanor, I never want to set eyes on that accursed portrait again!'

* * *

Stunned by the fall, Jean-Paul Villemot was in no position to resist arrest. Jonathan Bale helped him to his feet and took a firm grip on him. Christopher, meanwhile, returned the horse to the stable. All three of them then set off. With a man either side of him, Villemot had no chance of escape. He felt betrayed.

'I thought you were my friend, Christopher,' he said.

'I am,' replied the other. 'That's why I want to help you to get out of this mess. You only made it worse by running away.'

'I did not kill Sir Martin!'

'Then why act as if you did?'

'Because of you,' said Bale, 'Mr Redmayne was arrested and taken into custody. They thought he was your accomplice.'

Villemot was chastened. It was something that Lady Lingoe had failed to mention to him. 'This is true?'

'Yes,' confirmed Christopher. 'The officers who called at my house thought I was distracting them so that you could get away. I spent a couple of hours in Newgate Prison.'

'I am sorry, Christopher. Is my fault.'

'I survived.'

'What about Lady Lingoe?' asked the other with sudden fear. 'I hope that she will not suffer.'

Bale was blunt. 'She took in a fugitive from justice.'

'Unwittingly, I think,' said Christopher, 'and that makes all the difference. I see no reason to mention her name at all and I'm sure that Jonathan agrees with me.' The constable gave a reluctant nod. 'Your friend is quite safe, Monsieur.'

The Frenchman was grateful. 'Thank you, Christopher.'

'What we have to do is to prove your innocence.'

'I will tell them. I will explain that it was not me.'

'It's not quite as simple as that,' said Christopher. 'There's evidence against you. The fact is that you were seen near Sir Martin's house around the time of the murder. And you were very excitable when you returned to your studio. I was there, remember. You were extremely rude to me.'

'I know. I came to make my peace with you. I apologise.'

'It will take much more than an apology to satisfy the court. It may well be that only one thing will persuade a judge that you were not guilty of the crime.'

'And what is that?'

'We have to catch the man who *did* stab Sir Martin to death.'

'Who is he?'

'We have no idea at the moment,' admitted Christopher, 'but we won't rest until we find out. It's not the first time that Jonathan and I have saved someone from the gallows.'

'True enough, Mr Redmayne,' said Bale.

'Rely on us, Monsieur.'

'If you're really innocent, we'll help you cheat the hangman.'

As the trio walked on, Villemot ran a hand around his throat.

Emile was horrified by the turn of events. When he heard that his master had been imprisoned in Newgate, he tried to visit him but was turned away and told to come back the following day. Returning to the rooms in Covent Garden, he reflected on how completely things had changed in such a short space of time. Instead of being the valet of the most famous artist in London, he was employed by a man accused of a heinous crime. Instead of having a job for life, he faced the threat of summary dismissal. Instead of looking forward to moving to the new house, he might have to sneak home to Paris in disgrace.

Villemot had not committed murder. Of that Emile was certain. But he was equally certain that his master would not be the first innocent man to be hanged by mistake. As an artist, his nationality was in his favour, suggesting a flair and passion felt to be lacking in the more reserved English. As a prisoner, however, his French manners and accent would be a serious disadvantage, attracting scorn from the turnkeys and other prisoners, and prejudicing the jury against what they would perceive as a wicked foreigner.

The problem had all started with Araminta Culthorpe. She was not the first beautiful woman to sit for her portrait but she had a quality that the others had lacked, a purity that set her apart and lent her face its spiritual glow. Emile went over to the easel and threw back the piece of cloth, staring in wonder at Araminta's face, neck and shoulders. She was truly captivating. Even with his long experience of painting young and gorgeous ladies, Villemot had been deeply moved by her presence in the studio.

It was late before Emile retired to bed, having tried to console himself with several glasses of wine. Once his eyes closed, he was dead to the world. The studio was unguarded.

The intruder came with great stealth, entering the house by means of a window at the rear and climbing the stairs with furtive steps. When he reached the rooms rented by Villemot, he first made certain that the valet was asleep then went into the studio and closed the door soundlessly behind him. Knowing that the floor was littered with objects, he took the precaution of lighting a candle. It enabled him to step between the scattered items and reach the easel without colliding with anything.

Here was the moment for which he had been waiting, the act of revelation that would deliver his beloved Araminta into his hands. Taking hold of the cloth, he threw it back and held the candle close to illumine the painting. His eyes widened in amazement and his heart began to pound. What he beheld was quite beyond belief.

Chapter Six

Work began early on the site of the new house. Oblivious to the fact that the person who had commissioned it was now in custody, Samuel Littlejohn was there to supervise his men and to help them unload the building materials that arrived by cart. He understood the importance of setting a good example for the others. Instead of standing apart and barking orders at them, therefore, he was quite ready to get his hands dirty from time to time by working alongside them. His combination of industry and cordiality won him the respect of his men and none of them tried to slack in his employ.

Littlejohn had just unloaded the last of the bricks when Christopher Redmayne came into view, riding his horse at a trot. The builder gave him a cheery wave then removed his hat and ran his sleeve across a perspiring brow.

'Good morning, Mr Redmayne!' he said.

'And to you, Sam.'

'There's precious little for you to see, I fear. Give us a week and we'll have made some real progress.'

'Unfortunately, I can't do that,' said Christopher, dismounting from his horse. 'I've come to call a halt to any work on the house.'

Littlejohn was wounded. 'A halt?'

'I fear so.'

'Aren't you satisfied with what we are doing?'

'I'm eminently satisfied. The fault lies elsewhere.'

There was no point in shilly-shallying. The builder deserved the truth and Christopher gave it to him as quickly and concisely as he could. Littlejohn was shocked to hear what had happened. He broke off to order his men to stop work then he searched for more detail.

'You say that Mr Villemot is not guilty?'

'He swears it, Sam, and I believe him.'

'Then why was he arrested?'

'It seems that he was in the wrong place at the wrong time.'

'What was he doing there?' asked Littlejohn.

'Monsieur Villemot claims that it was pure accident that he was in the vicinity of Sir Martin's residence. Two witnesses saw him at the rear of the house,' said Christopher, 'and that was where the killer gained access to the garden. Apparently, the gate was unlocked.'

'Was that usual, sir?'

'It was very unusual, Sam. Like any wealthy man, Sir Martin Culthorpe was careful to protect his property. A high wall encloses the garden and that gate is invariably locked.'

'Yet you still think that Mr Villemot is innocent?'

'Yes, I do.'

'I wish I had your confidence,' said Littlejohn, doubtfully, 'but I don't like the sound of what I've heard. A warrant would not be issued unless there was other evidence that we don't yet know about. I admire your loyalty to Mr Villemot but I choose to keep an open mind.'

'That's fair enough, Sam.'

'I did warn you something might go awry with this contract.'

'Nobody could have foreseen that our client would be accused of murder,' said Christopher. 'I know that you look askance at the French but even you must concede that they are not, by nature, inclined to stab people to death.'

'I never suggested that they were, sir.'

'But you were worried.'

'Foreign clients always worry me,' confessed the builder.

'This one may give you a pleasant surprise. When he's released from prison, work can begin at once on the house.'

Littlejohn was philosophical. 'I'll believe that when I see it,' he said with quiet resignation. 'Thank you, Mr Redmayne – it was good of you to come. I'd better go and pass on the sad news to the men.'

'Tell them not to lose hope.'

'I'll tell them to prepare for the worst. It's more honest.'

Putting his hat on again, the builder moved away. Christopher was about to mount his horse when he saw a rider approaching. He did not at first recognise the diminutive figure. It was only when the man pulled his mount to a halt that Christopher realised that it was Emile, the French valet.

'I am glad to find you, M'sieur,' said Emile, anxiously. 'I go to your house. The old man, he say you come here.'

'That would be Jacob, my servant.'

'I do not know who else to tell.'

'Tell what?'

'Is very bad.'

'You're not making much sense, Emile,' said Christopher. 'I can see that you're upset. Why not try to calm down before you speak? If there's a problem, I'll be glad to help.' Emile nodded gratefully. 'Now, let's go through it very slowly, shall we? What is so very bad?'

'I am afraid to tell him.'

'Who – Monsieur Villemot?'

'*Oui, m'sieur. C'est terrible.*'

'Why?'

'The portrait he paint...'

'The one of Lady Culthorpe?'

'Yes,' said Emile in despair. 'It was stolen.'

* * *

Henry Redmayne was not accustomed to being up so early in the morning and he was decidedly liverish. Still in his garish dressing gown, a garment that swept the floor as he moved, he was unshaven and without his wig. He regarded his visitor through a bleary eye.

'Death and hell and furies!' he shouted. 'What the devil has brought you here at this ungodly hour, Elkannah?'

'I needed to speak with you.'

'Could you not delay conversation until a more fitting time of day? This is most inconsiderate. I'm never fully awake until noon.'

'My business will not brook delay,' said Elkannah Prout.

'What does it concern?'

'Araminta.'

'Ah!' The name brought Henry to life. 'Now she is the one person in the world for whom I would willingly drag myself out of bed at the crack of dawn. I'd go without sleep for a month for Araminta.'

'I'm glad that she arouses a philanthropic impulse.'

'There's *nothing* I would not do for her, Elkannah.'

'Then bestow upon her the greatest gift you have to offer.'

'I've already done that,' said Henry, dreamily. 'I've given her my exclusive and undivided love.'

'Araminta would prefer your forbearance,' said Prout. 'At a time like this, she needs to be left alone to mourn in peace. I want you to join with me and stop your reckless courtship of her.'

Henry was disdainful. 'That's a strange entreaty on the lips of the man who first devised the Society to which all four of us were willing signatories,' he said. 'I spy your intent here, Elkannah. Because you have no chance of enjoying Araminta's charms, you want to prevent others from doing so.'

'I merely want her protected from your unsavoury attentions.'

'There's nothing unsavoury about me,' said Henry, pouting.

'Sir Martin's death weighs heavily with me,' said Prout, head down and hands clasped tight. 'It brought me to my senses. Like you, I disguised my licentiousness behind the many tokens of love I sent to Araminta. When she was single, such gifts were simply a nuisance to her. Now that she is a widow, they would be a source of torment.' He grabbed his friend's arm. 'Leave her be, Henry!'

'She needs me.'

'She needs respect and freedom from this persecution.'

'Nobody respects Araminta more than I do,' said Henry, 'and nobody has persecuted her less.' He shook his arm to detach Prout's hand from it. 'You are being very noble and I applaud you for it, but there are two reasons why I am unable to follow your example.'

Prout was critical. 'The first is your desire to win that bet.'

'No, Elkannah. I care nothing for the money. I'll gladly give it away to the deserving poor, if, that is, I did not myself happen to qualify for membership of that group of needy recipients. The first reason is this – I adore Araminta. To step aside now,' argued Henry, 'would be a repudiation of my love and that would be an act of treachery. The second and more pressing reason is one that you can surely guess.'

'If you do not go after her, others will.'

'Jocelyn and Sir Willard are even now making their plans.'

'I'll speak to each one in turn and urge him to stop.'

'You'll get the same answer,' warned Henry. 'They'll not budge an inch from their declared ambition – and neither will I.' He crossed to the door and opened it. 'I bid you good day, Elkannah.'

'Think over what I told you,' said Prout, crossing to the door.

'My ears are deaf to such petitions.'

They did, however, pick up the sound of the doorbell. It was rung with such vigour that that everyone in the house heard it. A servant opened the front door and Henry's brother came into the hall without waiting for an invitation.

'Christopher!' he exclaimed. 'What means this violent entry?'

'Up at this time?' said the other in surprise. 'I thought I'd have to roust you out of your bed.'

'Why – has something dreadful happened?'

'It has indeed, Henry.'

'Our father has died? The Tower of London has burned to the ground? Your beloved Susan Cheever has run off with a one-legged Spanish sailor?'

'Spare me your drollery.'

'Only a catastrophe of such proportions could make you try to burst our eardrums with the doorbell.' He indicated his companion. 'You know Elkannah, I believe.'

'We've met,' said Christopher, giving the man a respectful nod.

'Your servant,' replied Prout.

'Forgive my intemperance, sir, but I need to speak to my brother as a matter of urgency. He knows only too well why I must do that.'

'For the life of me,' said Henry, 'I do not. Enlighten me.'

'I am talking about a portrait of Lady Culthorpe.'

Prout's ears pricked up. 'Araminta?'

'Yes,' said Christopher. 'I must discuss it with Henry.'

'It's a subject in which I, too, have an interest.'

'Then you must stay, Elkannah,' said Henry, glad to have a shield between himself and his brother's anger. 'Let us go back into the drawing room where we can talk quietly.'

He led the way out of the hall, then closed the door behind his guests. Christopher did not mince his words. Taking off his hat, he confronted his brother with a blunt accusation.

'The portrait has been stolen and I am looking at the thief,' he said. 'I've never been so ashamed of you in all my life, Henry, and given your long career of drunkenness and debauchery, that's a bold claim. I'm revolted by the thought that my brother is nothing more than a common criminal.'

'Is this true?' asked Prout. 'You stole that portrait?'

'No!' retorted Henry. 'Until this very moment, I did not even know that it had been taken. Where did you glean this intelligence, Christopher?'

'I spoke with Monsieur Villemot's valet.'

'Is he *certain* the portrait is missing?'

'Emile would not make a mistake like that,' said Christopher, keeping his brother under close scrutiny. 'As soon as he went into the studio this morning, he saw that it was gone.'

'Where was it kept?'

'On an easel near the window.'

Henry gulped. 'Who would dare to steal it?'

'You are the prime suspect, Henry. The last time we met, you swore that you'd acquire that portrait of Lady Culthorpe by whatever means were necessary. Now I know what those means were.'

'This is unpardonable of you,' said Prout.

'By rights, you should be arrested,' added Christopher.

'But I've done nothing wrong,' bleated Henry, flapping his hands. 'Do you really think I'm capable of such a dastardly act?'

'Yes,' said the two men in unison.

'Then you cut me to the quick. My life has not been without its occasional irregularity – what gentleman's has not? – but I would never stoop to theft or any other crime.' He thrust out his chest. 'I am a model of a law-abiding citizen.'

'If you had no designs on the portrait,' said Christopher, 'why did you bother to go to the house yesterday?'

Henry gulped again. 'What do you mean?'

'I've just come from there. According to the maid, someone who fits your description to the last detail called at the house yesterday evening and claimed that he had left something in Monsieur Villemot's studio by mistake.' Henry's eyelids flickered. 'Since nobody was there, the maid obligingly showed the visitor into the studio. Luckily, she had the sense to stay with him.'

'What did you do then, Henry?' Prout challenged.

'I was not even there!' cried Henry.

'The maid got a close look at you,' said Christopher.

'Then I must have a double.'

'Your double did not stay long in the studio. Once he had reclaimed what he said was a handkerchief that had fallen from his sleeve, he took a peep under the cloth on the easel. Your motive was crystal clear,' said Christopher, sombrely. 'It was a reconnaissance expedition. You contrived to get inside the house in order to take your bearings, and you checked to see where the portrait was so that you could return at night and spirit it away.'

'Where is it?' demanded Prout.

'Return it immediately or face arrest,' Christopher put in.

'I'll have you arrested in any case. This is abominable.'

'But I do not have that portrait!' bellowed Henry. 'How many times must I tell you? Search the house, if you do not believe me. Turn the whole place upside down and look in every corner. You are quite correct, Christopher,' he said, displaying both palms in an attempt at mollifying him. 'I did make some foolish boasts with regard to that painting of Araminta, and I did hope that I might somehow purchase it from the artist. Wiser counsels prevailed and I backed off.'

'Before or after your visit to the house?' asked Christopher.

'I did not go anywhere near it.'

'That's a blatant lie,' said Prout, jabbing the air with a finger. 'I spoke to Jocelyn yesterday evening and he told me that he met you standing outside Monsieur Villemot's lodging.'

'I was strolling down the street by pure chance,' said Henry, thrown on the defensive. 'It's only a few minutes away from here so there's nothing sinister in the fact that I was there. I often use that street as a short cut to Covent Garden. Jocelyn, however,' he went on, seizing on the opportunity to escape the interrogation, 'went there for a reason. He offered money for the portrait of Araminta and admitted as much. There's your thief, Christopher,' he continued. 'Instead of hounding your innocent brother, talk to Jocelyn Kidbrooke.'

'I'll need his address.'

'You shall have it – along with that of Sir Willard Grail.'

'Why is that?'

'Because he must be suspected as well,' said Henry. 'They are both men in the grip of an obsession with Araminta. Neither of them would hesitate to steal the portrait. Am I right, Elkannah?'

'They would both dearly love to possess it,' confirmed Prout.

'So I am in the clear. I require an apology, Christopher.'

'You'll not get one until the truth of the matter has been established,' said his brother. 'And there is still the question of why you inveigled yourself into that studio.'

'But that was not me. Nor could it have been Jocelyn, for he's too fat and misshapen. Sir Willard, on the other hand,' he said, 'is a very different proposition. He's younger than me but – to the eyes of some ignorant little maid – he could pass for Henry Redmayne, especially in bad light. Elkannah?'

'Yes,' said Prout, thinking it over. 'He could do so.'

'He even apes some of my gestures.'

'That he does, to be sure.'

'There you are, Christopher. Now stop looking at me as if I had just stolen His Majesty's entire art collection. Jocelyn and Sir Willard are the true suspects here.' He pulled himself up to his full height. 'I am vindicated.'

'Not yet, Henry,' warned his brother. 'There's a lot more to come out about this little adventure and I'm sure that you will be implicated in the crime in some way or other.'

'But I'm the victim of it. I coveted that portrait.'

'So did we all,' murmured Prout.

'Araminta must be found. I'll join forces with you to recover her.'

'No, thank you,' said Christopher. 'I choose to work with Jonathan Bale. His integrity is not in doubt.'

'That sour-faced imbecile has no place in this search.'

'He most certainly does, Henry. We are not just looking for someone who stole a painting. We are hunting the killer of Sir Martin Culthorpe. The two crimes are inextricably linked. I have an interest here,' he declared. 'Lady Culthorpe lost a husband and, as a result, I have been deprived of a client. Sir Martin, alas, is beyond recall but Jean-Paul Villemot is not. I mean to prove his innocence and recover the portrait he painted. Jonathan has volunteered to help me.'

'Who is the fellow?' asked Prout.

'A dull-witted constable with a Puritan conscience,' said Henry with a sneer. 'He's an odious creature.'

'I like him,' said Christopher.

'There's nothing remotely likeable about the ugly devil.'

'There are many things, Henry. For a start, I like his essential goodness. After dealing with you, I find it uplifting. Jonathan would never trick his way into someone's lodging by pretending to have left a handkerchief there.' His gaze was cold and unwavering. 'Couldn't you have invented a better excuse than that?'

Until he was imprisoned, Jean-Paul Villemot had never known that such squalor and degradation existed. He had seen poverty in the back streets of Paris where women sold their bodies to feed their children, and where there was a pervading stink of despair. None of it compared with the sustained nightmare that was Newgate. It seemed as if the most violent, foul-mouthed, desolate, God-forsaken human beings on earth had been gathered there. The noise was deafening, the stench unbearable and the food inedible. Everyone inside the prison was filthy and depraved. He could not decide if the prisoners or the turnkeys were the more corrupt.

Villemot had important concessions. In return for payment, he was given a single cell and that isolated him from attack. But it did not rescue him from the jeering of his captors or from the pandemonium in the nearby cells. He was kept awake all night by the howls of pain, the forlorn pleas, the screams of violated women and the sound of bruising fights. He had paid for wine but it tasted like vinegar. He had asked for visitors but he was told to wait until the next day. Sympathy was nowhere to be found. Villemot was treated less like someone whose guilt was uncertain than a condemned man biding his time before he ascended the gallows.

His cell gave him neither comfort nor privacy. It was small, fetid and covered in dank straw. When Villemot was shoved into it, a rat had scurried out. Through the iron bars of the gate, the turnkeys could keep him under constant surveillance. He was horror-struck at the thought of relieving himself in a wooden pail that was pitted by age and stained by long usage. For a man of the artist's delicate sensibilities, Newgate Prison was pure torture.

Morning brought the same sickening reek and the same unceasing tumult but it also brought his first visitor. When he saw Emile being led along the corridor by a turnkey, Villemot flung himself at the bars.

'*Emile!*' he exclaimed. '*Enfin!*'

'*Bonjour, M'sieur Villemot.*'

'None of that,' decreed the turnkey. 'You speak English or you speak nothing. Talk in that turkey-gobble and, for all I know, you could be plotting an escape.' He folded his arms. 'English.'

He loomed over Emile who was plainly intimidated by his presence. Fastidious by nature, the valet was disgusted by everything he saw, heard and smelled. He was appalled to see his master in such a place and gave him an affectionate handshake through the bars.

'How are you, sir?' he enquired.

'I am glad to see the friendly face at last, Emile.'

'You do not belong.'

'Then why did you help to put me here?'

'M. Redmayne ask the question – I tell truth.'

'Lie for me next time,' said Villemot. 'Protect your master.'

'I am sorry.'

'I could have got away.'

'They look for you, sir. You not run forever.'

'I'd do anything to keep out of this hell-hole.'

'It's cosy when you get used to it,' said the turnkey with a snigger. 'You'll come to like it here in time.'

'Never!' Villemot turned to the valet. 'It is so bad.'

'I speak to Mr Redmayne this morning. He tell me he will get you out of here soon.'

'What can he do?'

'He want to help, sir.'

'That's what he says but can I trust him?'

'I think so. He tell me he has the friend who is the constable.'

'I met him.' Villemot fingered the lump on the back of his head. 'His name is Jonathan Bale. Because of him, I was almost killed when I was thrown from a horse. Why should he help me? Jean-Paul Villemot is nothing to him.'

'You are, sir.'

'Am I?'

'The new house, it is in M'sieur Bale's parish.'

'It may never be built now.'

'Do not say that. You will get out somehow.'

'Yes,' said the turnkey. 'You'll get out, Villymott. We'll see to that. We'll even provide the cart to take you to the hangman.'

'It is no jest!' snapped Villemot.

'Don't you shout at me, you lousy French dunghill!'

'I want to talk to my friend.'

'Two minutes – that is all.'

'But I have a lot to tell him.'

The turnkey grinned provocatively at him. 'You'll have to speak fast, then, won't you?'

'What can I do, sir?' said Emile.

'Go to the lady.'

'Mr Redmayne helps you.'

'He has no power – the lady does. Tell her where I am.'

'Yes, sir.'

'Go straight to the house.'

'What do I say?'

Villemot was explicit. 'Beg her to get me out of here!'

The response had been overwhelming. As word of the murder spread ever wider, letters of condolence, tributes and flowers were delivered in abundance to the house. Dozens of visitors came to pay their respects and offer their sympathy. Though it was very tiring to cope with it all, Araminta Culthorpe was glad to have something to occupy her mind. Having dealt with another batch of callers that morning, she settled down in the drawing room to go through the piles of letters that had accumulated.

Eleanor Ryle assisted her, noting each sender's name before passing the missive over to her. She picked up another from the pile.

'Mr Henry Redmayne,' she announced.

'Throw it away!'

'But it's a poem.'

'It always is,' sighed Araminta. 'Destroy it.'

'You don't know what he's written, m'lady.'

'I know exactly what he's written and I've no wish to read a word of it. Anything that bears his execrable name must be torn up.'

'Yet you read that letter sent by his brother.'

'That was different,' said Araminta, her voice softening at once. 'Christopher Redmayne is a true gentleman. His commiserations were sincere and heart-felt. What he wrote touched me. Henry Redmayne, however,' she said, sharply, 'has sent a poem that contains the same flowery language and the same unsought declaration of love as all the others he's written. It's both hurtful and vexing. Tear up his letter.'

Eleanor obeyed her, putting the pieces of paper aside on the table. She reached for the next letter and unfolded it.

'Mr Elkannah Prout.' At the sound of the name, her mistress hesitated. 'Shall I tear up this one as well?'

'No,' decided Araminta. 'I'll read it.' The letter was handed over to her. 'And I'm glad that I did,' she went on as she scanned the neat calligraphy. 'Mr Prout is very kind. His words bring real comfort. He's also apologised for any earlier correspondence he sent me and done so handsomely. Elkannah Prout was acquainted with my husband and says kind things about him.' She put the letter aside. 'Next?'

'Lady Lingoe.'

Araminta was checked. 'Lady *Hester* Lingoe?'

'Yes,' said Eleanor. 'She has a fine hand.'

'But she hardly knew Sir Martin. Her husband, on the other hand, certainly did – he's an ambassador who travels all over Europe.' She took the letter and glanced at it. 'Wait,' said Araminta, looking up. 'I've just realised why she may have felt impelled to write.'

'Oh?'

'Lady Lingoe and I have something in common – we both had our portraits painted by Monsieur Villemot. I remember my husband remarking on it.'

'Did he see the portrait of Lady Lingoe?'

'Sir Martin forbade me to do so.'

'Why was that?'

'He said that it was not a suitable example of the artist's work. Besides, I was there to sit for my own portrait, not to look at what Monsieur Villemot had done for his other ladies.'

Eleanor was curious. 'Does he only paint ladies?'

'For the most part,' said Araminta. 'That's how he made his name. His excellence is not in question. He has done portraits of members of the French royal family and was feted in his own country, yet he preferred to live and work here.'

'I wonder why, m'lady.'

'He told me that he adores England.'

'But he has a wife in Paris, does he not?'

'Yes, Eleanor – I'd rather forgotten about her.'

'It seems that *he* forgot about her as well,' said the maid.

'I'm mightily afraid that he did.'

'How will she feel when she hears about her husband?'

'Poor thing!' said Araminta with a surge of compassion. 'I've been so bound up in my own misery that I've not spared a thought for anyone else's suffering. Madame Villemot will be horrified. What the husband did was utterly detestable,' she continued, grimacing at the memory, 'but I can still feel sympathy for the wife. She was not to blame. Madame Villemot is another victim of this tragedy.'

'It may be some time before the news reaches her.'

'Yes, Eleanor – it will tear her life apart as it has sundered mine. No matter for that,' she said, holding back tears. 'We must make an effort to carry on as best we may.' She looked down at the letter. 'Let me see what Lady Lingoe has to say.' Her face soon crumpled. 'Good heavens!' she exclaimed.

'What's wrong?' said Eleanor.

'It's what Lady Lingoe has written in her letter. According to her,' said Araminta, upset and bewildered, 'Monsieur Villemot did not commit the crime at all. She claims that he's innocent.'

Lady Hester Lingoe had always liked Emile. She found him attentive and amusing. He was an educated man. To relieve the boredom she inevitably felt while sitting for long periods in the studio, Emile had read the poems of Catullus to her in the original Latin, and he had found other ways to stave off tedium. She was less pleased with what he said to her now. His account of what had happened made her roam around the library of her house like a restless animal.

'I had no idea that he had been arrested,' she said in dismay. 'I ordered a horse to be saddled for him. Nobody told me that the animal had been returned to the stable. It's my fault,' she admitted, slapping her thigh. 'I should have known that

Christopher Redmayne did not believe me. He was too astute. When I allowed Monsieur Villemot to leave the house, I let him fall straight into Mr Redmayne's hands.'

'He wants to help, Lady Lingoe.'

'Locking up your master in prison is not my idea of help.'

'He help you as well,' Emile reminded her.

'All that he did to me was to pester me with questions.'

'You were hiding my master. That is against law. Monsieur Redmayne, he does not get his friend, the constable, to arrest you.'

'That's a small mercy, I suppose,' she conceded. 'It would have been humiliating to be hauled before a magistrate even though he would never have dared to impose a sentence on me. My husband is an important man. We have friends in high places.'

'What can they do for my master?'

'We shall see, Emile. To begin with, I'll appoint a lawyer to defend him and to make sure that he's treated properly in Newgate.'

'He wants to get out *now*.'

'That's more difficult to arrange.'

'Is frightening in there.'

'I can imagine.'

She stopped to consider the situation and Emile had his first opportunity to look around the library. He loved its classical style and its array of leather-bound books. He also liked the attire of a Roman priestess that she was wearing. It gave her allure and distinction. Most of the English ladies whose portraits had been painted by his master had been either shy and reticent or haughty and garrulous. Lady Hester Lingoe fitted neither of these categories. She was unique. Shrewd, perceptive and friendly, she was a woman of real character.

'I need more time to think,' she said, conscious that he was waiting for her to speak. 'I'll be in touch, Emile.'

'Thank you, m'lady.'

'When will you be seeing Monsieur Villemot again?'

'Soon.'

'Tell him that he is in my thoughts.'

'I will,' said Emile with a smile. 'My master will like that.'

Sarah Bale was delighted to see him again and she became almost girlish. Christopher Redmayne always had that effect on her. For his part, he was pleased to be given the customary warm welcome and to answer the battery of questions that she fired at him. After making some polite enquiries after her children, Christopher was rescued by Bale. The constable eased his wife into the kitchen.

'Mr Redmayne came to see me, my love,' he told her, gently, 'and not to listen to your gossip.'

'Is he going to ask you to make another model?'

'I doubt it.'

'Offer to do so, Jonathan,' she said. 'Don't hold back.'

'We've other things to talk about, Sarah.'

After kissing her on the forehead, he went out and closed the kitchen door behind him. He and Christopher went into the little parlour. Bale moved some toy soldiers from a chair so that his visitor could sit down. He put the soldiers on a table. Christopher peered at them with interest.

'Did you make those?'

Bale smiled. 'As a matter of fact, I did, sir.'

'I thought so,' said Christopher with a grin. 'Who else would build his children a New Model Army?'

'I served under Oliver Cromwell and I'm proud of the fact.'

'You've a right to be so, Jonathan. You were on the winning side at the battle of Worcester and that's a memory you'll cherish. But,' he went on, 'that's all past. We are subjects of a King once more.'

'You know my views where His Majesty is concerned,' said Bale, 'so I'll not spoil our friendship by giving them to you again. Something has happened, hasn't it?'

'Yes – the portrait of Lady Culthorpe has been stolen.'

Bale started. 'Who took it?'

'That's for us to find out.'

'Did you have anyone in mind?'

'Yes,' said Christopher, thinking of his brother but determined to keep his name out of the discussion. 'There are two people who might bear close examination. We must recover that portrait.'

'Does the lady herself know that it's been stolen?'

'No, Jonathan, and she must never find out. It would distress her even more if she realised that her likeness was in the hands of a thief. Lady Culthorpe doesn't know what occurred and neither does Monsieur Villemot.'

'Why?' asked Bale. 'The artist ought to be told.'

'His valet is terrified of the way he would respond,' said Christopher. 'His master has a temper – I've seen him flare up with my own eyes. While he's away, Emile is in charge of the studio. It's his responsibility to protect the paintings.'

'Especially the one of Lady Culthorpe.'

'Emile told me that he would rather have lost all the other paintings in the studio.'

'Does that include the portrait of Lady Lingoe?'

'It does, Jonathan. I know that you'd be saddened if that had been stolen,' he teased. 'The portrait had a special meaning for you.'

Bale sniffed. 'It made me wonder what goes on in an artist's studio,' he said, dourly.

'You'll have to put that question to Lady Lingoe herself.'

'No, thank you, sir – I'd rather not meet her at all.'

'You'd be quite safe. She dresses as a Roman priestess.'

'I'll keep my distance from her, dressed or undressed.'

'One thing is certain,' said Christopher. 'Whoever stole that other portrait, it was not Lady Lingoe. I begin to think that it may be the same person who killed Sir Martin Culthorpe.'

'He could have stolen it without resorting to murder.'

'That depends on his motive. If he was spellbound by Lady Culthorpe's beauty, he could have been driven to kill the husband in order to get closer to her.'

'She's in mourning.'

'That's why he has to be patient,' said Christopher. 'Since he can't even see her while she's brooding on her loss, he would have wanted to look upon her in some way.'

'The portrait.'

'Why else would he take it?'

Bale fell silent, deep in contemplation. His brow was rutted, his lips pursed, his eyes staring into space. Christopher looked down at the toy soldiers. They had been made with love for Bale's two sons so that they could play out various battles. Each soldier had been carved and painted with precision. To a doting father, the soldiers were every bit as important as Villemot's portraits were to the artist. Christopher could see how deeply wounded Bale would be by the theft of his handiwork. Over the time he had worked on the miniature figures, he would have built up a close relationship with them.

'I wonder if we are mistaken,' said Bale, suddenly.

'Mistaken?'

'I very much doubt if the thief was also the killer.'

'You reason?'

'I deal with crime every day, Mr Redmayne. In my experience, a man who commits murder has only one thought in mind and that is to get far away from the place where the deed was done. I do not think that he would stay in London so that he could steal a portrait.'

'If he'd taken flight,' said Christopher, 'he'd have given himself away. Better to stay here and keep out of sight. A city as large as London has many hiding places.'

'I still say the thief is not the killer.'

'But the two must be connected in some way.'

'It's possible,' said Bale, 'but it may not be the case at all. For the sake of argument, suppose that Lady Culthorpe has nothing to do with what happened to her husband.'

'Lust is a powerful motive, Jonathan.'

'So is greed, so is envy, so is hatred. Sir Martin was known for his kindness but even the kindest of men have enemies. Someone may have wanted to strike him down out of sheer malice. Remember this,' he went on. 'The murder was planned. It was no accident. The killer must have known that Sir Martin went for a stroll in his garden at certain times of the day. He must have contrived a means of getting the key to the garden gate.'

'I realise that,' said Christopher. 'The problem is that the person who could help us most is the one who is out of our reach.'

'Lady Araminta Culthorpe.'

'She would know about Sir Martin's habits and be able to tell us who had the keys to that gate. Without realising it, Lady Culthorpe probably has lots of information that would be useful to us but we could not possibly approach her at a time like this.'

'When is the funeral?'

'Very soon, I should imagine.'

'Then we must wait until it's over.'

'There's one way we might ensure her assistance.'

'What's that, sir?'

'By finding that portrait,' said Christopher. 'Because Sir Martin commissioned it, it's a last memento of her husband. If we tell her that we recovered it from the thief, she'll be extremely grateful.'

'How do we track it down?'

'I'm not entirely sure.'

'You told me you had two suspects in mind, sir.'

'I hoped that we might question one each.'

'Who are they?'

'They're friends of my brother.' Bale sniffed again. 'Yes, yes, I know you think they're Henry's fellow libertines and that may turn out to be true. What we have to decide is whether or not one of them is also a thief and a killer.'

'He'll not be both, Mr Redmayne, mark my words.'

'I bow to your superior instincts.'

'Who are these gentlemen?'

'One is Sir Willard Grail and the other, Jocelyn Kidbrooke.'

'I do not like the sound of that title,' said Bale, curling a lip, 'unless, of course, it was awarded by the Lord Protector.'

'Sir Willard comes from Cavalier stock.'

'Then I'll take the other gentleman, if it's all the same to you.'

'Jocelyn Kidbrooke made his money in trade,' said Christopher, 'and bought his way into society. My brother describes him as serious-minded but amiable. That might just mean that he loaned Henry some money. Kidbrooke fell in with my brother in order to secure an introduction to His Majesty's circle.'

'What am I to ask him, Mr Redmayne?'

'You might begin by saying that you know he made a substantial offer for that portrait. His interest in it is clear.'

'Did your brother think him capable of stealing it?'

'Not in person, perhaps, but he might hire someone to do it.' Taking a piece of paper from his pocket, Christopher handed it over. 'This is Kidbrooke's address,' he said. 'Like so many men – Henry, alas, among them – he's besotted with Lady Culthorpe. That's why I need to warn you about something.'

'And what's that, sir?'

'Jocelyn Kidbrooke is married.'

Bale stiffened. 'He has a wife yet pursues another woman?'

'So it appears.'

'That's a betrayal of his marriage vows.'

'It's something else you might raise with him,' said Christopher.

Despair came in waves. Though she immersed herself in work, there were times when Araminta Culthorpe simply could not keep dejection at bay. Coming when she least expected it, it washed over her and left her drenched with misery as she was forcibly reminded of the gruesome discovery she had made in the garden. With one thrust of a dagger, her husband had been murdered and her happiness taken away. The future looked bleak and empty. Araminta did not know if she would have the courage to face it.

'Bear up, m'lady,' said Eleanor Ryle.

'I've no strength left to do it.'

'Then you need to rest. You've not had a proper sleep since the day it happened. Go to bed, m'lady. Things may not look so daunting when you've had a good, long sleep.'

'I've tried to sleep,' said Araminta, 'but my mind is too full of phantoms when I lie down. I remember what I saw in the garden and the horror starts all over again. The only way I can block it out is by keeping myself busy.'

'But you're close to exhaustion, m'lady.'

'So are you, Eleanor. You've hardly left my side for days. It's a terrible strain on you. I can see how weary you are.' She stifled a yawn. 'Every ounce of energy has been drained out of us.'

'As long as you want me, I'll stay by you.'

'Thank you.'

Seated beside each other, they were in Araminta's bedchamber. The strain of a long day had told on both of them but it was Araminta who was drooping. She was fighting to stay awake. Eleanor offered the same advice once again.

'Go to bed, m'lady,' she urged. 'Why suffer all this pain? Let me help you off with your clothes.'

'No, Eleanor – you are the one who needs to sleep.'

'How can I when I have to attend to you?'

'Leave me,' said Araminta, touching her hand in a gesture of gratitude. 'You've done more than enough. I can manage without you now.'

'I want to help you keep sad thoughts away, m'lady.'

'They'll come again and again, whatever you do.'

'Then you must have someone to share your grief.'

'It's time for me to be on my own,' decided Araminta, getting up and pulling Eleanor gently after her. She ushered the maid towards the door. 'There are some things even you can't share,' she said. 'I've imposed on you enough.'

'You could never do that,' said Eleanor, gravely.

'Off you go now.'

'No, m'lady – my place is here.'

Araminta was firm. 'I'm telling you to leave,' she said. 'I may not be able to sleep but you certainly will. I can see the fatigue in your face. Go to bed, Eleanor. I do not wish to see you for hours.'

'What if you should need me?'

'I'll have to manage without you.' Araminta opened the door and waved her out. 'Don't try to slip back in again because I'll lock the door. Away with you, girl – you've earned a rest.'

'Will you promise me that—'

'I'll promise you nothing apart from this,' said the other, cutting her off before she could finish her sentence. 'I can manage by myself. I *have* to manage, Eleanor. That's what my life will be about from now on.' She forced a smile then closed the door. 'Goodbye.'

Eleanor heard the key turn in the lock. She was both worried and relieved, sorry to leave her mistress alone but glad to be spared the constant stress of looking after her. While the prospect of rest was enticing, she was not ready to yield to it. The maid was prompted by a higher priority than her own comfort. Tripping along the corridor, she went down the backstairs until she came to her own room.

She let herself in, poured water from the jug into the china basin then gathered it up in her palms to sprinkle her face. It was cold but refreshing. After drying her face, she looked in the mirror and saw how gaunt she was. She hardly recognised herself. Eleanor did not worry about her appearance. Finding her cloak, she put it on before leaving the room and going along a passageway. Making sure that nobody saw her, she opened a side door, went out swiftly and hurried away from the house.

Chapter Seven

Christopher Redmayne had met several of his brother's friends before and they tended to be as shameless and profligate as Henry. They also bore the indelible imprint of decadence. Expecting to see another unconscionable rake, Christopher was startled to find that Sir Willard Grail had none of the telltale signs of a sybarite. He was tall, well-favoured and looked remarkably wholesome. His boyish smile made him seem even younger than he really was. Sir Willard's attire was flamboyant without being gaudy. He was affable and unaffected.

'Henry's brother, are you?' he said, weighing his visitor up. 'Nobody would ever guess it to look at you. I believe you're a famous architect.'

'No, Sir Willard – I've yet to rise in my profession.'

'It's only a matter of time, I'm sure. Having no inclination or capacity for hard work, I always admire those who do and you are obviously a Trojan in your chosen field.'

'Work is never onerous when you enjoy it,' said Christopher.

'So I believe.'

They were in the hall of Sir Willard's home near Shoreditch, an elegant house, designed by a disciple of Inigo Jones, which would have fitted into Covent Garden without a hint of incongruity. It was close enough to the city to allow easy access yet sufficiently distant to give it a sense of isolation. It was a place where Lady Grail could live in style and comfort while her husband pursued pleasures elsewhere.

'I'm glad that we finally met,' said Sir Willard, 'though I'm bound to observe that you seem to have gone out of your way to make my acquaintance.'

'I came on private business, Sir Willard. Given its nature, you might wish to discuss it somewhere other than in your hall.'

'To what does it relate?'

'Lady Culthorpe.'

'Perhaps we'd better step in here,' said the other, smoothly, taking Christopher into the drawing room before closing the door firmly behind them. 'You know Araminta?'

'I've had the pleasure of meeting her.'

'Then you must be as enthralled as the rest of us.'

'She's a very beautiful lady, Sir Willard.'

'Araminta is quite incomparable. But you do not need to be told that. We all worship her. Your brother has been sending poems to her for months.'

Christopher stared. 'Henry has no talent for poetry.'

'That might explain why he met with such a cold response. He once showed me a sonnet he penned in praise of her,' said Sir Willard with a laugh. 'It beggared description. Shakespeare has no rival in the Navy Office, I do assure you.' He met Christopher's gaze. 'Now, then, what exactly has brought you to my door?'

'The theft of Lady Culthorpe's portrait.'

Sir Willard's eyes narrowed. 'The *theft*?'

'It was stolen some time during last night.'

'How do you know?'

'Monsieur Villemot's valet sought me out to tell me,' explained Christopher. 'Since his master is at present in Newgate, it fell to Emile to guard his property. The loss of the portrait has struck him like a thunderbolt.'

'Why did the valet turn to you, Mr Redmayne?'

'I've designed a house for Monsieur Villemot.'

'Of course,' said Sir Willard. 'I should have remembered that. What a pity the house will never be built!'

'I'm confident that it will.'

'Even though its owner will soon be dangling from the gallows?'

'I don't accept that he committed the murder,' said Christopher, resolutely, 'and I'll strain every nerve to prove his innocence.'

Sir Willard grinned. 'By Jove!' he exclaimed. 'I was much mistaken in you. There *is* a resemblance to your brother, after all. You have Henry's boldness, his wild-eyed passion and his readiness to pursue a lost cause.'

'Trying to rescue Monsieur Villemot is not a lost cause.'

'The man is patently guilty.'

'Not in my eyes, Sir Willard.'

'Then perhaps it's time to buy some spectacles.'

'I've been in this position before,' said Christopher, 'and on that occasion I also saved someone who had been judged guilty before he was even brought to trial. His name was Henry Redmayne. I'm sure that he's told you the story of how he evaded the noose.'

'Many times,' replied Sir Willard, 'though he's never mentioned your name in his account. He prefers to claim all the credit for himself, but that's ever his way.'

He gave a dismissive gesture with his hand that Christopher recognised as belonging to his brother, and there were other indications – a shrug, a nod, a facial expression – that Sir Willard had picked up some of Henry's characteristic actions. What Christopher could not believe was that, even by candlelight, Sir Willard could be mistaken for Henry. He was of similar height and build but his age, fair complexion and handsome features set him clearly apart.

'I'm sad to hear that Araminta's portrait has gone astray,' said Sir Willard, 'and I'm grateful that you rode all this way to tell me.'

'I'm not here merely to impart news.'

'No?'

'I came in search of your help,' said Christopher. 'I wondered if you could suggest the name of anyone who would covet that portrait enough to steal it.'

Sir Willard laughed again. 'That's a very naïve question,' he pointed out. 'I can suggest the names of at least a hundred men who would yearn for that painting. I'm one of them and, since you saw Araminta in the flesh, your name could probably be added to that list.'

'Very few people even knew that the portrait was in hand.'

'Then that cuts down the number appreciably.'

'Does anyone come to mind, Sir Willard?'

'Yes,' said the other.

'I've already taxed Henry with regard to the matter.'

'It's just the sort of madcap thing he'd do. Jocelyn Kidbrooke is another potential art thief, and you'd have to bring Elkannah Prout into the reckoning.'

'I'd discount him,' said Christopher.

'Why?'

'As it happens, I met Mr Prout earlier today at my brother's house. He did not strike me as the kind of man who would lower himself to such an act.'

'Nevertheless, he was a member of the Society.'

'Society?'

'I'll leave your brother to divulge any details of it,' said Sir Willard, discreetly, 'if he so decides, that is. By the way, what made you tax Henry with the crime?'

'Someone called at the studio the previous evening,' said Christopher. 'My guess is that he watched the house until the valet left – Emile told me that he went out for a time – then he tricked the maid into letting him in so that he could see the premises from the inside. He also took the opportunity to have a sly look at Lady Culthorpe's portrait.'

'Did the maid give you a description of the man?'

'It was her description that sent me haring off to Bedford Street.'

'Then your brother must be the thief.' He snapped his fingers in a way that was reminiscent of Henry yet again. 'The crime is solved. Have him arrested and repossess the painting.'

'He does not have it, Sir Willard.'

'Then a confederate is hiding it for him.'

'No,' said Christopher, 'there are rare moments in his life when Henry actually tells the truth – or, at least, enough of it to give the semblance of truth. He did not steal that portrait. Of that I have not the slightest doubt.'

'He could still have visited the house yesterday.'

'I mean to look into that more closely.'

'Take the maid to Bedford Street to identify your brother.'

'I've thought of an easier way than that,' said Christopher. 'But I've taken up too much of your time already. You've already answered the question I was bound to ask.'

'You thought that *I* might have been the thief, didn't you?'

'It did cross my mind.'

'Well, don't let it do so again,' said Sir Willard, testily. 'Much as I'd love to own that portrait, I have a distinct handicap – there's nowhere that I could safely keep it. I could hardly suggest to my wife that I hang it in the library to encourage me to read more.' He gave a cold smile. 'Stay away from my house in future, Mr Redmayne.'

'I'll gladly do so unless I have cause to return.'

'There *is* no cause. Now continue on your way and catch him. Catch the villain who stole Araminta from that studio and send him off to prison where he belongs.'

'Henry is no culprit, nor is Mr Prout. I absolve both of them.'

'Then turn your gaze elsewhere.'

'To whom?'

'The most obvious suspect, man – Jocelyn Kidbrooke.'

* * *

Jonathan Bale was spared the prospect of a long walk across London. Thanks to information passed on by Christopher from his brother, the constable knew where to find Jocelyn Kidbrooke at a certain time of the day. He would be in his habitual coffee house. It was not a place that Bale entered willingly. In his view, coffee houses were either gambling dens or places where idle, over-dressed, wealthy individuals met to drink coffee, smoke, talk, argue, discuss political matters or boast of their latest conquests. He was alarmed by the spread of these exclusively male institutions. The first coffee house had been opened in Holborn in 1650. Now, some twenty years later, there were well over a hundred of them in the capital. Bale regretted the fact.

He got there early and lurked in the anteroom so that he could intercept Kidbrooke on his arrival. Finding his way blocked, the newcomer was resentful.

'Out of my way, fellow,' he ordered.

'Mr Jocelyn Kidbrooke?'

'Who wants to know?'

'My name is Jonathan Bale and I crave a few words with you.'

'I've no time for chatter, Mr Bale,' said Kidbrooke, trying to brush past him. He felt a strong hand on his arm. 'Let me go, damn you!'

'Not until you agree to talk to me, sir.'

'We've nothing to say to each other.'

'It concerns Lady Culthorpe.'

Kidbrooke's resistance weakened. Through the open door of the coffee house, he could see his friends and hear their merry banter as they sat around the large common table at the heart of the room. Eager to join them, he was held back by curiosity.

'You have news of Araminta?' he asked.

'I have sad tidings of her portrait,' said Bale, releasing him. 'It was stolen last night from the artist's studio.'

Kidbrooke was impassive. 'Really?'

'You do not seem surprised.'

'Very little surprises me, Mr Bale.'

'Did you expect the portrait to be taken?'

'It was the only means of acquiring it,' said Kidbrooke, flatly. 'I tried to buy it but my generous offer was turned down.'

'Why did you want to buy a painting that was unfinished?'

'I can see that you have never laid eyes on Araminta.'

'True,' said Bale.

'Then you've missed one of the wonders of the world.'

'I'm a married man, sir.'

'For a smile from Araminta, you'd divorce your wife.'

'Is that how you feel about the lady, sir?'

'My feelings are my business.'

'Did you steal her portrait?'

'No,' said Kidbrooke, reacting angrily to the bluntness of the question. 'How dare you have the audacity even to ask that!'

'You admit that you wanted it.'

'That does not mean I was ready to steal it.'

'May I ask where you were when the crime was committed?'

'You may ask, Mr Bale, but I've no intention of telling you. I came here to commune with friends, not to be accused of a crime.'

'Where would you have kept it, sir?'

'What?'

'The portrait,' said Bale. 'If you'd been able to buy it, where would you have hidden it? Your wife would hardly approve. Do you have such little care of Mrs Kidbrooke that you'd smuggle a painting of a beautiful woman into your house?'

Kidbrooke was infuriated. 'I'll not be censored by you!'

'You face a higher critic than me, sir.' Bale looked upwards. 'You entered holy matrimony in His sight. Does that mean nothing to you?'

'My private life does not concern you.'

'It does when a crime is committed.'

'But I was not the thief, you insolent dog!'

'You might have hired one to do the business for you.'

'That's a slanderous suggestion!'

'I have to look at every possibility, sir.'

'Then look elsewhere,' snarled Kidbrooke, 'and let me go to enjoy some civilised company in place of this brash interrogation.' When he tried to move, Bale's hand held him fast again. 'Unhand me, sir!'

'We are not done yet, Mr Kidbrooke,' said Bale, steadfastly. 'I have something important to put to you. The thief will surely know how many people would like to own that portrait.'

'So?'

'Supposing that he offered to sell it to you?'

'You're hurting my arm.'

Bale let him go. 'Would you buy it from him?' he pressed. 'Knowing that you'd be receiving stolen goods, would you pay to have that painting of Lady Culthorpe?'

Jocelyn Kidbrooke was silent but a shifty look had come into his eyes. It was time to go. Bale had his answer.

Christopher Redmayne rode back to his house in Fetter Lane where he expected to meet with Jonathan Bale so they could trade information about their respective visits. But it was not his friend who had called to see the architect. Jacob passed on the news.

'A young lady is waiting for you, Mr Redmayne,' he said.

'Did she give her name?'

'She refused to do so, sir.'

'What does she want?'

'I've no idea,' said Jacob, 'but she insisted on seeing you. The young lady is in the drawing room. She's very pretty.'

There was the faintest touch of reproach in his voice. Knowing how close his master was to Susan Cheever, the old man felt it improper for him to be entertaining another young lady in her absence. Christopher quashed his suspicions at once.

'She is not here by invitation, Jacob, I promise you.'

'Very good, sir.'

Walking past the servant, he opened the door to the drawing room and went in. The young woman leapt to her feet at once. Though extremely pretty, she was also tense and uncertain.

'Mr Redmayne?' she asked.

'Yes.'

'*Christopher* Redmayne?'

'The very same,' he said, appraising her. 'May I ask your name?'

'Eleanor Ryle, sir,' she said. 'I work for Lady Culthorpe.'

He was taken aback. 'Lady Culthorpe sent you here?'

'No, Mr Redmayne – I came of my own accord. She doesn't even know that I'm here and she might be very cross with me if she did. I can't stay, sir. I have to be back in case Lady Culthorpe needs me, but I felt that I had to come.' Having gabbled the words, she paused for breath. 'I hope I've done the right thing.'

'At least, sit down while you're here, Miss Ryle,' he offered. When she resumed her seat, he took the chair opposite her. 'Why exactly did you want to see me?'

'It was because of your letter, sir – the one you wrote to Lady Culthorpe. She found it very moving. I took the trouble to read it myself and that was how I got your address.' She chewed her lip. 'I was touched by what you wrote. I felt you were a person I could trust. That's not true of some of the men who sent letters of condolence.'

'Are you referring to my brother?'

'Lady Culthorpe would not even read the verses he sent.'

'From what I hear, he's been harassing her for some time with his foolish attempts at poetry. I'll speak to him about it,' promised Christopher. 'So you came here solely on the strength of my letter?'

'No, sir,' she said. 'It was what Lady Lingoe wrote about you.'

'Oh – what was that?'

'She sent her condolences to Lady Culthorpe but she also claimed that Mr Villemot did not commit the murder. She knows the gentleman well and swears he is innocent. Lady

Lingoe mentioned you in her letter. She said that you agreed with her and were determined to clear his name.'

'That's true, Miss Ryle.'

'Then I'd like to help.'

'I'd be grateful for any assistance.'

'I'm doing it for Lady Culthorpe's sake,' said Eleanor, playing nervously with the edge of her cloak. 'I can't bear to see her suffering so much. She's in agony, Mr Redmayne, even though she tries to hide it. If it goes on like this, it will make her ill. Imagine what it must have been like for her to find Sir Martin the way she did.'

'It must have been excruciating,' said Christopher. 'And while she was tottering from that blow, she was hit by another. The man arrested for the murder is none other than the artist who's been painting her portrait.'

'That really hurt her.'

'Understandably.'

'In her heart,' said Eleanor, 'I *know* that Lady Culthorpe doesn't believe he could do such a thing, but the evidence is against him.'

'At the moment,' he said. 'That could well change.'

'Nothing could bring Sir Martin back, sir, but it would make his death so much easier to bear if Mr Villemot was not the killer. My mistress liked him. Whenever she got back from a sitting, she told me how thoughtful and caring he was.'

'That's exactly how I found him, Miss Ryle.'

'Why would he do something that would cause her so much pain and misery? That's what puzzles me. It set my mind thinking.'

'I'm glad that it did.'

'I came to tell you what I know, Mr Redmayne. I spend each and every day with Lady Culthorpe. Because I hate to see her like this, I've picked up every scrap of information I can about the crime. Ask me anything you want.'

'Monsieur Villemot was seen at the house by two witnesses,'

he recalled. 'Do you happen to know who they were?'

'One of them was Dirk, the coachman.'

'How would he have recognised him?'

'He drove Lady Culthorpe to the studio every day,' she replied. 'A couple of times, Sir Martin went with her but it was Dirk who looked after her from then on. Monsieur Villemot came to the front door to welcome her. The coachman would have got a close look at him.'

'And he saw him again at Sir Martin's house?'

'Yes, Mr Redmayne, he did. The stable block is at the rear of the garden. After dropping Lady Culthorpe at the front door, he drove around to the back. Dirk swears that he saw Monsieur Villemot, sitting astride his horse.'

'What about the second witness?'

'That was Jamie, the stable lad,' she said. 'He was walking past the garden gate when Monsieur Villemot came out. He didn't know him by sight, of course, but he described him so well that it simply has to be him.'

Christopher was alarmed. 'Are you sure that Monsieur Villemot was *in* the garden?'

'Jamie took his Bible oath.'

'Was the garden gate open or shut?'

'Wide open.'

'And was Monsieur Villemot running when he came out?'

'I don't think so,' said Eleanor. 'I only know what the butler told me. He says that Jamie is very trustworthy. He wouldn't make up a story like that.'

Christopher was disturbed. The artist had admitted riding past the house at the crucial time but he had never mentioned that he actually went into the garden. That was damning evidence. It was ironic. Eleanor had come in the hope of helping to prove Villemot's innocence but her information had so far only confirmed his probable guilt.

'How many keys are there to the garden gate?'

'That's what the officers wanted to know.'

'And?'

'There are three, it seems. Sir Martin had one, so did the head gardener and the third was kept in the house.'

'So how could Monsieur Villemot have got hold of one?'

'I can't say.' Worried about the time, she stood up abruptly. 'I'd better go, sir, or they'll start to miss me.' She paused. 'But there is one last thing,' she remembered. 'I don't think this is anything to do with what happened but I thought I ought to tell you.'

'Go on,' he said, getting up from his seat.

'Sir Martin was very fond of his garden. He spent a lot of time there. A couple of weeks before he was killed, Sir Martin had an argument with one of the gardeners and dismissed him.'

'Do you know what the argument was about?'

'No, sir,' she answered.

'What was the man's name?'

'Abel Paskins.'

'Thank you, Miss Ryle – that could turn out to be important.'

'I must leave now – it's a long walk.'

He was amazed. 'You came all this way on foot?'

'Yes, Mr Redmayne.'

'Well, you'll certainly not have to walk back.' He opened the door and called, 'Jacob!'

The old man appeared from the kitchen. 'Yes, Mr Redmayne?'

'This is Miss Eleanor Ryle. She's Lady Culthorpe's maid and has taken great pains to provide me with valuable intelligence about the murder. I want her to ride back to Westminster.'

'I'll get Nigel to saddle the other horse.'

'But I've never ridden before,' she protested.

'The lad will look after you, Miss,' said Jacob. 'All you have to do is to sit tight and let Nigel tug you along on a lead rein.'

Christopher smiled. 'Would you rather *walk* all the way back?'

'No, sir,' she said.

'Then it's settled. Jacob will arrange everything.'

Catching his master's eye, the servant shot him a look of apology before going out. He regretted making a false assumption about him. Christopher kept thinking about the gardener.

'This man who was dismissed – Abel Paskins...'

'Yes, sir?'

'I suppose you have no idea where he went?'

'I do, as a matter of fact,' said Eleanor, helpfully. 'I asked Mr Rushton – he's the butler. Mr Rushton likes to keep a close watch on everyone who's employed at the house.'

From the way that she pronounced the butler's name, Christopher had the impression that he was rather more to her than a colleague on the domestic staff. Eleanor's fondness for the man was apparent. Everything she told Christopher had come from the butler.

'So where is Abel Paskins?' he asked.

'He's working for a Mr Foxwell in Chelsea.'

'Mr Foxwell?'

'Yes,' she said. 'Mr Cuthbert Foxwell.'

It was the second time within an hour that Jocelyn Kidbrooke had been deprived of pleasure at the coffee house and he was embittered. Instead of being able to sit at the common table and revel with the others, he was taken aside by Elkannah Prout.

'We must agree to a pact, Jocelyn,' said his friend.

'The only pact I favour is one which commits all of us to entering a coffee house for the sole purpose of enjoyment.'

'I appeal to your conscience.'

'When I come in here,' said Kidbrooke, 'I leave it at the door.'

'So do the rest of us but this is a special case.'

'Do as you wish, Elkannah. That's your privilege. But you have no right to force the rest of us to imitate your folly.'

'It's not folly,' retorted Prout. 'It's an act of clemency. I've persuaded Henry to agree to the pact. I'd hoped you'd join us.'

'Confound your pact! Have a cup of coffee with the rest of

us, man, and forget about serious matters. Wear a smile again –
you were always wont to do so.'

'How can one smile at a funeral, Jocelyn?'

'How can one be miserable in a coffee house?'

Prout relaxed slightly and even managed a ghost of a smile.
He had chosen the wrong place to broach such a solemn subject
but he did not give up. After gritting his teeth, he tried once
more.

'It's a simple request, Jocelyn,' he said. 'In two days' time, Sir
Martin Culthorpe is to be buried. Will you consent to stay away
from the funeral?'

'No, Elkannah.'

'You have no place there and neither do the rest of us.'

'I neither consent to stay away nor to go,' said Kidbrooke.
'I'll make the decision on the day itself and not have it made for
me. If you and Henry shy away like frightened horses, that's
your affair.'

'Sir Willard will also see sense in the pact.'

'Then let him accept it. I'll have no rival at the graveside.'

'It would be a cruelty to Araminta to go.'

'How else can I get close to her?'

'You would not be wanted.'

'Stop browbeating me,' complained Kidbrooke. 'You're the
second person to snap at my heels about Araminta and I'll not
endure it. First, I am accused of stealing that portrait of her and
now you try to force me to sign a pact. I'll have none of it.'

Prout was interested. 'What's this about the portrait?'

'An oafish constable named Bale stopped me at the door and
had the effrontery to ask me if I was a thief.'

'According to Henry, you did offer to buy it.'

'I would have thought that was proof of my good intentions,'
said Kidbrooke. 'Why offer money for something if I intended
to take it by stealth?'

'Was the constable persuaded?'

'I don't think he had brain enough to comprehend logic.

When such men are in charge of law and order, how can we wonder that London is awash with crime?'

'Who did steal that portrait of Araminta?'

'I wish I knew, Elkannah. Were you the thief in the night?'

'No,' replied the other, indignantly. 'I told you – I've withdrawn from the Society so I am no longer at the mercy of the same imperatives.'

'Are you saying that you've lost interest in Araminta?'

'No man who has seen her could do that. I just respect her right to mourn her husband without being bothered by any of us.'

'Would you like to own that portrait?'

'That's neither here nor there.'

'You're prevaricating,' said Kidbrooke, digging his ribs with a finger. 'Be honest, man. Did you or did you not covet it?'

'I did,' conceded Prout.

'There you are – you're as bad as the rest of us.'

'No, Jocelyn, I'm not. I wanted it but knew that I could never have it. The portrait belongs to Araminta and it would be an act of cruelty to take it away from her.'

'Who would do such a thing – Henry?'

'He vehemently denies the charge.'

'Sir Willard?'

'I'd not put it past him.'

'A few days ago, I'd not have put it past Elkannah Prout. You were always in the forefront of the chase. But now,' said Kidbrooke, 'you've lost your nerve.'

'I've lost nothing. What I did was to gain a moral sense.'

'Has it robbed you of your love of coffee?'

'No,' said Prout, inhaling the aroma with a smile. 'I'll join you in a cup or two this minute. As for our pact...'

'*Your* pact, Elkannah,' said the other, slipping a companionable arm around his shoulders. 'It has no power to restrain me. Stay away from the funeral, if you wish. I answer to my own desires.'

* * *

When Jonathan Bale arrived at the house, Christopher took him into the study and first listened to his report before giving one of his own. They agreed that neither Sir Willard Grail nor Jocelyn Kidbrooke had stolen the portrait, but that both would be likely to pay handsomely for it were the painting to be offered to them. Bale grew quite excited when he heard about the visit of Eleanor Ryle. It was an unexpected bonus to get such valuable information from someone inside the Culthorpe household. He was shaken by the revelation that Villemot had been seen leaving the garden around the time when the crime was committed, but he rallied when he heard about Abel Paskins.

'We must find him, sir,' said Bale.

'That's my office, Jonathan. I'll save your legs by riding there. Not that I have a horse at present,' he added, 'but I will before too long.' He picked up a sheaf of papers from the table. 'Take a look at these sketches and tell me who the subject is.'

'An easy question, sir,' said Bale, glancing at them. 'It's your brother, Henry.'

'You recognise him?'

'Clearly.'

'Then let's see if someone else does as well,' said Christopher, looking over his friend's shoulder at the sketches. 'I can conjure buildings out of the air and create a wonderful garden with deft strokes of my pencil, but I'm no Jean-Paul Villemot. He can distil the essence of a person. I can only capture a faint likeness.'

'It's more than a likeness, Mr Redmayne.'

'I hope that's enough.'

'When did you do the drawings?' asked Bale, handing them back so that Christopher could slip them into a portfolio. 'And what did your brother think of them?'

'I did them a year ago at Henry's request. He picked out the best one to send to a lady with whom he'd become acquainted. My brother blamed me when it was returned in tiny pieces.' He moved to the door. 'Come, Jonathan – you are about to meet Matilda.'

'Is she the lady who tore up the sketch?'

'No, she's the maid at Monsieur Villemot's lodging.'

They set out together and maintained a good pace until they reached Covent Garden. When they got to the house, Emile saw them from the upstairs window and came down to open the door.

'You bring good news?' he asked, hopefully.

'Not yet,' said Christopher, 'but we soon will.'

'I see my master in the prison. Is terrible place.'

'It's intended to be,' said Bale.

'He ask me to tell Lady Lingoe where he was. She will help.'

'So will we, Emile,' said Christopher. 'We're here to speak to Matilda but there's something I must ask you first.'

'What is it?'

'You told me that you went out for a walk yesterday evening. Someone must have seen you because that's when he persuaded the maid to let him into the studio. How long were you away?'

Emile shrugged. 'An hour?'

'You walked for an hour in the dark?' said Bale. 'I should take more care, sir. It's not safe to be on the streets at that time. London is a dangerous city.'

'We learn that, my master and me.'

'May we come inside?' requested Christopher.

Emile stood back to let them into the passageway. 'I fetch Matilda for you,' he said.

He walked a few yards and tapped on a door. The maid's head soon emerged. At the sight of the strapping constable, she drew back slightly. Christopher beckoned to her.

'Could we have a moment of your time, Matilda?' He held up the portfolio. 'I want you to look at something.'

'If you wish, Mr Redmayne,' she said, coming towards him.

'Do you remember that gentleman who called yesterday?'

'Yes, I do.'

'Did he look anything like this?'

He took out the sketches and handed them over. Matilda was

a short, fat, young woman who was worried by the thought that she had mistakenly allowed the stranger to enter the house. At the time, he had seemed so friendly and plausible. She was less sure about him now. As she peered at the drawings with great concentration, Emile stood beside her. He was not impressed.

'These are not by the good artist,' he said.

Christopher smiled. 'I'm the first to admit that.'

'Oh!' cried Emile in embarrassment, 'I did not know that they are yours, Mr Redmayne. I am sorry.'

'You made an honest judgement. Stand by it.' He turned to Matilda, who was gazing hard at one sketch. 'Was that the man?'

'I think so.'

'Close to my height and a few years older?'

'He kept moving his hands.'

'Like this?' said Christopher, gesticulating in a manner typical of his brother. 'Is that what you mean?'

'Yes, Mr Redmayne.'

'Look at all the sketches – be certain.'

'I am certain,' she said, holding two of the sketches side by side. 'This is the man who called here yesterday.'

'Thank you, Matilda.'

'You know this man?' asked Emile.

'Yes,' replied Christopher, putting the drawings back into the portfolio. 'Unfortunately, I know him only too well.'

Since she was no horsewoman, the ride back to Westminster was both frightening and uncomfortable for Eleanor Ryle but it got her there much quicker than her own feet could have done so. Nigel, the fresh-faced young servant who had accompanied her, helped her down from the saddle. She thanked him profusely before running to the house. In her estimation, she had been away for the best part of two hours and feared that her mistress might have called for her in the interim.

Admitted through the side door by one of the kitchen maids, she scampered up the backstairs and along the corridor to Lady

Culthorpe's bedchamber. Eleanor was relieved to see that the door was firmly shut. Leaning against the wall opposite, she tried to catch her breath. She did not regret what she had done. Like her mistress, she had lingering doubts about Jean-Paul Villemot's guilt and she felt a *frisson* of pleasure when she recalled the artist's suggestion that she should wear the exquisite blue dress at a sitting in place of Lady Culthorpe. He had noticed her. During the few seconds they had met, Villemot had observed that her figure and deportment were similar to those of her mistress. That simple act of recognition meant so much to Eleanor. It made her *want* him to be innocent of the crime.

The door of the bedchamber suddenly opened and Araminta stood before her. With a squeal of surprise, Eleanor stood away from the wall and gave an obedient smile.

'I hope you haven't been waiting there all this time,' said Araminta with concern.

'No, m'lady.'

'What have you been doing?'

'I went for a little walk,' said the maid. 'We've been trapped in the house so long that I felt the need of some fresh air.'

'An excellent idea – there's no need to entomb ourselves here.'

'Did you get any sleep, m'lady?'

'Yes, I did, for an hour or so.'

'Oh, I'm so pleased.'

'It's left me feeling drowsier than ever.'

'Perhaps you should go back to bed.'

'No,' said Araminta, 'I feel the need to stretch my legs. Fresh air will do me good. Let's take a turn around the garden.'

'The garden?'

'Yes, Eleanor.'

'Are you sure that you're ready for that, m'lady?' said the other, thinking about Lady Culthorpe's last venture into the garden. 'I don't want you to upset yourself.'

'I need to go,' decided Araminta. 'A dreadful event may have taken place there but I'll not bar myself on that account. My husband adored his garden and he'd want me to enjoy it to the full. In any case, I have another reason for wanting to see it.'

'What was that, m'lady?'

'It was where Sir Martin proposed to me,' confided the other, a distant smile touching her face. 'So it will always be a very special place to me. Come, Eleanor. The garden will revive happier memories.'

'As long as it does not trouble you in any way.'

'We will soon find out,' said Araminta.

The ritual of dressing to go out was a long and laborious one for Henry Redmayne. Every detail had to be right, every colour had to match, every article of clothing had to blend into a dazzling whole. After a final ten minutes spent on choosing the best hat, he was ready to depart but, when he opened the front door, his brother was bearing down on the house with Jonathan Bale beside him. Henry shivered with apprehension. Recovering quickly, he sought a means of escape.

'I'm sorry, Christopher,' he said, holding up a hand. 'I can see that you've come on urgent business. Whatever it is, it will have to wait until the morrow. I have an appointment with His Majesty at the palace and he must not be kept waiting.'

Christopher was direct. 'I don't think the King would be pleased to know that he was consorting with a thief.'

'What are you talking about?'

'That portrait.'

'I did not steal it,' said Henry. 'I'd swear on the biggest Bible in Christendom. I'd even do so before our esteemed father and there's no more solemn oath than that. Now, let me get on my way.'

'No, sir,' said Bale, obstructing him.

'You've no right to stop me.'

'And you've no right to tell us lies, Mr Redmayne. I am not as close to King Charles as you but I do hear gossip about him from time to time, and I am certain that he's not even in London.'

'That's true,' said Christopher. 'I read it in the newspaper. His Majesty is visiting Oxford. No more flimsy excuses, Henry. Invite us in so that we may settle this matter.'

'It already *is* settled – I'm not a thief.'

'We are talking about the visit you paid to the house yesterday.'

'That wasn't me, Christopher.'

'The maid believes that it was,'

Henry was incensed. 'Do you accept the word of an ignorant slattern over mine?'

'Yes,' said Christopher, tapping the portfolio. 'We showed Matilda those sketches I did of you. She recognised you.'

'And she is no ignorant slattern, sir,' said Bale. 'The girl has good eyesight. Even by the light of a candle, you are very distinctive.'

'If you still persist in denying it, Henry, there's an easy solution. Now that you no longer have to rush off to the palace, you can step along to Monsieur Villemot's lodging with us and let Matilda take a proper look at you.' Christopher held out an arm. 'Shall we do that?'

Henry Redmayne was like a trapped animal. Caught at the threshold, he could not get free. What made his discomfort more intense was that Bale was there to enjoy it. They had met before in the course of Henry's previous indiscretions and the constable had always seized the chance to deliver a lecture at him on morality. Henry could not bear that. He looked for a compromise.

'Very well,' he said with a grandiloquent gesture, 'perhaps my curiosity did get the better of me. There's no harm in that.'

'You entered that house under false pretences,' said Bale.

'I'm prepared to discuss this misunderstanding with my brother, Mr Bale, but not if you are party to the conversation.

Your presence would inhibit me. This is an occasion for filial confidences.'

Bale looked at Christopher and they had a silent discussion. At length, and with reluctance, Bale agreed to withdraw, touching the brim of his hat in farewell. Henry took his brother into the house and guided him into the drawing room. Sweeping off his hat, he conjured up an expression of remorse.

'I did visit the house,' he confessed, 'and it was wrong of me to do so. But I was desperate to see that portrait of Araminta and it seemed like the only way.'

'Short of stealing it, that is,' said Christopher.

'I did not take the portrait and there's an end to it.'

'Far from it, Henry – I fancy we are just at the beginning. I spoke to Sir Willard Grail earlier and he mentioned an association to which you and he belong. What exactly is it?'

'Harmless fun among friends,' said Henry, airily.

'I don't think that wheedling your way into someone else's property can be classed as harmless fun. Matilda has been blaming herself for letting you in ever since. I could see it in her face,' said Christopher. 'But for her, that portrait would not have been stolen.'

'I told you – I had nothing to do with the theft.'

'We'll come back to that. First, tell me about this society.'

'It was Elkannah's notion,' said Henry, trying to shift responsibility on to someone else. 'I was against it from the start but the others cajoled me into it, and I was as entranced by Araminta as any of them. Under pressure from the others, I joined the group.'

'And what was its purpose?' There was an awkward pause. 'Come along, Henry. I know that it pertained to Lady Culthorpe so you might as well be honest about it. What was its name?'

'The Society for the Capture of Araminta's Maidenhood.'

Christopher was shocked. 'That's disgraceful!'

'It was only meant in jest.'

'Well, the jest has so far led to the murder of her husband and the theft of her portrait. What other amusement is your iniquitous society going to offer?'

'Do not be so harsh on me, Christopher.'

'A round of applause seems inappropriate.'

'I expect you to appreciate your brother's position.'

'Allying yourself with your companions in corruption in a bid to deflower an innocent young woman!' said Christopher. 'That's your position. I'm not surprised that you or Sir Willard were drawn into this hideous scheme, but I expected more of Mr Prout. He struck me as a man with some sense of honour.'

'Yet he proposed that we set up the Society in the first place.'

'Indeed?'

'Elkannah even drew up the articles of association and nominated the amount of money that was to be involved.'

'*Money?*' Christopher's voice was rich with disgust. 'There was money at stake here? What sort of degenerates are you that you should gamble on the loss of a lady's virtue?'

'It was not like that, Christopher.'

'What other construction can I put upon it?'

'Think about Susan Cheever.'

'Don't you dare mention Susan's name in this context,' said Christopher, pulsing with fury as he grabbed his brother by the shoulders to shake him hard. 'Keep her out of it.'

In the interests of safety, Henry stepped back out of his brother's reach, smoothing the wrinkles in his coat and adjusting the wig that had been shaken down over one eye. Seeing how irate his brother was, he measured his words.

'You have just proved my point, Christopher,' he said.

'What point?'

'Love is a ruthless emotion. When once it gets hold of us, we are driven to extremes by violent passion. I only had to mention your beloved and you flew at me.'

'You deserved it, Henry.'

'I also deserve a fair hearing. The Society was conceived

during a drinking bout in a tavern, and I subscribed too hastily to its rules. As soon as I began to court Araminta Jewell, as she then was, I shed my lustful feelings and became instead madly in love.'

'But still in pursuit of that purse.'

'It was a foolish game, played out among friends.'

'Four confirmed rakes, stalking their prey.'

'Not in my case,' argued Henry. 'I felt about Araminta as you feel about Susan.' He jumped back smartly as Christopher threatened him with a bunched fist. 'As you wish,' he added, quickly. 'If the comparison offends you, I'll keep her name out of it. I simply ask you to admit one thing. Is it not true that someone in the grip of passion will do anything to secure the favours of his inamorata?'

'No, Henry, respect and gentlemanly restraint hold him back.'

'Well, it was not so with me. I was desperate to see that portrait of Araminta. The thought that it was only a few streets away burned into my brain like a hot iron.'

'So you decided to steal it.'

'I only wanted to *look* at it.'

'So that you'd be able to find it in the dark later that night.'

'The thought never occurred to me.'

'Be honest,' said Christopher, advancing on him. 'You cannot hide behind the excuse of blind passion then claim you were able to control it. If it took you as far as the house, it would have made you want to possess that portrait.' Henry began to jabber. 'Give me a straight answer, man. This is important. Lady Culthorpe has lost a husband. Why did you set out to increase her misery by taking that portrait of her from the studio?'

'That was not my intention,' said Henry.

'Then what was it?' Christopher grabbed him again. 'We are trying to solve a murder and vindicate an innocent man. That portrait holds great significance so I need to know what happened to it. Now, will you tell me or do I have to beat the truth of you?'

'You're crumpling my new coat!' protested Henry.

'If you don't tell me what happened, I'll tear everything in your wardrobe to shreds. Now, speak. For the sake of Lady Culthorpe, I must recover that portrait. Where, in God's name, is it?'

'I don't know.'

'You're lying again.'

'I don't know,' repeated Henry. 'It was not there.'

Christopher released him. 'So you did go back at night?'

'Yes – but only to *look* at it.'

'In the dark?'

'I'd lit a candle. I was a true votary. I had an overpowering desire to worship at her altar. That was all. I wanted to gaze lovingly upon Araminta's beauty.'

'Then bring it back here as a trophy. Is this what it's come to, Henry?' asked his brother with revulsion. 'A man is brutally killed and the only way you try to console the widow you profess to love is to break into a house and steal her portrait.'

'It was not there, Christopher,' said the other, meekly. 'Araminta has disappeared. When I saw it earlier, the portrait was standing on the easel beside the window.'

'And that's exactly where I caught a glimpse of it.'

'It had been replaced.'

'By what?'

'I blush to tell you.'

'By *what*, Henry?'

'A portrait of Lady Hester Lingoe.'

Chapter Eight

Henry Redmayne collapsed into a chair. He cut a sorry figure. Dressed in his finery for an evening with friends, he was now totally deflated. His body drooped and his shoulders sagged. With his long, thin, sad face hollowed by despair and framed by his wig, he looked like a giant spaniel bemoaning the death of its master. Notwithstanding his rage, Christopher felt some sympathy for him. He had bullied the truth out of his brother and left him in disarray.

'Are you sure that Lady Culthorpe's portrait was not there?'

'Yes,' mumbled Henry.

'It could have been somewhere else in the studio.'

'I searched, Christopher. I looked at every painting in the room and there was no sign of Araminta. Someone had got there before me. I only came to gaze in wonder. The rogue went there to steal.'

'So did you,' said Christopher. 'You swore to me that you'd have that portrait as your own by whatever means were necessary.'

'I did,' admitted Henry, 'and, at the time, I meant it. When I set out from here last night, I planned to spirit it away and hang it in my bedchamber. But when I got there, Christopher, when I entered the studio where Araminta had sat, when I thought how deeply wounded she would be by the disappearance of her portrait, I realised that I could simply not take it. I was overwhelmed with remorse.'

'Ha! That must have been a novel sensation for you.'

'Laugh at me, if you must. I deserve it. I know that my erratic way of life invites your sarcasm. But something good happened to me in that studio, something that surprised me as much as it would have surprised our dear father. I discovered that I had a conscience.'

'It's a pity you didn't make the startling discovery earlier,' said Christopher. 'It would have stopped you committing the crime.'

'I'm not a thief. I lack the nerve and ruthlessness.'

'You had enough of both to break into someone else's property. You were trespassing, Henry. That, too, is against the law. The wonder is that you got in and out without being seen by anyone.'

'I must thank the maid for that.'

'Matilda?' gasped Christopher. 'She was your accomplice?'

'Yes,' said Henry, 'without even realising it. If you've met her, you know what a plump, unlovely, slow-witted creature she is. Matilda had never before had a gentleman heap praise upon her.'

'So you took advantage of her.'

'All I had to do was to pay her a few pretty compliments and she surrendered to my charm. When she explained that the family she served were away from the house, I told her to leave a window open for me so that I could visit her at night.'

'That was cruel, Henry.'

'I made no promises. I only said that I would *try* to call on her.'

'Without ever intending to do so.'

'Do you blame me?' said Henry, pompously. 'Where assignations are concerned, I have the highest standards. She met none of them.'

'But she lay in bed all night awaiting you. That's a brutal way to treat any woman,' Christopher admonished. 'No wonder Matilda looked so crestfallen when I saw her earlier. You not only raised false hopes in her breast, you made her an unwitting accessory to a crime.'

'I had to get into the house somehow.'

'Yes – by cunning and duplicity.'

'It was no more than a means to an end.'

'A reprehensible means to an ignoble end. Really, Henry,' said the other with consternation. 'Each new revelation makes me wonder what kind of monster I have as a brother. Do you have no moral sense at all? The only honest course of action for me is to have you placed under arrest.'

'On what charge?'

'I can think of three or four at least.'

'I did not break into that house – the window was left open for me. And I stole nothing from that studio. I could not have done so. I felt the sharp prick of my conscience.'

'I rejoice to hear that you have one,' said Christopher. 'Until now you've been governed by a sharp prick of another kind – the one you dangled in front of that gullible maid by way of enticement. I've heard enough,' he added, moving to the door. 'Tell the rest of the revolting story to a magistrate.'

'No!' yelled Henry, jumping to his feet and rushing to stop his brother. 'Don't do that, I beg you. I acknowledge that I did wrong and I've been haunted by guilt ever since. I want to repair my fault. Teach me how I can make amends.'

'A ten-year penance would not be enough.'

'I implore you, Christopher. Hold off out of brotherly love. Do you really want to see me branded as a criminal?'

'That's what you are, Henry.'

'Could you write the letter that would tell our father so? Think how much sorrow it would bring him. The old gentlemen would be distraught. Spare him that agony.'

It was a telling argument and it made Christopher pause. Unlike his brother, he kept up a regular correspondence with their father and he spent much of his letters trying to present any news about Henry in a favourable light. He did not want the venerable dean of Gloucester Cathedral to know just how wayward and unchristian an existence his elder son led. To confront him with the full horror of what Henry had done would cause him immense pain.

'Give me a chance,' pleaded Henry. 'I'll do absolutely anything to make up for my misdemeanours.'

'Anything?'

'Nominate it and it shall be done.'

'The first thing you must do is offer recompense to Matilda.'

Henry blanched. '*Sleep* with that plain-faced tub of flesh?'

'No,' said Christopher. 'I'd not inflict that ordeal on any woman but an apology would not come amiss. And a gift of some sort might help to take away the bitter taste of your callous betrayal.'

'Matilda shall have both with some honey-tongued flattery to make her feel like the Queen of the May.'

'An apology and a gift will suffice.'

'What else?'

'Resolve to help Lady Culthorpe instead of hurting her. Send no more of your unwelcome poetry to her.'

'But I slaved over those verses.'

'To ill effect from what I hear,' said Christopher. 'Your poems offend her, Henry. She did not even read the last one you sent.'

'I refuse to believe that.'

'I had it from an impeccable source – her maid, Eleanor Ryle.'

Henry's face ignited. 'You know her maid?'

'She came to see me.'

'How is Araminta? Is she bearing up? Has she mentioned me?'

'Only with distaste,' said Christopher. 'Everything you've done so far has incurred her displeasure. If you want to win her approval, there are two simple ways.'

'Tell me what they are and I'll do both instantly.'

'The chief one is to leave her alone, Henry – no more letters, no more verses, no more communication from you of any kind.'

'But I want to express my condolences.'

'I've just told you the most effective way to do it. The second thing you must do is to assist me. If we can prove that Monsieur Villemot is innocent, we'll remove a whole dimension of Lady Culthorpe's grief.'

'What if he's guilty?'

'Then he'll pay the penalty for his crime. But I'm convinced that he was not the killer and I'm not alone in that belief. Lady Lingoe also has complete faith in his innocence.'

Henry laughed. 'It's the first time that Hester has been troubled by the concept of innocence,' he said. 'You should have seen the portrait for which she sat.'

'I did see it, Henry. I thought it tastefully done.'

'It was – I could taste her as soon as I looked at it.'

'Even though you claim you've dedicated yourself elsewhere?'

'Hester and Araminta cannot be mentioned in the same breath,' said Henry, reprovingly. 'One arouses carnal desire while the other attracts only the purest love.'

'I don't recall any mention of the purest love in the title of the infamous society of which you were a member.' Henry was cowed. 'But let's not dwell on that. The person we must think of now is the one who's wrongly imprisoned in Newgate. You know better than anyone how that feels. You were once wrongly accused of murder.'

'It was a ghastly experience. The place is a common sewer.'

'Then help to get Monsieur Villemot out of it.'

'How?'

'You are acquainted with more people than anyone else in London,' said Christopher, 'and those you've never met you somehow seem to know about.'

'Only if they belong to the aristocracy or the gentry,' said Henry with a lordly tilt of his chin. 'I deal with the elite of society. I have no truck with the lower orders.'

'Does the name of Foxwell mean anything to you?'

'Partner it with another and it might. I could list half-a-dozen Foxwells and still not give you the fellow you want.'

'This gentlemen is called Cuthbert Foxwell.'

'Living in Chelsea?'

'Yes, Henry – do you know him?'

'Not in person but Sir Willard Grail knows him very well.'

'Does he?'

'He ought to – Cuthbert Foxwell is his brother-in-law.'

Sir Willard Grail sipped his wine and gave a smile of satisfaction. He was seated at a table in the corner of a tavern. Elkannah Prout was beside him. He tasted his own wine before returning to the argument.

'You must join us in this pact,' he said.

'I'll not be dictated to by anybody, Elkannah.'

'Keep away from that funeral.'

'I'd intended to until you tried to make it mandatory. My instinct now is to go. In a congregation of that size, I'd hardly be noticed.'

'That's not the point, Sir Willard.'

'What is?'

'You should stay away as a mark of respect.'

'Araminta will not know if I'm there or not,' said Sir Willard, 'so she will be quite unaware of any supposed respect I'm showing.'

'I didn't expect you to be so obstinate,' said Prout, irritably. 'When I put the idea of a pact to him, Henry agreed to it immediately.'

'What of Jocelyn?'

Prout scowled. 'He was less forthcoming.'

'I'll wager that he dismissed the notion out of hand. Jocelyn Kidbrooke and I are cut from the same cloth. We are free agents. We do not like being told what to do.'

'You both subscribed willingly enough the articles of the Society and they imposed certain restrictions on you.'

'We were united by a common purpose – to court Araminta and win the ultimate favour from her. Her marriage made that aim more ambiguous,' said Sir Willard, drinking his wine. 'The murder of her husband removed what might have proved a fatal handicap.'

'It left me with no stomach for the contest,' said Prout.

'Then stop trying to influence those of us still engaged in it.'

'Attending that funeral would be wrong, Sir Willard.'

'That's a judgement each of us must make for himself.'

'Can you be so heartless?'

'Yes, Elkannah,' said the other. 'I can and so could you a week ago. You may have been converted on the road to Damascus but the rest of us remain committed to our common objective. There was a time when you were the most pitiless and cold-blooded member of the Society. We took our lead from you.'

'I confess it freely and am deeply ashamed.'

'Shame is not an emotion with which I am familiar, and nor is Jocelyn. From what I know of him, he'll not only be at that funeral, he'll probably contrive to act as a pallbearer.'

'At least, Henry Redmayne has scruples.'

'They may lose him the prize,' said Sir Willard. 'By the way, did I tell you that I was accosted by his brother earlier today?'

'Christopher?'

'He seemed to think that I might have stolen that portrait.'

'You are not the only suspect,' said Prout. 'I was there when he accused Henry of the theft. Jocelyn, too, has been questioned.'

'What – by Christopher Redmayne?'

'A parish constable lay in wait for him at the coffee house – a boorish fellow who demanded to know if Jocelyn had the portrait.'

'Who was this constable?'

'He's a friend of Henry's brother. They've worked together before to solve various crimes and had a measure of success. Christopher is tenacious and so is Bale.'

'Is that his name?'

'So I hear – Jonathan Bale. His heavy-handed questioning

really upset Jocelyn and it takes a lot to do that. Christopher Redmayne and this constable are clearly determined to recover that portrait.'

'To be honest, I thought it *had* been taken by Jocelyn.'

'He denies it hotly.'

'What about Henry?'

'His denials were even more fervent. Since none of we four has that portrait of Araminta,' said Prout, thoughtfully, 'then only one conclusion can be drawn. Someone else stole it.'

Sir Willard's envy glowed. 'Who the devil is he?'

Wearing the blue dress and reclining on the couch, Araminta Culthorpe did not seem to have a care in the world. She looked happy, composed and thoroughly at ease with herself. The portrait was a study in unimpaired beauty and contentment. Though he had looked at it many times, the man never tired of his scrutiny. When he set the painting up on the table once more, he examined every last detail of Araminta's face, hair and shoulders. Her soft, white, delicate arms held him in thrall. Her dainty hands had their own delight for him. It was over an hour before he had seen his fill. Pulling the cloth down over the portrait, he put it back carefully in its hiding place.

Araminta had lapsed back into melancholy. She sat beside the table in the drawing room and stared in silence at the paper in front of her. It contained the provisional list of mourners who would attend the funeral but she saw none of the names. Her mind was on the life that lay ahead and it was not appealing. When her husband was lowered into his grave, Araminta's high hopes and bold plans for their marriage would go with him. It was depressing.

Coming into the room, Eleanor Ryle sensed the problem at once.

'Try not to brood, m'lady,' she said, crossing over to stand beside her mistress. 'Only this afternoon, you were beginning to shake off sad thoughts. We had that walk in the garden.'

'I know, Eleanor, and it restored me.'

'You took such an interest in it.'

'I have to, now that my husband is not here. That garden is a sacred duty I've inherited. I'll keep it exactly as Sir Martin would have wished.'

'He would not have wanted you to fret like this.'

'It's much more than fretting,' said Araminta. 'I feel a great emptiness inside me. And I'm so listless. I've no strength to cope with the demands made on me.'

'That's why you've got people like me to help,' said Eleanor, a hand on her shoulder. 'Have you been looking at that list of guests? You've no need to trouble with that. I've spoken to Mr Rushton. He'll make sure that everyone is taken care of, m'lady.'

'It's the service itself that worries me.'

'You've family and friends to carry you through it.'

'I'm not sure if I shall be able to bear up.'

'Yes, you will – for Sir Martin's sake.'

'Of course,' said Araminta, sitting upright. 'I'm doing it for his sake. I must stop thinking of myself and turn all my thoughts to him. What would my husband expect of me – that's what I must consider.'

She addressed herself to the list and started to go through it. Glad to see her mistress's spirit restored, Eleanor sat beside her. It was only when Araminta had been through all the names that her sadness returned.

'What if one of them should come?' she asked.

'One of whom?'

'Henry Redmayne and those other men who bothered me.'

'I'm sure they'll be considerate enough to stay away, m'lady.'

'It's so strange,' mused Araminta. 'Mr Redmayne and his silly poems were so objectionable yet his brother was charming. I could not believe they belonged to the same family. One is an idle fop and the other, a well-mannered and diligent young man.

And he must have great talent as an architect or Monsieur Villemot would never have employed him.' She let out a gasp. 'Oh dear!'

'What ails you, m'lady?'

'I've just remembered him – locked away in that prison.'

'If he's guilty, that's where he should be.'

'But what if he's not, Eleanor? That's what worries me. I got quite close to Monsieur Villemot. I liked him. I respected him as an artist. He had a wonderful career ahead of him and was having a new house built so that he and his wife could live in London.' She pursed her lips in thought. 'Why put all that in jeopardy?'

'It does seem rather reckless,' said the maid.

'He could never hope to get away with it.'

'Then perhaps he was not the killer, after all.'

'I'd *love* to believe that,' said Araminta. 'I'd love to believe he could be exonerated and set free.'

'Perhaps that will happen, m'lady.'

'How? He's imprisoned in a foreign country with nobody to help him. Even if he were innocent of the crime, how would we ever know?'

Eleanor thought of her visit to Christopher Redmayne.

The meeting took place in the prison sergeant's office. Lady Hester Lingoe had commandeered it with the help of a generous bribe, but even her money and position were not enough to ensure a private conversation with the prisoner. A turnkey was there throughout and his presence set precise limits on their freedom of expression. When they first met, therefore, all that Jean-Paul Villemot felt able to do was to touch her hand in gratitude.

'Thank you,' he said. 'Thank you so much for coming.'

'Did my lawyer visit you?'

'Yes, he did. He had me moved to a larger cell.'

'A single one, I trust.'

'I am all alone – apart from the rats.'

'It must be intolerable.'

'They treat me bad.'

'Then I'll make a formal complaint about that.'

Lady Lingoe held the pomander to her nose and inhaled deeply. Even in the prison sergeant's office, the offensive odours were evident and Villemot was embarrassed by the fact that his clothing was giving off an unpleasant smell. He looked worn and desperate. For her part, Lady Lingoe had shed the costume of a Roman priestess and put on more conventional apparel. In the drab little room, she looked like a beacon of light and he dared to nurse hopes again.

'Get me out of here!' he begged.

'That may take a little time, Jean-Paul.'

'I did not kill this man.'

'I know that,' she said with a fond smile. 'We have to gather evidence to prove it. Mr Redmayne is doing all he can to help you.'

'But he handed me over to the magistrate.'

'It was for your own good.'

'Good?' he echoed with a mirthless laugh. 'This is *good*?'

'Put some trust in Christopher Redmayne,' she advised. 'That's what I've decided to do. He's eager to build that house for you, Jean-Paul. He has an incentive to get you released – and so have I.'

Unseen by the turnkey, she touched the artist's hand again then she held the pomander to her nostrils. Thrilled to see a friend, Villemot was frustrated by the watchful presence of a third person. It made for halting and unsatisfactory exchange.

'I've brought food and wine for you,' she said.

'*Merci beaucoup!*'

'My lawyer will come to see you every day.'

'You are the only person I wish to see, Hester!'

'I hope we can meet in more propitious circumstances next time, Jean-Paul.' She glanced around. 'This is hardly the ideal place for a tête-à-tête.'

'I am living in the privy.'

'How sordid!'

'The noise, it drives me mad.'

'Hold fast – we will do everything in our power to save you.'

'And if you *fail*?'

Lady Lingoe could not hide her fear. For one vital second, the mask of reassurance slipped from her face and Villemot saw that she was as frightened as he was. She recovered her air of imperturbability and produced a dazzling smile.

'We'll not fail, Jean-Paul,' she said. 'You mean too much to us.'

It was still light when Christopher Redmayne reached the house in Chelsea and he was able to see the extensive gardens in which it stood. In the previous century, Chelsea had been known as a village of palaces because Henry VIII and some of the leading men of the day had maintained splendid houses there. It was still a place to catch the eye of an architect. Cuthbert Foxwell's mansion was not as large or palatial as many others but its clear signs of French influence aroused Christopher's interest. He noted features that he had incorporated into the design for the Villemot residence.

When he rang the doorbell, he was invited into the house and introduced himself to its owner. Cuthbert Foxwell was a short, slim, round-shouldered man in his late thirties with a book under his arm. After conducting his visitor into the library, he looked at him over the top of his spectacles.

'To what do I owe the pleasure of your company, sir?' he asked.

'I believe that you are Sir Willard Grail's brother-in-law.'

'I have that honour. Do you know Sir Willard?'

'My brother is a close friend of his,' said Christopher.

'Redmayne...Redmayne...' Foxwell's memory was jogged. 'I thought I'd heard that name before. Sir Willard has mentioned it to me. I can't say that I see much of my brother-in-law,' he continued. 'We have no mutual interests – apart from my wife, that is. Sir Willard is a man of the world while I'm more parochial in outlook. I think he looks upon me as a country yokel.'

'You're hardly that, Mr Foxwell,' said Christopher with a gesture towards the bookshelves. 'You have a magnificent library here.'

'I'm bookish by nature and account myself a true scholar.'

'You obviously have a passion for the garden as well.'

'I do indeed, Mr Redmayne.'

'It's on that subject that I came to speak to you.'

'Tell me more, dear sir.'

When they had sat down, Christopher told him about the murder and the arrest of Jean-Paul Villemot. He explained that he believed in the Frenchman's innocence and was bent on proving it. Foxwell was impressed with the clarity of his report and the earnest manner in which it was delivered.

'This is all very intriguing,' he said, 'but I do not see how your researches can have brought you to Chelsea.'

'I came to look for a gardener.'

'We have a small team of them here, Mr Redmayne, and they are kept very busy. Gardens are a joy to behold when they are well-tended. If you neglect them, however,' he counselled, 'you'll soon end up with a wilderness.'

'One of your gardeners once worked for Sir Martin Culthorpe.'

'Did he? That's news to me.'

'He may have concealed the fact from you, Mr Foxwell. I gather that he left Sir Martin's employ under something of a cloud.'

'What was the man's name?'

'Paskins – Abel Paskins.'

'I remember him – a sturdy, hard-working fellow.'

'Is he here at the moment, by any chance?' said Christopher.

'I'm afraid not.'

'You dismissed him?'

'No, Mr Redmayne – he left of his own accord. At least, that's what I thought at the time. I later learned that he'd been poached.'

'By whom?'

'A friend of my brother-in-law,' said Foxwell. 'To be frank with you, I was rather put out. When you have guests in the house, you do not expect one of them to tempt a gardener away. For that's what happened,' he continued. 'When Sir Willard and his friend arrived, we entertained them as we saw fit. I showed them around the garden.'

'Was Abel Paskins there at the time?'

'He was. I saw Sir Willard's friend chatting to him.'

'Then the gardener left you.'

'I think he was lured away by the promise of more money.'

'What was the name of your guest?'

'It was my brother-in-law who invited him. He was not the sort of person to whom I could ever take – a portly man who looked as if he caroused too much, and who only remembered that he had a wife on Sunday when they went to church. In fact,' said Foxwell, 'he was a very disagreeable fellow altogether.'

'Did he have a name?'

'Jocelyn Kidbrooke.'

Henry Redmayne was not given to making apologies. He had certainly never been compelled to tender one to a roly-poly maid with an unappetising face. But his brother had ordered him to do so and it was the only way he could appease Christopher. To that end, he asked a servant to gather a basket of flowers from the garden then set out with it on his arm. Reaching the house, it took him a long time before he could pluck up the courage to ring the bell. While he waited for the door to open, he rehearsed his apology and manufactured his most ingratiating smile.

Matilda opened the door to be greeted by the daunting sight

of a gentleman in fashionable attire. The maid had been crying and her eyes were still moist. Strands of straggly hair hung down over her forehead. She was so overwhelmed by her ostentatious visitor that she dropped a curtsey by instinct.

'How are you, Matilda?' asked Henry, solicitously.

Recognising his voice, she let out a yelp of pain and tried to close the door. He stuck out a foot to hold it open. Matilda was cowering with a mixture of fear and anguish. Tears began to explore the periphery of her fat cheeks.

'I've brought you a gift,' he said, holding up the basket. 'Do you see? These are for you – by way of an apology.'

Matilda regarded the flowers warily. When she saw what a large and colourful variety had been gathered, she slowly began to relax. Her caution gave way to pleasure and she was soon beaming. When she opened the door wide, Henry gave her the basket.

'Thank you, kind sir,' she said.

'I am sorry that I was unable to come to you last night.'

'I waited and waited.'

'Circumstances beyond my control intervened,' he said. Seeing her look of incomprehension, he supplied his excuse in plain terms. 'My wife came home unexpectedly.'

'Oh!' she cried. 'I didn't know you were married, sir.'

'I forgot that I was when I looked upon *you*, Matilda.' Her cheeks turned crimson. 'Alas, I was unable to fulfil my promise.'

'I left the window open all night long, sir,' she said in a hoarse whisper. 'If they ever find out, I'll get the blame.'

'For what?'

'A thief crept into the house.'

'Never!'

'He stole a portrait from the studio upstairs. He couldn't have done that if the window had been locked. It was all my fault.'

'No,' said Henry, altruistically, 'I absolve you of any blame. I was the culprit, Matilda. That window was open because of me.

You need have no qualms about it. The responsibility is entirely mine.'

'But I don't even know your name, sir.'

'It's perhaps better that you never do.'

Clutching the basket to her bosom, she beamed hopefully. 'Shall I see you again, sir?' she enquired, coyly.

'One day, perhaps,' said Henry, gallantly. 'One glorious day.'

Then he flitted gratefully away into the gathering twilight.

Darkness was falling by the time he reached Addle Hill. Christopher was glad that he had made the effort to ride to Chelsea and back. He was now calling on Jonathan Bale to apprise him of what had happened since they parted. He was always glad to visit the little house when the whole family was at home. He was as fond of Sarah Bale as she of him, and he liked the two boys. It did not trouble the architect that Oliver and Richard had been named after the Lord Protector and his son. They were two lively, friendly, fun-loving lads. Whenever he met them, Christopher found himself wondering if he and Susan would ever have such a contented family.

When his wife had taken the children into the kitchen, Bale invited his visitor to sit down then perched on a stool that he had made when first married. It seemed too small for his bulk but it held his weight without any difficulty.

'I'm sorry that you had to leave us earlier on,' said Christopher, 'but my brother would not have been so open in your company.'

'Did you get the truth out of him, sir?'

'Little by little.'

'I long to hear it.'

Christopher gave him a brief description of what had occurred at the house in Bedford Street, picking out only the salient points. Since his friend already had a low opinion of his brother, he saw no point in revealing that Henry had coaxed the maid into leaving the window open for him at night. Bale would despise him even more and would insist that legal action be taken against him for attempted theft. Christopher preferred to keep his brother out of prison so that he could be of assistance to them, and so that their father could be spared the shock of learning about the antics of his elder son.

Bale was interested to hear about the visit to Chelsea.

'The gardener was poached?' he said. 'I wonder why.'

'I can think of one good reason – he would know about Sir Martin Culthorpe's regular visits to his garden.'

'And he'd have some idea how to get the key to that gate.'

'There's also the fact that Abel Paskins might have had a score to settle with his old employer,' said Christopher. 'I think it significant that, when he found a new position with Mr Foxwell, he took care to say nothing about having worked for Sir Martin.'

'The person we must look at is the one who recruited him, sir.'

'Jocelyn Kidbrooke.'

'He's not the nicest man you'll meet.'

'You said that he was rude and quick-tempered.'

'He treated me with disdain,' said Bale, 'and he had the look of a man who treats the law likewise.'

'If he's part of Henry's circle, he'll not qualify for holy orders, we can take that for granted. My brother always describes his friends as belonging to a merry gang.'

'That's not what I'd call them, Mr Redmayne.'

'Nor me, Jonathan,' said Christopher. 'They pursue pleasure as huntsmen pursue a fox, and they care nothing for the damage they may do in the course of the chase.'

'Shall I speak to Mr Kidbrooke again, sir?'

'No, I think it's my turn. As Henry's brother, I may at least get some civility out of him. On second thoughts,' he went on, 'it might be better if I got Henry to approach him on our behalf. We don't want to arouse his suspicions. My brother is the best person to tackle Kidbrooke.'

Bale was surprised. 'Would he agree to help us?'

'I've no doubt about that.'

'But Jocelyn Kidbrooke is his friend.'

'Henry owes me a very large favour,' said Christopher, thinking of the way he had suppressed details of his brother's peccadilloes. 'Let me put it more strongly – he's in no position to refuse.'

'How close are the two men?'

'Very close.'

'They dine and drink and go to the theatre together?'

Christopher sighed. 'Oh, I think they do much more than that.'

'He was a parish constable, a blundering fool named Jonathan Bale.'

'I know the rogue,' said Henry Redmayne.

'Then you know how stubborn he can be.'

'Stubborn, stupid and far too inquisitive.'

'The man had the gall to ask me if I stole that portrait,' said Jocelyn Kidbrooke with a snort. 'I almost knocked him down for his impudence. What's the world coming to when one can't have a coffee with friends without being set upon by some idiot like that?'

'Bale is no idiot. I'd clear him of that charge.'

'Wait until he comes calling on you.'

'He already has, Jocelyn,' said the other, 'on more than one occasion. He has no need to accuse me of being a thief. My brother has already done that. Ask Elkannah – he was there at the time.'

After an evening spent at a tavern, the two men were being driven in Kidbrooke's coach through the echoing streets of London. Both had imbibed heavily and their speech was slightly slurred, but, as far as they were concerned, there was a long way to go yet before they would even think of retiring for the night. Henry still felt raw after his abrasive encounter with

Christopher and was relieved that no legal action would be taken against him. Jocelyn Kidbrooke had other preoccupations.

'I'm glad you mention Elkannah,' he said, pausing to inhale snuff from a silver box. 'What's all this balderdash about a pact?'

'He thinks we should stay away from the funeral.'

'And you agreed?'

'Only to get rid of Elkannah,' said Henry. 'He kept on and on at me so I pretended to concur.'

'He badgered me as well and I daresay that Sir Willard was also his victim. I liked the fellow *before* he developed a conscience. He's beginning to sound horribly like a priest now.'

'He'll come back to us in time. What did you say to him?'

'I spurned his nonsensical pact.'

'Does that mean that you intend to go to Sir Martins' funeral?'

'I wouldn't miss a chance to see Araminta for anything.'

'You won't see much of her, Jocelyn. She'll be swathed in black and surrounded by mourners.'

'But I'd be in the same church as her, breathing the same air.'

'It is a temptation,' confessed Henry. As the coach began to slow, he glanced through the window. 'Here we are at last. I hope that my luck changes tonight. The cards have been unkind to me all week.'

'I'm not here to gamble,' said Kidbrooke.

When the coach came to a halt, they got out and walked uncertainly towards the portico of a tall, elegant house. The front door opened before they even reached it and they went into the building and down a corridor. Henry peeled off into the first room they came to, looking for an empty chair at one of the card tables and sniffing the strong aroma of tobacco smoke. Because he was a regular visitor to the house, he was given a cordial welcome and a free glass of wine. His fingers itched to touch the cards again.

Jocelyn Kidbrooke, meanwhile, had gone to a room at the

back of the house. Large, luxurious and only half-lit by candelabra, it was watched over by a buxom woman in her fifties with a beauty spot on one cheek. Powder had been used in liberal amounts to disguise her raddled face, and arching black eyebrows had been painted on in such a way that she seemed to be in a permanent state of astonishment. The sight of a new customer brought her to life. As she laughed aloud, her breasts wobbled and her jowls shook.

'Mr Kidbrooke,' she gushed, embracing him familiarly. She indicated the array of attractive young women, reclining seductively on sofas as they tried to catch the newcomer's attention. 'Whom will you choose tonight, sir?'

Jocelyn Kidbrooke ran an expert eye over the painted ladies. 'The one who looks most like Araminta,' he murmured.

In his master's absence, Emile did not slack. He attended to his duties with even more alacrity. When he had eaten his breakfast, he washed the dishes, fed the cat, made his bed, cleaned all three rooms, taking care, as he did so, to leave the studio almost exactly as it was when Jean-Paul Villemot departed. Believing that the artist was innocent, he was less convinced that anyone would be able to rescue him from the menace of the English judicial system. For his visit to Newgate that morning, he was taking food, wine and the fresh clothing that his master had requested.

Clemence gave him a yawn of farewell then started to clean herself. Carrying the supplies in a basket, Emile went downstairs. Matilda was cleaning one of the windows, humming to herself as she did so. One of the late daffodils from a Bedford Street garden was pinned to her frock. Emile came up behind her.

'*Bonjour*,' he said.

'Oh!' she exclaimed, breaking off and turning around. 'I didn't see you there, sir – good morning.'

'You sound happy.'

'I am very happy.'

'I like your flower.'

'So do I,' she said, touching the daffodil.

'Who was the man who calls last night?'

'What man?'

'I see him through the window. He dress well.'

'Oh, that gentleman,' she said, not wishing to confide in Emile. 'He was asking directions from me.' She looked at the basket. 'Are you going to see Mr Villemot?'

'Yes, Matilda.'

'Tell him that I don't believe he did the crime.'

'Thank you, I will.'

'He likes women so much. He'd never do anything to hurt one.'

'I know that.'

She moved nearer. 'Have you found that missing portrait yet?'

'No, Matilda – not yet.'

'What a terrible thing to do, stealing it like that.'

Emile gave a shrug. 'London, it has bad people.'

'It has good ones as well, sir. We're not all thieves.' She felt an upsurge of guilt as she remembered leaving the window open. 'I'd do anything to get that portrait back.'

'We get it somehow.'

'Mr Villemot must have been so upset when you told him.'

'He does not know,' said Emile. 'It would be unkind. He has the trouble enough.'

'He ought to be told.'

'The painting, we find it before he come.'

Matilda was optimistic. 'He is coming back, then?'

'I hope so. I pray for him. He is the great artist,' said the little Frenchman with pride. 'He *must* come back.'

Bright sunshine bathed the garden and made it glow with morning freshness. Under a cloudless blue sky, the full colour of the flowers, trees, shrubs and lawns came out, turning the whole scene into a triumph of natural beauty. Seated at her bedroom window, Araminta Culthorpe gazed down on it with sadness. She was still wearing her dressing gown as Eleanor brushed her mistress's hair.

'Nature can be so cruel at times,' observed Araminta.

'Cruel?'

'When my heart is full of sorrow, it gives us the most glorious day in weeks. Part of me wants to be out there, revelling in this weather, but another part holds me back.'

'There's nothing to stop you going into the garden,' said Eleanor.

'Yes, there is – it would be inappropriate.'

'We went for a walk in it yesterday, m'lady.'

'That was only a test,' said Araminta. 'I had to find out if I could face the garden after what happened out there.'

'And you did.'

'To venture out now would be an indulgence. Our guests would frown upon it and they would be right to do so. I must mourn my husband indoors.'

'The garden will wait for you,' said Eleanor.

She brushed on with slow, careful, measured strokes, wishing that her own hair were as long and silken. Everything about her mistress was so perfect that it reminded her of her own imperfections. Yet there had been a moment when she was asked to be Araminta Culthorpe, to impersonate her in such a way that Villemot could finish the portrait. The artist had seen enough similarity between the two women to select Eleanor as his model. That thought still had the power to excite her.

'What are you thinking?' asked Araminta.

'Nothing, m'lady.'

'I saw your reflection in the window – you were smiling.'

'I was thinking how lovely your hair was,' said Eleanor.

'Your mind was not on me. It was elsewhere.' She turned round and took the brush from the maid. 'Now, tell me what you were thinking. Come on, Eleanor – I'll not be angry.'

'It's more likely to make you miserable.'

'Why?'

'I was thinking about Mr Villemot.'

'Then why did you smile like that?' Araminta read the look in her eyes. 'Ah, I see. You wanted to sit for him in his studio.'

'I was being selfish, m'lady. I apologise.'

'There's no need. You've not only shared my loss, you've had one of your own to bewail. You were deprived of a privilege. I understand. I'm glad that you can have such a pleasant memory about Monsieur Villemot when I've had so many black ones.'

'It won't happen again.'

'You're entitled to your own thoughts, Eleanor.'

'I'm here to serve you, m'lady.'

'And so you have,' said Araminta, thankfully. 'Since my husband died, you've kept me alive. Without you beside me, I'd have perished from grief.'

'Call on me at any time of the day or night.'

'That's what I have done. It's been a real trial for you.'

'I'm not important,' said Eleanor, humbly. 'But you are.'

Putting the brush aside, Araminta took hold of her hands and squeezed them hard in a gesture of affection and gratitude. Then she swung round to look out at the garden again.

'I'm ready to get dressed now, Eleanor.'

'Very good, m'lady.'

Picking up the hairbrush, the maid took it across to the dressing table. She moved on to one of the large wardrobes that stood against the far wall. Made of walnut, it was catching the sun and shining with the brilliance of a mirror. Eleanor opened the door. The first thing she saw was the blue dress that she would have worn as the model and she could not resist taking it out and holding it against herself. She felt a pang of remorse when she recalled that the dress belonged to a vanished time. There was no place for it now.

Hanging it back in the wardrobe, she took out the black

mourning dress that Araminta had been wearing since her husband's death. It felt cold and heavy in her hands. Eleanor was sad. There would be no more colour in either of their lives for a long time.

When Jacob let him into the house, he could not understand how a man who did the same domestic tasks as he could remain so trim and spotless. Emile was as neat and well-groomed as ever. The old man showed him into the study and left him alone with Christopher.

'*Bonjour*, Emile,' said the architect.

'*Bonjour, m'sieur.*'

'I was hoping to see you today.'

Emile was morose. 'I have been to the prison.'

'I intend to pay Monsieur Villemot a visit myself today,' said Christopher. 'How did you find him?'

'Is very unhappy.'

'We're doing our utmost to get your master out of there.'

'Lady Lingoe, she help.'

'Oh?'

'She have him put in better cell.'

'Lady Lingoe has been there?' asked Christopher in amazement.

'Yesterday.'

'That's a real testament to the quality of her friendship. Newgate is no place for a lady like her. That stink is nauseous.'

'I still feel sick.'

'Sit down and tell me all about it,' said Christopher, waving him to a chair. 'Is there anything I can take Monsieur Villemot? Does he have enough to eat and drink? What about clothing?'

Emile sat on the edge of a chair and related everything that had passed between him and his master. He felt it a great injustice that they were not allowed to converse in their native language. The visit had obviously shaken him up badly.

'Did you tell him about the portrait?' said Christopher.

'*Non, m'sieur.*'

'He'll have to know sooner or later.'

'We find it,' said Emile.

'We've not had much success in doing that so far, but I'm not without hope. Only a handful of people even knew that Lady Culthorpe was having her portrait painted. I am working through them one by one.'

'Thank you.'

'Apart from anything else,' said Christopher. 'It was a superb piece of work – unlike my own artistic efforts.'

'Everything my master paint, is very good.'

'His brushwork is amazing. I've never seen anything like it.'

Emile smiled. 'He is the best.'

'His reputation goes before him.'

'Nobody paints the ladies as he does.'

'I don't suppose they do,' said Christopher as an image of the nude Lady Lingoe popped into his mind. 'He's able to delineate the character of his subjects.' Emile looked blank. 'I'm sorry – that's a difficult word for you. What I mean is that we see people as they really are in his paintings.'

'He is the artist – he look for the truth.'

'He certainly found it in Lady Culthorpe's case.'

'He like her.'

'It's impossible not to do that, Emile.'

'He not kill her husband.'

'You don't have to persuade me,' said Christopher. 'The more I reflect on this whole business, the more certain I am of his innocence. The one thing that troubles me, however, is why he went into that garden on the day of the murder. Has he said anything to you about that? Did he tell you what he was doing at the house in the first place?'

'He ride past, m'sieur.'

'He didn't ride past – that's the problem. For some unknown reason, he dismounted from his horse and went into the garden. There's a witness who saw him coming out of the gate.'

'This man, he tell the lie.'

'I don't think so, Emile. He's given a sworn statement.'

'What is that?'

'He took his oath before a magistrate,' said Christopher. 'He's prepared to stand up in court and tell the judge what he saw. We have to make sure that it doesn't reach that stage.'

'How you do that?'

'By working hard to find the man who *did* murder Sir Martin.'

'You know who he is?'

'We have a suspect in mind.'

'Arrest him!' demanded Emile.

'That's not possible as yet,' explained Christopher. 'We have to gather more evidence before we can apprehend the man. That will take a lot of time and effort. Monsieur Villemot will have to be patient.'

'Is bad in there – very bad.'

'I know. I've been in Newgate before.'

'All he want is to live here quiet and paint.'

'I hope that he's eager to occupy his new house as well. It would be dreadful if this unfortunate experience were to rob him of his desire to stay in England. Has he said anything to you on that subject?'

Emile was puzzled. 'Subject?'

'Does your master want to go back to France?'

'*Non*!'

'You sound very positive about that.'

'He stay here.'

'That's gratifying to know and it will make me redouble my efforts on his behalf. But I'm concerned about you as well as Monsieur Villemot.'

'Me?'

'Yes, Emile,' said Christopher. 'You must be quite bewildered by everything that's happened. Your master is put in prison and you are left alone in his lodging. The next thing that happens is that a portrait is stolen from the studio next to the room where you sleep.'

'Clemence, she let me down.'

'Clemence?'

'She is the cat, m'sieur. She should have waked me.'

'Does she sleep in the studio?'

'Yes.'

'Then she should have heard an intruder.'

Emile gave a nod of assent. Having come for reassurance, he looked gloomier than ever. He got to his feet and bid Christopher farewell. The architect walked him to the front door.

'Cheer up, Emile,' he said. 'We'll get him released soon.'

'You think?'

'I know – as long as he promises to stay in England.'

'He must stay.'

'He wouldn't spend so much money on that new house if he did not intend to put down roots and bring Monique over. That's something else I meant to raise with you,' he added. 'Have you written to his wife to tell her what's happened?'

'Who?'

'Monique – his wife.'

The words spilled out before Emile could stop them coming. 'He is not married, m'sieur.'

Chapter Nine

It was mid-morning before Elkannah Prout called on the house in Bedford Street and he fully expected to have to wait while his friend was summoned from his bedchamber. In fact, Henry Redmayne was already up and had breakfasted, shaved and dressed. Moreover, he had a zest about him that was unheard of at that time of day.

'Good morning, Elkannah,' he said, cheerily.

'You are uncommonly happy this morning.'

'I'm exultant.'

'For what reason?'

'The best reason in the world,' said Henry. 'When I looked in the mirror this morning, I saw a fine gentleman who was tall, handsome and extravagantly in love. The very thought that I inhabit the same city as Araminta made me feel elated.'

'We all share that elation,' said Prout, quietly, 'though it's tempered by the fact that Araminta is in mourning. I adore her as much as anyone but the tragic change in her circumstances has made me look at her in a different way.'

'There's only *one* way to look at her.'

Prout did not share his laugh. 'Vulgarity is out of place, Henry.'

'None of this solemnity,' ordered the other, taking him into the drawing room. 'I'll not let anyone put me out of countenance today. Last night, Dame Fortune finally remembered my name.'

'You won at cards?'

'Repeatedly. I had the Midas touch. I was able to repay my loan from Jocelyn and I have an equal sum to give to you.'

'There's no hurry to settle that debt.'

'But the money is here.'

'Keep it, Henry. If you are having a run of luck at last, keep what you owe me and invest it at the card table to win even more. I know that feeling of success. When it courses through your veins, you have to take full advantage of it.'

'Then I shall – thank you.'

They sat down opposite each other. Since he had to go to the Navy Office that afternoon, Henry was dressed more soberly than when gadding about town with his cronies. Though his job was largely a sinecure, he was called upon to put in an appearance from time to time and to be seen to do some nominal work. Elkannah Prout, by contrast, was a man of inherited wealth, who had been able to retire from the legal profession and devote himself entirely to pleasure. He was a generous friend and he had often helped Henry out of financial difficulties in the past. Prout now had a serious air about him.

Henry was guarded. 'I hope you haven't come here to talk about that pact, Elkannah,' he said.

'Not at all.'

'I know that you've been hounding Jocelyn and Sir Willard on that score, and I also know that they rebuffed you.'

'Quite rightly,' said Prout. 'I acted too rashly. It was foolish of me to try to tell them how to behave. They are a law unto themselves and I should have accepted that.'

'I'm relieved to hear you taking a more tolerant view.'

'You were the only person willing to see any merit in the pact, Henry, and I wanted to express my thanks in a tangible way. There's racing at Newmarket tomorrow,' he went on. 'If the Navy Office can spare you, those winnings you collected at the card table last night may be doubled or trebled at the racecourse.'

'It's a tempting offer.'

'I shall put it to Jocelyn and Sir Willard.'

'Then they'll view it in the same cynical way as me.'

'Why cynical?'

'We are not blind, Elkannah,' said Henry with a grin. 'You've not abandoned your pact at all. You are simply presenting it to us in disguise. If we go to Newmarket tomorrow, we'd be unable to attend Sir Martin's funeral. That's your ruse. You wish to get the three of us out of London.'

'I feel that I owe it to Araminta to do so.'

'Then your feelings do not accord with mine.'

'How so?'

'I grieve with her,' said Henry, trying to sound dignified. 'I share her misery. Tomorrow will be the most trying day of Araminta's young life. It would be callous to spend it enjoying myself at the races.'

'You intend to break our pact, then?'

'Only minutes ago, you declared it impractical.'

'The principle holds, Henry.'

'It will be something to reflect on as you journey to Newmarket.'

'Do you plan to sneak off to the funeral behind my back?'

'I will do what I will do,' said Henry, grandly.

'Then you are just as bad as the others.'

'We are all four banded together in this, Elkannah.'

'Do not include me,' said Prout, firmly. 'I renounce the Society and all it stands for. My devotion to Araminta remains unaltered but it prompts me to move in a different direction.'

'To Newmarket – so that you can bet on horses.'

'That was merely a device to keep you away from her tomorrow.'

'Why not admit that at the start?'

'You disappoint me, Henry.'

'There's nothing I can do about that. Allow me to give you a word of warning. Do not even think of inviting Jocelyn or Sir

Willard to join you tomorrow. They will laugh in your faces.'

Prout got to his feet. 'Is that what *you* are doing?'

'No, Elkannah.'

'I know mockery when I hear it.'

'I'm giving you sound advice.'

'What you are doing is to betray the promise you gave me. You agreed to stay away from Araminta tomorrow.'

'And I may still do so,' said Henry, getting up from his chair.

'No,' said Prout, angrily. 'I see you for what you are. You, Jocelyn and Sir Willard have signed a pact of your own. The three of you are plotting to be there tomorrow to get a glimpse of her even though she will be consumed with sorrow.'

'There's no plot, Elkannah.'

'I looked upon you as a friend.'

'I remain one still.'

'Not when you deceive me like this.'

'It's you who wilfully misunderstands me.'

'I've seen far too much of Henry Redmayne to misunderstand him. You tell me that you grieve with Araminta but that did not hinder you from spending half the night at the card table. Is that the way you share her misery?'

'Why this sudden piety?'

'I know you for what you are.'

'A devotee of pleasure in all its forms.'

'A weak-willed degenerate.'

'I patterned myself on you,' rejoined Henry. 'There was not a rake in the whole of the capital who could touch Elkannah Prout for drinking, gambling and whoring. You gave the lead that I followed. Yet now you've lost your appetite for vice,' he continued, 'you portray yourself as a paragon of virtue.'

'I just felt that it was time to make a stand.'

'We preferred you as you were.'

'That's your prerogative.'

'Come back to us, Elkannah.'

'Not while the three of you scheme against me.'

'But we've not been doing that.'

'There's nothing I despise as much as disloyalty, Henry, and that's what you've displayed. I take back my former suggestion.' He held out his hand. 'Please repay the money you owe me.'

'When I have the chance to make it work for me?'

'Yes,' said Prout, nastily. 'And look to borrow nothing more from my purse. I'll not lend a single penny to you ever again.'

Henry was alarmed. 'That's too harsh, Elkannah.'

'It's a fit penalty for a traitor.'

'But you have ever been my most reliable banker.'

'Not any more, Henry.' Prout snapped his fingers. 'Pay up!'

After his brief imprisonment there, Christopher Redmayne knew all about the multiple indignities of Newgate. As a result, he returned to the place with some trepidation. Because he had helped to capture and hand over Jean-Paul Villemot, he was no longer suspected of aiding the escape of a fugitive and was safe from arrest. That fact brought him no comfort as he walked reluctantly towards the prison. Once inside, he feared that they would somehow find a means of keeping him there.

Destroyed by the Great Fire, the prison had been completely rebuilt and it was slowly nearing completion. The structure had a splendour to gladden the heart of any architect yet it did not even attract a glance from Christopher. Behind the imposing exterior, he knew, was a world of suffering, hunger and darkness of the soul. As he entered the great portal, he felt an instant tremor. The man who conducted him to Villemot's cell insisted on staying to listen to the conversation. When he saw that he had a visitor, the artist flung himself at the bars.

'Christopher!' he cried.

'How are you, Monsieur Villemot?'

'I am not well, my friend.'

'If you are ill, I can arrange for a doctor to visit.'

'The illness, it is not in my body,' said Villemot, tapping his skull with a finger. 'It is up here – in the head.'

'Are you in pain?'

'My thoughts leave me in agony.'

Christopher was disturbed by his appearance. The Frenchman was haggard with anxiety and loss of sleep. His eyes were darting and his body twitching. He slapped a hand to his temple as if suffering severe pain. Christopher feared that he might have picked up one of the many diseases that were so rife in the prison. Foul water and lack of sanitation made an already noxious environment far worse. Even the healthiest prisoner could succumb to the powerful compound of infections. In spite of a good constitution, Villemot might easily have fallen prey to a form of brain fever. In its later stages, it would make him rant and rave as it was patently doing to some of those who were contributing to the daily tumult in the other cells.

'Emile came to see me,' said Villemot.

'Yes, I spoke to him earlier.'

'He says you are trying to get me out of here.'

'Indeed, I am,' said Christopher, 'and I'm not alone in my efforts. Jonathan Bale, whom you met, is helping me a great deal and I've called on the services of my brother, Henry.'

'What can he do?'

'He knows people. He can open doors for me.'

'Then let him open this door,' yelled Villemot, shaking it with such violence that it rattled aloud. 'I lose my mind in here.'

'Emile told me that you had another visitor, one who must have been shocked by your condition. Lady Lingoe came to see you.'

'She brought food and drink.'

'So did I,' said Christopher. 'I left them with the prison sergeant. Let me know if they don't reach you.'

'I am not worried about food. I hate being locked up.'

'I know. I felt the same and I was only behind bars for a short time. It's that sense of helplessness, of being at the mercy of others.'

'Set me free!' begged the other.

'We are working hard to do so, Monsieur Villemot.'

'I am an artist. I paint things of beauty. In here, everything is ugly. Is frightening. I look ugly myself.'

It was true. Even though he had put on the fresh clothing that his valet had brought, Villemot looked dirty, crumpled and beaten. The prison stench had burrowed its way into his garments and pieces of damp straw were sticking to his shoes and breeches. Christopher's desire to rescue him was intensified.

'Before I can get you out,' he said, 'I need your help.'

'What can I do?'

'Tell me what happened the day you went to that house.'

'I've already done that, Christopher.'

'No, you didn't. You told me only part of the story and I need to know every last detail. Why did you go into the garden?'

'I did not,' said Villemot, defensively.

'You were seen coming out of there,' said Christopher, 'so there's no point in denying it. A reliable witness will stand up in court and tell the judge that you were in that garden.'

'It was only for a second.'

'So you *were* there?'

Villemot kept him waiting for an answer. 'I put my head in,' he said, eventually, 'that is all, Christopher.'

'Why didn't you tell me this before?'

'Is not important.'

'It's very important,' argued Christopher. 'It could mean the difference between life and death. If all that you did was to look at the house, they have no case against you. Since you were seen coming out of the garden – the very place where Sir Martin was killed – then you do have questions to answer.'

'I was there one or two minutes at most.'

'Why?'

'The garden gate, it was open.'

'But why did you go through it?'

'I was curious.'

'Are you in the habit of trespassing on other people's property out of curiosity?'

Villemot tensed. 'You make fun of me.'

'I'm asking exactly what will be asked in court.'

'It must never get that far.'

'Then give me some real help, Monsieur Villemot. I am on your side. Why do you keep holding things back from me?'

Drawing back from the bars, the artist retreated to a corner of his cell and sulked. He studied Christopher warily. It took time for him to reach the decision to trust his visitor. When he did so, he took a step towards him.

'Araminta – Lady Culthorpe – she talk a lot about it.'

'The garden?'

'Sir Martin spent much money.'

'He obviously derived great pleasure from it.'

'I was curious,' said Villemot. 'When I see the gate open, I wanted to look at this famous garden for myself.'

'Wasn't there an easier way to do that?' asked Christopher.

'Easier way?'

'All you had to do was to express an interest and I'm sure that Lady Culthorpe would have invited you to the house. Instead of which, you sneak in there like a criminal.'

'I am no criminal!' shouted Villemot.

'Calm down, calm down.'

'I do nothing wrong.'

'There's no need to get so angry, Monsieur Villemot.'

'Then do not call me names.'

'I'm sorry,' said Christopher. 'I am simply telling you how it looks to an impartial observer. A man is stabbed to death in his garden. You are seen leaving it. A plea of curiosity is not an adequate defence. We need more.'

'What more is there?'

'You still haven't admitted why you went near the house.'

'I was riding past.'

'But what took you to Westminster?'

'I wanted some fresh air.'

'There are plenty of others places you could have gone.'

Villemot shrugged. 'I go for a ride. I find myself in Westminster.'

'You're hiding something from me.'

'What am I hiding?'

'I think that you followed Lady Culthorpe's carriage when it took her home that day.' The Frenchman's eyes flashed but he held his tongue. 'When she had been dropped off at the front door of the house, the coachman drove around to the stable block. He saw you there. His name is Dirk and he's another reliable witness. So,' said Christopher, patiently, 'let's have no more pretence. Did you follow that carriage to Westminster?'

There was a long pause before Villemot grunted his reply. 'Yes.'

'Was that out of curiosity as well?'

'Yes.'

'Or was it because you'd grown so fond of Lady Culthorpe?'

'No!' snapped Villemot.

'Is that what took you there?'

Spinning on his heel, the artist retreated to the farthest corner of his cell and kept his back to his visitor. His shoulders were heaving and his feet shuffling. Christopher gave him plenty of time before he returned to his questioning.

'What happened afterwards?' he asked. 'When you came out of the garden, where did you go?'

'Back to the studio.'

'But you didn't. When I called in there, Emile said that you'd been away for a couple of hours. Was your valet lying?'

Another lengthy pause ensued. 'No, he was not.'

'So where did you go?'

'I tell you already,' said Villemot, rounding on him. 'I go for the ride. I often go for the ride. You can ask Emile.'

'Did something happen in the course of the ride?'

'Why do you say that?'

'Did it, Monsieur Villemot?'

'No.'

'Then why were you so upset when you got back?'

'I was not upset.'

'I was there,' said Christopher, tiring of his evasion. 'I saw you with my own eyes. And if you were not upset, why did you come to my house the next day to apologise for your behaviour?' He fixed the artist with a stare. 'Or are you going to deny that as well?'

Villemot chewed his lip. 'I was annoyed, Christopher,' he said. 'While I was out riding, I have the argument with someone and it annoyed me. That was why I was rude to you.'

'With whom did you have the argument?'

'A man I meet in the park.'

'What was the argument about?'

'I do not remember.'

'If it annoyed you that much, you'd be certain to remember.'

'Why do you keep on at me like this?' demanded Villemot, banging the bars with his fists. 'You say you wish to help yet you do not believe what I tell you.'

'There's still too much missing. I need more detail.'

'Do you never ride your horse for the pleasure?'

'Of course I do.'

'Can you always remember where you went and what you saw?'

'I'd remember a heated argument in a park.'

'It was all over in a moment.'

'What did you do with the rest of the time?'

'The rest?' repeated the other.

'You were out of the studio for two hours,' Christopher reminded him. 'Take out your brief visit to Sir Martin's garden and your even briefer argument with some unnamed person in the park and that still leaves a large amount of time.' He put his face close to the bars. 'Why are you so afraid to tell me where you went?'

'Get me out of this place,' whispered Villemot.

'That's precisely what I'm trying to do.'

'Get me out soon or you will be to blame.'

'Blame?' said Christopher.

'Yes, my friend – for my death.'

'What are you trying to tell me?'

'If I stay here much longer, I will kill myself.'

He meant what he said. The visit was over.

Sir Willard Grail was leaving his house when he saw his brother-in-law riding towards him. He waited until Cuthbert Foxwell had dismounted before exchanging a greeting with him. A servant came to take away the horse. Foxwell was panting and beads of perspiration stood out on his brow.

'A ride like that always tires me,' he said, removing his hat to use its brim as a fan. 'I'm an indifferent horseman, Sir Willard.'

'My sister married you for your other virtues, Cuthbert. I don't think that she values horsemanship in a husband overmuch. Like you, she's a restful creature.'

'I'm hoping that she had a good rest here, Sir Willard.'

'She did – and she was wonderful company for my wife. Barbara is always welcome here and so are you.'

'Thank you.'

'It's odd how relationships subtly alter, isn't it?' said Sir Willard. 'When we were children, Barbara was always the elder sister who kept me firmly in line. I was terrified of her.'

Foxwell grinned. 'How could you be?'

'Compared to me, she was so big, strong and formidable.'

'Yet she has such a sweet disposition.'

Sir Willard laughed. 'It wasn't quite so sweet when we were growing up,' he said. 'I think I was fourteen before my sister realised that she could not order me around any more. That's when the first subtle change occurred. Instead of bullying me, Barbara learned to get her way by the black art of female persuasion.'

'I'll listen to no more of this,' said Foxwell, pleasantly. 'My wife is the closest thing to perfection that I've ever met and I'll not hear a word against her. I'm just grateful that when we ride home this afternoon, we'll do so in our coach. I'd not have enjoyed a journey both ways in the saddle.'

Foxwell's wife had visited her brother for a few days and her husband had come to collect her. The irony was that she had seen far more of Lady Grail than of Sir Willard but she was habituated to that by now. Her brother did not spend a great deal of time at home.

'You'll not be joining us for dinner, then?' said Foxwell.

'I've business to attend to in the city.'

'That's a pity, Sir Willard. I'd have appreciated a talk with you.'

'Another time.'

'You always put me off.'

'We have so little to say to each other, Cuthbert.'

'I set that down to lack of practice.'

'Different interests are bound to keep us apart.'

'Yet you knew I was coming to dinner today.'

'Yes,' lied Sir Willard, 'and I'd intended to join you but I've been called away unexpectedly. You'll have a splendid time with the ladies and you can sample the skills of our new cook.'

'I look forward to that.'

Cuthbert Foxwell wanted to administer a mild rebuke but he felt unable to do so. Though Sir Willard was younger than him, he always found him faintly intimidating. Much as he disapproved of the way that he neglected his wife, Foxwell was unable to even broach the subject. The contrast between the two families was stark. In the ten years of their marriage, Foxwell and his wife had grown steadily closer and disliked being apart. Sir Willard and Lady Grail, however, were rarely together for any length of time, even though their marriage was of much shorter duration. His brother-in-law had his suspicions about the business in the city that always took Sir Willard away but he did not dare to voice them to the ladies.

'Incidentally,' he said, using a handkerchief to mop up the last of the sweat, 'do you, by any chance, remember that gardener of mine who was stolen away from me?'

'Gardener?'

'Fellow by the name of Abel Paskins.'

'You can't expect me to know the names of gardeners, Cuthbert,' said Sir Willard, scornfully. 'Underlings are underlings. If you give them the dignity of a name, they tend to get above themselves.'

'Your friend did not think so.'

'What friend?'

'Mr Kidbrooke.'

'Ah, now I'm with you,' said the other with a chuckle. 'It was that time I called in with Jocelyn. You kindly showed us around your garden.'

'Had I known that I'd lose a good man in the process, I'd not have bothered. Paskins had vision. He knew how to make the best of a garden. He designed and built that rockery for me.'

'That's what impressed Jocelyn so much.'

'Did he have to take the fellow away from me?'

'It was force of habit, Cuthbert.'

'Does he make a habit of collecting other people's gardeners?'

'No,' said Sir Willard, 'but he acts decisively when he sees something that he wants. Jocelyn Kidbrooke is known for it.'

'I found him rather disagreeable.'

'He's a good man at heart.'

'I take your word for it,' said Foxwell, 'for I saw no evidence of it. But the reason I mention Paskins is this – did you know that he used to work for Sir Martin Culthorpe?'

'I did not,' said Sir Willard, nonchalantly, 'and I'm not sure that I care.' He concealed his interest behind a lazy smile. 'Were you aware of that when you first employed him?'

'No, it came as a complete surprise.'

'When did you learn about this?'

'Only yesterday,' said Foxwell. 'I had a visit from a young man whom I think you may know – Christopher Redmayne.'

'I know and like his brother much better.'

'He was trying to find out where Abel Paskins was.'

'Why on earth should he do that?'

'I'm not at liberty to say, Sir Willard.'

'You can tell me, surely.'

'Before he left, Mr Redmayne asked me to treat everything he had told me in the strictest confidence and I gave him my word.'

'I'm your brother-in-law, Cuthbert. There should be no secrets between us. Why is he so interested in a gardener?'

'My lips are sealed,' said Foxwell. 'What I will tell you, however, is that, no matter how long it takes, he'll track the man down. Mr Redmayne is very determined.'

'That was only one of his faults,' complained Sir Willard.

'He's set himself a difficult task – I hope he succeeds.'

'Since you won't tell me what that task is, I can make no comment. Go on in and meet the ladies, Cuthbert. My business will not wait.' He walked towards the horse that was saddled and waiting for him then he stopped. 'What was that gardener's name again?'

'Abel Paskins.'

Intending to do some work that afternoon, Henry Redmayne dined at home for a change and allowed himself only one glass of wine. In the days when Sir William Batten had been Surveyor to the Navy, tippling was the order of the day and Henry had joined in the merriment with gusto, if only to hear Sir William's ripe language booming across the tavern like a broadside. Things were somewhat different now. He was expected to have a degree of sobriety when he was at the Navy Office.

He was still eating his meal when his brother arrived. As Christopher was shown into the dining room, Henry almost choked on a piece of chicken.

'You've no cause to upbraid me,' he said, spluttering. 'I did what you commanded, Christopher. I gave that moon-faced maid a basket of flowers and soothed her ruffled feathers with an apology.'

'I'm glad to hear it, Henry.'

'What's more, I've resolved to stay away from the funeral.'

'A commendable decision.'

'You've no need to harry me further.'

'Yes, I have,' said Christopher. 'I need to talk to you about your friends.' He sat down at the table and helped himself to a slice of pie. 'How well do you know them?'

'As well as any man can know his boon companions.'

'Could there be a killer among them?'

'Unthinkable!'

'I'm forced to explore the realms of the unthinkable.' He chewed then swallowed the pie. 'This is good, Henry.' He cut himself another slice. 'I think I'll have some more.'

'I didn't know that you were coming to dinner.'

'I didn't know I'd have the good fortune to find you at home.'

'What do you want?'

'Information. Tell me about Sir Willard Grail.'

'You've met the fellow.'

'He kept me very much at arm's length. What is he really like?'

'He's like so many of my acquaintances – he's an impecunious aristocrat who married for money and who chose a wife who would not be too inquisitive about the way he spent his time. In character, Sir Willard is a younger version of Henry Redmayne.'

'Another strutting peacock, you mean?'

'An urbane, intelligent, harmless fellow of good breeding who has a fondness for the luxuries of life.'

'Some of those luxuries being the favours of Lady Culthorpe.'

'That would be the ultimate indulgence.'

'Would Sir Willard kill to achieve it?'

'No,' said Henry with emphasis, 'and I'm absolutely certain that he did not murder Sir Martin.'

'Are you?'

'At the time when the crime was committed, Sir Willard was dining at Locket's with Elkannah and me. You can eliminate all three of us, Christopher.'

'What about Jocelyn Kidbrooke?'

'He didn't turn up that day.'

'Was he supposed to?'

'Oh, yes,' replied Henry, nibbling a piece of bread. 'When we formed our Society, we agreed to dine together once a week to compare the progress each of us had made with regard to Araminta. Jocelyn let us down.'

'Did he say why?'

'He claimed that he dined with his wife.'

'Did you believe him?'

'Not for one second,' said Henry. 'Jocelyn spends as little time at home as possible. He leaves early and gets back late. Take last night, for instance,' he added. 'It would have been almost one in the morning when he went back to the house. His coach dropped me off here well past midnight. And there's another thing...'

'Go on.'

Christopher had to wait until Henry had finished the last mouthful. His brother washed it down with a sip of wine, then surveyed the table to see if anything else tempted him.

'According to Sir Willard – and he's always unnervingly well-informed about such matters – Jocelyn's wife is not even in London at the moment. She's visiting her family in Hampshire.'

'So why did he lie to you?'

'Why else but to go peering at Araminta through his telescope?'

'He has a telescope?'

'He bought it for that sole purpose. All that the rest of us have had to sustain us are distant glimpses of her. Jocelyn has been able to bring her much nearer through his infernal instrument.'

'So at the time of the murder,' said Christopher, eager to confirm the fact, 'Jocelyn Kidbrooke missed an opportunity to dine with friends because of a more urgent appointment?'

'Yes, Christopher.'

'That appointment could have been in Sir Martin's garden.'

'It could but I doubt very much that it was.'

'Why?'

'Wait until you meet him,' said Henry. 'He's too fat and slow to be a likely assassin – though strangely enough, Elkannah did make a comment to that effect,' he continued as a memory surfaced. 'It was over that meal we had in Locket's.'

'What did Mr Prout say?'

'Only that Jocelyn was so bedazzled by Araminta's charms that he would kill to make her his own.' He flapped a hand. 'Elkannah was only speaking metaphorically. He knew as well as I did that Jocelyn would be incapable of such a deed.'

'I wonder,' said Christopher.

'His passions run deep but they would not provoke him to commit a murder. To begin with, Jocelyn would have had no means of getting inside that garden.'

'Abel Paskins might have helped him.'

'Who?'

'The gardener who was dismissed by Sir Martin Culthorpe.'

Christopher told him how he had first heard about the man and how he had driven to Chelsea in the hope of meeting him. The news that Kidbrooke had blatantly poached the gardener from his last employer made Henry forget all about his dinner. He began to revise his opinion of his friend.

'Paskins could have told him everything he needed to know.'

'Especially how to get into that garden.'

'Jocelyn – the killer?' He shook his head. 'I can't believe it.'

'Why was he so keen to engage Abel Paskins? Why did he fail to turn up for dinner that day? What use did he put that telescope to?' asked Christopher. 'Is he simply a man in the grip of an obsession or was he driven by uncontrollable jealousy to stab the husband of the woman he pursued? I need you to find out, Henry.'

'Me?'

'You're an intimate of his. If you make casual enquiries, he'll give you some answers. If I try to approach him, Mr Kidbrooke will be curt and defensive. That's what happened when Jonathan Bale talked to him.'

'Bale would make anyone curt and defensive.'

'Find out what he was really doing on the day of the murder.'

'He's unlikely to volunteer the information.'

'Then dig it out of him by more devious means,' said his brother. 'As long as you don't alert him to the fact that we have the gravest suspicions about him.'

'I'm not sure that I'm equal to the task, Christopher.'

'You have to be. You still have much to do to make amends for the way you tried to steal that portrait. Any magistrate who heard what you did would clap you in prison at once.'

'Not prison again, *please* – it so disagrees with my complexion.'

'It's driven Monsieur Villemot to thoughts of suicide.'

'That could be a sign of guilt,' said Henry, pensively. 'He'd rather take his own life than face the hangman in front of a baying crowd. Perhaps you are wrong about Jocelyn. What if the real killer is the man they have already arrested for the crime?'

'Monsieur Villemot is innocent – I swear it.'

'I feel the same about Jocelyn. 'Sdeath, I spent the whole evening with him yesterday. I cannot get my brain to accept that I was revelling with a cold-blooded killer.'

'I've no proof that Mr Kidbrooke *is* guilty,' said Christopher, 'or that Abel Paskins is in any way involved in the crime. It may be that they are not. But it's an avenue I must explore for the sake of Monsieur Villemot. About it, Henry.'

'I'm working at the Navy Office this afternoon.'

'Seek out your friend at the earliest opportunity.'

'I need to think this over.'

Christopher was authoritative. 'I've thought it over for you. Do as you're told or there'll be repercussions.'

'Would you really turn me over to the law?'

'Yes, Henry!' His stern expression melted into a smile. 'But if you do help me and Jonathan to find the killer, I'll sing your praises to Lady Culthorpe and wipe away her painful memory of those mawkish verses you felt moved to write.'

Henry was wounded. 'I put my heart and soul into every line,' he said, piteously. 'I expected Araminta to swoon at the sheer magic of my words. I discern a small flaw in her character at last – Araminta has no appreciation of a master poet's craft.'

Christopher was tactful. 'Then send her no more examples of it.'

Emile was stroking the cat when he heard the coach rumble to a halt in the street below. Going to the window, he looked down to see Lady Lingoe being helped out of the vehicle by her footman. Clemence did not like being tossed on to a chair and she screeched her disapproval but Emile was already out of the room and descending the stairs. He opened the front door to admit his visitor, greeted her warmly then escorted her up to the studio. Lady Lingoe stood in the doorway and surveyed the room with a nostalgic smile.

'I spent so much time in here,' she said, fondly.

'It was the honour to see you here.'

'Things have changed for the worse since then, Emile. What I admired most about your master was that he was a free spirit, an artistic vagabond. He lived his life exactly as he chose.'

'Is very true.'

'Monsieur Villemot had such a healthy disdain for the

pointless restraints that society imposes upon the rest of us. It was a joy to be in his company.' Her face clouded. 'The free spirit has now been caged. I went to see him in Newgate.'

'He tell me, Lady Lingoe. He thank you.'

'It was disheartening to see him in such a squalid place.'

'He is hurting very much.'

'Can you blame him? He's locked up with the sweepings of London. It's like Bedlam in there.'

'I know. I tell Monsieur Redmayne.'

'*Christopher* Redmayne?'

'Yes. He say that he will go to the prison himself.'

'He'd be better employed trying to get your master out of there. The atmosphere in Newgate is so foul. When I got home, I had to change out of my clothes to get ride of the smell.'

'I do the same,' said Emile, fastidiously.

'When you spoke to Christopher Redmayne, did he give you any reason for hope?'

'A little – he say he has the suspect.'

'Did he tell you who it was?'

'No, Lady Lingoe, he give me no name.'

'At least, it sounds as if he's picked up a scent. I wonder who the man could be and how he managed to get away with the murder.'

'We will know one day.'

'Let it be one day soon,' she said with feeling. 'I do not think that Monsieur Villemot can stand those unspeakable conditions for much longer. I only got as far as the sergeant's office but that was enough to make me feel crushed. It must be soul-destroying to be locked away in one of the cells.'

'When I come out of there,' said Emile, 'I cry for my master.'

'I can well believe it. However,' she went on, looking around, 'I did not only come here to tell you about my visit to Newgate. I wanted to collect my portrait and take it back with me.'

'But you ask us to keep it here until Lord Lingoe come.'

'The case is altered, Emile. I was perfectly happy for it to remain here while Monsieur Villemot was able to look after it for me, but he's not able to do that now. I'd prefer to have it where I can see it.'

'Very well.'

'Could you find it for me, please?'

'Is here,' said Emile, crossing to the easel. 'You like to see?'

'Yes, please.' He lifted the cloth so that she could see the portrait and she viewed herself with a mixture of pleasure and regret. The circumstances in which it had been painted no longer existed and that clearly saddened her. 'Thank you, Emile.'

Lowering the cloth, he lifted the portrait to the ground.

'While I'm here,' she said, 'I'll take the opportunity to peep at the painting of Lady Culthorpe. Where is it?'

Emile became uneasy. 'You not want to see that.'

'Yes, I do.'

'Monsieur Villemot, maybe he not like it.'

'Of course he would. We were friends. He let me see whatever I wanted of his work. I'm sure that he wouldn't have the slightest objection to my looking at his latest portrait.'

'Is not finished.'

'Then let me see how far he managed to get.'

'Bad idea.'

'It's not an idea, Emile,' she said, asserting herself. 'It's a direct request. I intend to see that picture of Araminta Culthorpe and I'll not let a mere valet stand in my way. Now stop prevaricating and show me which one it is.'

'Is not here.'

'Why not?'

'The lady, she take it away.'

'You're lying to me,' she decided. 'She's in mourning. When a husband has been murdered, the last thing a wife would do is to worry about a portrait that is not even finished. Tell me the truth,' she demanded, imperiously. 'Where is it?'

'Is not here – that is the truth.'

'Then where have you put it?'

Emile licked dry lips. 'The portrait, it was stolen.'

'*Stolen!*'

'Monsieur Redmayne, he try to get it back.'

'Who took it?'

'He not know yet.'

'I'm glad I decided to retrieve my own portrait,' she said. 'The thought that it might have been stolen by a stranger so that he can gloat over it is quite outrageous.'

'It is. I am very upset.'

'What about the man who actually painted it? Your master will be mortified to hear what happened to it.'

'That is why I not tell him.'

'But he has a right to know, Emile.'

'We find it,' said the valet. 'Before he come out of the prison, we find it for him. He not be told it was ever missing. That would hurt Monsieur Villemot like the sword through the heart. I love him too much to do that to him.'

Sir Willard Grail considered the offer before giving a polite refusal.

'Thank you, Elkannah,' he said, 'I can think of nothing I'd enjoy more than a visit to Newmarket. On any other day but tomorrow, I'd have been delighted to accompany you.'

'But you have a funeral to attend.'

'I didn't say that.'

'You didn't need to say it,' said Prout, resignedly. 'I should have guessed that nothing would tear you away from that. Well, I have one consolation, I suppose. At least, you didn't laugh in my face.'

'Why on earth should I do that?'

'Henry assured me that you would.'

'Did you put the same suggestion to him?'

'Yes, I did, and I've been regretting it ever since.'

'Why?' asked Sir Willard. 'Was he contemptuous?'

'His behaviour was inexcusable,' said Prout, stiffly, 'and I no longer list him among my close friends.'

'Dear me! Was your conversation with him as bad as that?'

'It was worse, Sir Willard.'

They had met on their way to the coffee house and stepped into the anteroom so that they could talk in private. Like Henry Redmayne, Sir Willard had seen through the ruse immediately. The offer of a trip to Newmarket was a means of keeping him away from the funeral of Sir Martin Culthorpe. Though he had not decided if he would attend the latter, he had graciously declined the invitation.

'I daresay that you had the same response from Jocelyn,' said Sir Willard. 'He's the one person determined to be at that church.'

'I felt obliged to make the offer to him as well.'

'What did he say?'

'Nothing,' replied Prout. 'When I called at his house, he was not there. His butler told me that he had business in Richmond and would be away all day.'

Sir Willard was exasperated. 'Confound it!' he exclaimed. 'I was hoping to find him here. I need a word or two with Jocelyn Kidbrooke.'

'Have you fallen out with him?'

'No, Elkannah – but it may come to that.'

'Why?'

'It's a private matter regarding my brother-in-law.'

'And it threatens your friendship with Jocelyn?'

'Possibly.'

'What a turn of events!' observed Prout, drily. 'Not so long ago, all four of us were close companions, fellow pleasure-seekers and members of a Society whose very name defined our characters. Where has our warm friendship flown?' he asked. 'I have spurned Henry Redmayne. You are on the verge of a serious argument with Jocelyn Kidbrooke, and there's no common ground left between us.'

'All that will change once the funeral is over.'

'Do you believe that?'

'It's self-evident,' said Sir Willard. 'Until her husband is buried, Araminta cannot learn to live again and, until she does that, none of us can, in all conscience, make any overtures to her.'

'That was not your opinion a couple of days ago.'

'I've mellowed since then.'

'If only Jocelyn could have done so as well,' said Prout, 'but there was no chance of that. Of the four of us, he was always the most rabid and uncompromising in his desires.'

'That's precisely why Araminta will reject him.'

'Such over-eagerness would be very distressing to her.'

'Almost as distressing as Henry's crude attempts at poetry,' said Sir Willard with a laugh. 'When I read that sonnet of his, I began to wonder if English was his first tongue. He mangled the language.'

'This morning, he mangled our friendship.'

'Why are you so bitter about it, Elkannah?'

'Because he betrayed me,' said Prout, icily. 'He agreed to my pact at first, then threw it back in my face. That was unpardonable. I will be supremely happy if I never see Henry Redmayne again.'

The closer the funeral came, the more Araminta Culthorpe sank back into despair. Nothing could alleviate her suffering. The brevity of her marriage added a poignancy to the situation. Having been pursued and harassed by a number of suitors, she had found a decent, loving, caring man who neither pursued nor harassed her, offering her instead a respect and consideration that slowly drew her to him. Sir Martin Culthorpe was all that she had ever envisaged in a husband, and their life together had been blissful.

Now he was gone and the brutal manner of his demise made his death more shocking. He could never be replaced. Araminta could never again know that joy of discovery. She and her husband had been enlarged with a vision of each other. Such delight only happened once in a lifetime. In its wake, came a form of oblivion.

Occupied by these thoughts, Araminta sat in her bedchamber and tried to summon up the strength to face the ordeal on the morrow. All eyes would be on her. She would be tested to the limit.

Eleanor Ryle was seated beside her, watching her mistress's face gradually darken. She tried to lighten the mood of despondency with some light conversation.

'Mr Rushton says that everything is under control.'

'Good.'

'All that you need worry about is getting through the service,' said the maid. 'It's bound to be harrowing, m'lady, but I know you'll keep your composure somehow.'

'I'll try.'

'You'll be surrounded by people who love you.'

'That will bring comfort,' said Araminta. After a pause, she sat bolt upright to announce an important decision. 'I've been thinking about the portrait.'

'Is that wise?'

'It hasn't upset me, Eleanor. It did at first, I admit, because it had such painful associations. Then I tried to look at it from Monsieur Villemot's point of view. He was so excited by the commission. He brought such relish to his work.' A look of bewilderment came over her face. 'Monsieur Villemot wanted more than anything to finish that portrait. He told me that it would be his finest work since coming to England. Why should he do anything that might prevent him from completing it? That would be nonsensical.'

'I agree, m'lady.'

'He stood to gain nothing whatsoever by committing the crime,' said Araminta, 'yet he risked losing everything. Once I'd dwelt on that fact, I realised that I need no longer shun the portrait. It was not, after all, the work of a man who killed my husband.'

'Other people feel the same,' said Eleanor, thinking of her visit to Christopher Redmayne. 'I'm sure that they are doing whatever they can to prove his innocence.'

'It was as if a curse had suddenly been lifted off the portrait.'

'I'm glad you see it that way.'

'Since it was commissioned by Sir Martin, it ought to be here in our house. In time – God willing – Monsieur Villemot may even be in a position to finish it, though I can understand that he might want to have nothing more to do with it.'

'All that he wants at the moment is to be set free.'

'If he's truly innocent, that will surely happen.'

'What do you want me to do about the portrait, m'lady?'

'Go and fetch it.'

'Today?'

'Tomorrow,' said Araminta, decisively. 'Take the carriage to the studio and collect what is rightly mine.'

Christopher Redmayne was impatient. The evening was wearing on yet there was no sign of his brother. He feared that Henry might have forgotten his assignment and drifted off to a tavern with his friends. As he paced up and down the drawing room of his house, Christopher reprimanded himself for trusting so important a task to a person who was noted for his unreliability. Valuable time had been lost. Until they had more detail about Abel Paskins, neither Christopher nor Jonathan Bale could press ahead with their investigation into the murder and the theft of the portrait.

There was the additional problem of Jean-Paul Villemot. To a man of such pride and sensitivity, being under lock and key in Newgate was like being stretched on a rack of humiliation. He would not be able to withstand it indefinitely. His threat of suicide had not been an idle one. If he carried it out, his name would be added to the long list of prisoners who had taken their own lives to escape the shame of being thrown into Newgate.

Christopher did not want the artist's death on his conscience but the only way to avoid that was to establish his innocence. If he put his mind to it, Henry could play a crucial role in getting Villemot out of prison, but it appeared that he had once again been distracted by the more immediate pleasures of the city. His brother's first impulse was to visit Henry's favourite haunts and drag him out of the one into which he had selfishly rolled that evening. Christopher drew back from that course of action because he knew how quickly Henry could drink himself into incomprehensibility. An inebriated brother would be no use to him at all.

He was just about to give up all hope of seeing Henry that evening when he heard the clatter of hooves in the street. Someone pulled his horse to a halt and dismounted. When the doorbell rang, Jacob went to answer it. Leaving his horse in the care of the old servant, Henry Redmayne swept into the drawing room and took off his hat before giving a low bow. Christopher was astounded. He did not at first recognise his brother for he wore a peach-coloured suit of the finest silk and the most elaborate sartorial accessories. What confused Christopher was that his visitor's face was covered in white powder and marked with a large beauty spot.

'Is that *you*, Henry?' asked his brother, tentatively.

'As large as life, Christopher.'

'Why have you dressed like this?'

'I'll tell you in a moment,' said Henry. 'Meanwhile, prepare yourself for a disappointment.'

'You forgot all about speaking to Jocelyn Kidbrooke.'

'On the contrary, I rode to his house as soon as I'd finished at the Navy Office. But he was not there. He spent the day in Richmond.'

'Did you enquire about Abel Paskins?'

'That's the other disappointment.'

'Why?'

'The gardener left Jocelyn's staff days ago,' said Henry. 'Nobody at the house has any idea where Paskins might have gone. But do not worry,' he continued. 'As one trail goes cold, we pick up a scent elsewhere. Get changed, Christopher. Put on the most gaudy apparel that you possess.'

'Whatever for?'

'It will help us to blend in. Samson Dinley is a distant acquaintance of mine, though anyone less like the Biblical Samson it would be impossible to find. He's no strong man brought down by a woman, but a puny, prancing, pigeon-chested fellow. However,' said Henry, magnanimously, 'despicable as he is in many ways, Samson gave me the most valuable piece of information.'

'About what?'

'The missing portrait.'

'He knows where it is?'

'Samson saw it for himself.'

'Where?'

'At the place I'm about to take you, Christopher. But you'd not be admitted in that dull and workaday attire. Seek out the brightest thing in your wardrobe,' he urged, pushing his brother out of the room. 'You are about to have an experience that will set your mind racing. Araminta awaits us – dress up accordingly for her.'

Chapter Ten

Jean-Paul Villemot dreaded the approach of night. The day had been a trial but visits from Emile and Christopher Redmayne had acted as a welcome distraction and left him with the minor comforts of clean clothing and edible food. Natural light had also filtered into his cell. Although the narrow slit in the wall was too high for him to look out through, he was grateful for the sunshine that poked in and for the additional benediction of a whiff of fresh air that came in its wake. At night, one of them disappeared.

Newgate was plunged into darkness. Villemot had a candle in his cell but its flickering flame created only a small circle of light. He was lost in shadow, a hunched figure sitting against the wall as he listened to the nocturnal howls of the crazed, the sick and the violent. Noise was more intrusive at night, bruising his ears, battering on the iron bars and pressing in upon him with almost physical force. As the din built to a crescendo, he put his hands to his face in sheer dejection.

There was no way out. He admired Christopher Redmayne but he simply could not believe that the architect – albeit with the aid of a constable – would be able to secure his release from prison. There were strict limits to what Emile could do for him and even Lady Lingoe was only able to make his imprisonment marginally less hideous. Villemot was on his own, a renowned French artist who discovered that his fame, his nationality and his choice of profession only provoked derision in Newgate. Charged with murder, he was treated like the lowest criminal. It was degrading.

He was not only obsessed with his own suffering. His thoughts frequently turned to Araminta and to the torment that she was undergoing. Her pain would be intensified beyond endurance by the belief that the artist had stabbed her husband to death. Wanting her to think well of him, he was horrified that he was seen as the agent of her grief. Young, vulnerable and forlorn, Araminta would be locked in a prison of anguish. She had her own Newgate.

The notion of suicide had at first been too frightening to contemplate but it began to take on a seductive appeal. It would liberate him from his woes and save him from the strong possibility of being hanged in front of a jeering mob. The problem lay in deciding on a means of committing suicide that would be swift and effective. A razor was the obvious choice but he was not allowed to shave. The alternative was a dagger with a sharp blade. However, since a turnkey overheard every conversation he had, he could hardly instruct a friend to provide one for him.

Fire was a possibility, though a daunting one. Even if he managed to light the dank straw with his candle, it would be a slow, painful, lingering death. In any case, the smoke was likely to arouse suspicion before the fumes could take their effect on him. That left another potential way of departing the earth. Villemot could spurn one hangman by taking on the office himself. All that he needed was a ligature. In the gloom of his cell, he stripped to the waist and tore the sleeve off his shirt, looping it until it formed a noose. By way of experiment, he slipped it around his neck. It felt strong enough to dispatch him. He thought that it would be a merciful end.

Tearing the other sleeve from his shirt, he tied it to the noose then stood on tiptoe so that he could reach the highest point on the bars. With the noose around his neck, he slipped the end of the other sleeve through the bars, intending to use his own weight to throttle himself. His hands were shaking and he had difficulty tying the knot. By the time he finally succeeded, his heart was racing and his whole body was running with sweat. After offering up a silent prayer for the salvation of his soul, he kicked his legs forward and let the noose bite into his neck. The sudden pain made him gasp.

The attempt was soon over. As the turnkey walked past on patrol, he held up his lantern and saw the figure squirming in the cell.

'Oh, no you don't,' he said, unlocking the door and rushing in to cut Villemot down. 'You can't escape as easily as that, you French cur. You'll be hanged proper and I'll be there to cheer with the rest of 'em!'

Christopher Redmayne had been past the house hundreds of times without ever once asking himself what lay behind its front door. It was a large, high, nondescript building, only five minutes' walk from Fetter Lane, and they could see light blazing in some of the windows. He was relieved that it was night. Henry loved to disport himself in public but his younger brother felt far too conspicuous in the red doublet and matching petticoat breeches that he had put on. They belonged to his younger days when he was a more adventurous dresser. Christopher was pleased when they reached their destination.

'Let me do the talking,' suggested Henry.

'Why?'

'I speak the language.'

'Is this a foreign establishment?' said Christopher.

Henry laughed. 'Entirely foreign to you,' he replied. 'Brace yourself for a surprise, dear brother. You are about to enter Mother Pilgrim's domain.'

'What exactly is this place?'

'It's a Molly House.'

Christopher was alarmed. He had heard about such haunts of

effeminate young men and sodomites, and could not imagine why he had been brought there. He had no time to protest. Henry had already pulled the bell-rope and the front door swung open. Dressed in ornate livery, a black boy, no more than three feet in height, beckoned them in. They went into a large hall that was lit by candelabra and charged with a sweet perfume.

Fanny Pilgrim glided towards them. Tall, stately and with a blonde wig of enormous dimensions on her head, she wore a dress of such regal magnificence that it dazzled their eyes. She held an ivory fan in one hand and waved it beneath her chin. Henry beamed at her with unassailable confidence but Christopher felt far less comfortable. Though their hostess appeared to be a shapely woman, encrusted with jewellery of all kinds, the architect was certain that he was, in fact, looking at a man.

'Welcome, darlings,' said Fanny, her deep, rich voice confirming Christopher's diagnosis. 'What brought you to my house tonight?'

'A kind word from a friend,' said Henry.

'And who might that friend be?'

'Samson Dinley.'

'Ah, yes – dear Samson, our very own Delilah. You'll find her in one of our rooms. If you are recommended by Samson, you are doubly welcome.'

'Thank you, Mother Pilgrim.'

'To my friends, I am known as Fanny.'

'Then Fanny it shall be.'

She extended a gloved hand and, to Christopher's chagrin, his brother actually kissed it. The visitors had clearly passed some kind of test. Fanny Pilgrim's house provided a form of entertainment that was highly illegal, so any strangers had to be subjected to intense scrutiny before being allowed in. Henry's foppish manner and his friendship with a regular denizen of the house had got them admitted. Christopher found himself wishing that they had been turned away.

They were taken across the hall to a room that was dimly lit and filled with the excited babble of a dozen or more men and women. Some of the men were so garishly attired that they made Henry's suit look rather subdued. Their hair was brushed back from their forehead and combed into the high, curling waves of a woman's coiffure. They had made heavy use of cosmetics to paint their faces. The women were even more decorative, wearing beautiful dresses, exaggerated wigs, glittering jewellery and an abundance of powder and perfume. It took Christopher only a second to determine that all the occupants of the room were men.

'Why have we come?' he said, nudging his brother.

'To broaden your education.'

'We do not belong here, Henry.'

'Pretend to and all will soon be explained.'

A slim young woman in a scarlet gown came across to them and sized up Christopher with a roguish eye. She turned to Henry.

'You never told me how handsome your brother was,' said Samson Dinley with a titter. 'Has he been to a Molly House before?'

'No,' answered Henry.

'Then I'll take good care of him.'

Dinley's short, slight build and delicate features allowed him to assume the mantle of womanhood with comparative ease. His stance and gestures were genteel and ladylike. His voice was light and teasing. In the normal course of events, Christopher would have taken care to avoid such a person. That was not an option now – Samson Dinley was in a position to help them.

'Henry tells me you know where Lady Culthorpe's portrait is.'

'I do,' said Samson.

'Is it still here?'

'It will be on view upstairs any moment.'

'How did it come to be here?'

'What an inquisitive man you are, Christopher! I like that.'

'Are you sure that it's her?'

Dinley giggled. 'Darling,' he replied, arching an eyebrow, 'do you think any of us would ever make a mistake about Araminta? She is our goddess. We worship her. We love, honour and reverence her. She has the beauty to which we all aspire.'

'Araminta is an icon here,' explained Henry. 'Unbeknown to her, she has many acolytes in Fanny Pilgrim's house. Araminta is a true emblem of womanhood in all its glories. She's incomparable.'

'She carries all before her.'

'Did someone from here steal the portrait?' said Christopher.

'We have something far better than a portrait,' said Dinley, taking Christopher by the arm. 'We have Araminta in the flesh, a painting that moves and breathes as much as she herself. Come – let me show you.'

In spite of his misgivings, Christopher allowed himself to be led into the hall and up the wide staircase. Henry followed behind them. As they walked along the passageway, it was obvious from the noises emanating from every doorway that the rooms were occupied. Music was being played in one of them and Christopher caught a glimpse of two men dancing together. Samson Dinley stopped outside the room at the end of the passageway and rapped on it with his knuckles. It inched open.

'I've brought some friends to see Araminta,' he said.

An eye was applied to the crack between door and frame, and the visitors were subjected to a close inspection. Christopher was glad that the light from the candles was dim. He shrunk back slightly. Henry, on the other hand, took a bold step forward and grinned at the unseen gatekeeper. It seemed to impress the man because he opened the door and waved the three of them in.

Nothing had prepared the two brothers for what they were about to see and they were rendered speechless. The room was half-full of people who stood in a semi-circle around a large, gilded picture frame. Inside the frame, lolling on a couch and wearing a blue dress that shimmered in the candlelight, was a beautiful woman. She looked so much like the figure Christopher had seen in the portrait at the studio that he thought, for one startling instant, that it was Araminta. The resemblance was quite uncanny.

Henry felt it, too, craning his neck and blowing her a kiss. As they had been told, it was no mere painted likeness of Araminta but a creature of flesh and blood, capable of movement. As she adopted another pose, Christopher eased himself forward to get closer. The mirage before him slowly began to change. He could not only see the thick powder that had been used on the face, he realised that this woman was much older than Araminta. When their eyes locked for an instant, he realised something else as well and it sent him back to Henry's side. He spoke in his brother's ear.

'I'm leaving, Henry.'

'Why? Look on Araminta and understand why I love her.'

'That's not her,' said Christopher.

'It's close enough to persuade me.'

There was a collective cry of disappointment as Araminta got up from the couch and withdrew into a dressing room. Christopher pulled his brother out by the sleeve.

'We need to catch him when he leaves,' he said.

'Who?' asked Henry. 'All I saw was a vision of Araminta. She looks exactly as she did in that portrait at the studio.'

'Now we know who stole it.'

'Do we?'

'I got near enough to recognise her – it was Emile.'

Sir Willard Grail was carousing in the tavern with some friends when he saw Jocelyn Kidbrooke enter. Excusing himself from the table, he went across to confront him.

'I've been looking for you all day, Jocelyn,' he said.

'I had to go to Richmond.'

'So I was told.'

'What did you want me for?' said Kidbrooke. 'If you're after more money, Sir Willard, you're out of luck. I have none on me.'

'It's not your money I'm interested in – it's your garden.'

'Whatever for?'

'Buy me another drink and I'll tell you.'

He took Kidbrooke to a vacant table and they sat down. A waiter came to take the order. When the man had gone, Sir Willard let his anger show.

'Did you poach a gardener from my brother-in-law?'

'That's a private matter,' said Kidbrooke.

'If it involved Araminta, it's a very public matter. I spoke to Cuthbert earlier today. What you did to him still rankles. He adores his garden almost as much as he does his library.'

'He has every right to, Sir Willard – it's very impressive.'

'It was until you lured away one of his best gardeners.'

'I, too, have a garden.'

'That wasn't the reason you wanted Abel Paskins, was it?' said Sir Willard, accusingly. 'You discovered that the fellow once worked for Sir Martin Culthorpe.'

'Really? He never mentioned that to me.'

'He had no need to, Jocelyn – you already knew.'

'I did nothing of the kind.'

'You wanted Paskins because he could tell you things about Araminta and her husband that only someone who had worked at the house would know. You didn't employ a gardener – you were buying information.'

Kidbrooke smiled defiantly. 'What if I was?'

'It was a breach of the Society's articles.'

'There was no reference to a gardener in them.'

'We made a solemn agreement that we wouldn't try to bribe members of Araminta's household to act as spies,' said Sir Willard. 'Yet that's exactly what you did.'

'I deny that.'

'It's as plain as the nose on your face.'

'Perhaps you should take another look at those articles that Elkannah drew up for us. Specific mention was only made of *Araminta's* household, not of Sir Martin's. At the time when we formed the Society,' said Kidbrooke, 'she was not married and was living with her cousin here in London.'

'Don't try to wriggle out of this, Jocelyn. You violated the spirit of the articles and should forfeit your right to the purse.'

'It's not the purse I'm after, Sir Willard.'

'No, it's that poor, wounded, defenceless, grieving widow.'

'As for the spirit of the articles,' said Kidbrooke, 'that does not apply here. I did not try to bribe one of Sir Martin's gardeners. Abel Paskins had already left his employ.'

'Yes – he was working for my brother-in-law.'

'I made him a more attractive offer.'

'Then pumped him for intelligence about Araminta.'

'I may have asked him if he was aware of the way that the romance between Sir Martin and her had first developed, but I also wanted him to build a rockery in my garden. The one he constructed for Mr Foxwell,' he went on, 'was what first drew my attention to him.'

'You cheated, Jocelyn.'

'I simply made the most of my chances.'

'You broke the rules.'

'What would you have done in my place, Sir Willard?'

'Behaved more honourably.'

'I beg leave to question that,' said Kidbrooke, roundly. 'Had you known that Paskins had once worked for Sir Martin Culthorpe, you'd have whisked him away from under your brother-in-law's nose without a second thought. Am I correct?'

Sir Willard was spared the awkwardness of a reply by the return of the waiter with a bottle of wine. When he had poured it into the two glasses, he withdrew again. Kidbrooke lifted his glass.

'Let's drink as friends,' he encouraged.

'Very well,' said the other, picking up his glass. 'But I'll not forgive you for what you did, Jocelyn. You tried to gain an advantage over the rest of us by using corrupt means.'

'I admit that I tried.'

'And what did you learn?'

'That Sir Martin was right to dismiss Abel Paskins.'

'Why?'

'The fellow was surly and ungovernable. Left to himself, he worked well and hard but he insisted on having his own way. Also, he was forever complaining.'

'About what?'

'Whatever took his fancy – he thrived on argument.'

'Cuthbert had no trouble from the fellow.'

'Then he would have been welcome to have him back because I soon regretted tempting him away from Mr Foxwell.'

'When I called at your house, they said Paskins was not there.'

'That's quite true, Sir Willard.'

'Where is he?'

'I've no idea,' said Kidbrooke, resentfully. 'He left earlier this week without a word of explanation. Paskins has flown the coop.'

As soon as they got back to Christopher's house, he asked Jacob to pour three large glasses of brandy. The old man was perturbed when he saw his master return with his two companions but he masked his concern with his usual aplomb. Jacob was used to seeing Henry in flamboyant clothing but not with a painted face. It worried him. What really disturbed him was the sight of the little French valet with a powdered features and a woman's wig on his head. He was, however, spared the blue dress. Emile had changed out of that before leaving Mother Pilgrim's Molly House.

Left alone with their brandy, Christopher fired off a question.

'Why did you steal that portrait, Emile?' he challenged. 'Did you want to show it off to your friends at Fanny Pilgrim's?'

'I no steal it,' insisted Emile.

'Then what did you do?'

'I hide it so that nobody could take it away. Matilda, she warn me that this man go to the studio when I was not there. He look at the painting of Lady Culthorpe. He want it.'

'You can hardly blame the fellow,' said Henry, blithely, giving no hint that he was the man in question. 'Any portrait of Araminta would be like spun gold.'

'I was scared,' said the valet. 'I know what Monsieur Villemot would say if anyone steal it. So I hide it.'

'Where?'

'Under my bed.'

'In other words,' said Christopher, 'it's still in the house.'

'Yes.'

'Then why did you tell us it was stolen?'

'Because I want everyone to think that,' said Emile, tasting the brandy with gratitude. 'If they believe the portrait is not there, they will not come to the house.'

'That was very clever of you but it did mean that we were searching for a stolen painting that never actually went missing. You wasted our time, Emile, time that could have been devoted to helping to get Monsieur Villemot released from prison.'

'I sorry.'

'What made you decide to be Araminta?' said Henry.

'I look at the painting every day. She is so lovely.'

'You achieved a remarkable verisimilitude.' He saw that he had strayed beyond the bounds of the valet's English vocabulary. 'You looked just like her, Emile.'

'It was the tribute. I like her.'

'How long have you been going to Fanny Pilgrim?'

'Since we move to London.'

'Does your master know about this?' said Christopher.

'Oh, yes,' replied Emile as if the question was unnecessary. 'Of course, he did. I hide nothing from him.'

'And he didn't mind?'

'Monsieur Villemot is an artist. He believe in freedom.'

'I can think of better ways to exercise it.'

Henry sipped his drink. 'You take too narrow a view of the world, Christopher,' he said, 'and fail to appreciate its teeming variety. I'd not care to spend an evening among the catamites in a Molly House but I refuse to condemn those that do. Well, you met Samson,' he added. 'Have you ever seen a more feeble, confused, innocuous creature? I dislike his sin but pardon the sinner.'

'I'd prefer to put tonight's little escapade behind us, Henry,' said his brother. 'Now that we know the portrait is safe, one problem is solved. We can turn to the more pressing one of Monsieur Villemot's imprisonment.'

'We must get him out,' pleaded Emile, 'or he die.'

'I hate to say this but he's his own worst enemy. Instead of telling me what I need to know to mount his defence, he keeps holding back salient facts.'

'What sort of facts?' said Henry.

'He won't tell me where he went on the day of the murder.'

'You already know that. He went to Araminta's house.'

'But where did he go *afterwards*?' asked Christopher. 'He did not come back to the studio for two hours or more, and when he did, he was in a state of excitement.'

'If I'd been to her house, I'd be in a state of delirium.'

'He's hiding something from me, Henry, something that might prove his innocence. It's perverse,' said Christopher in exasperation. 'How can I help someone who keeps telling me lies?'

'What sort of lies?'

'To begin with, he told me that he was married and that he wanted the house built for him and his wife. But it turns out that there *is* no wife back in Paris.'

'How do you know?'

'Emile told me.'

The two brothers looked at the valet. Shifting in his seat, he took a long sip of his brandy. The resemblance to Araminta Culthorpe had vanished completely now. He was a weary, aging, bewildered, frightened little man.

'Why did he mislead me, Emile?' said Christopher. 'Why did he tell me that he has a wife in France?'

Emile looked hunted. He rolled the glass between his palms.

'I not tell you.'

'Why?'

'Ask him,' said Emile.

Elkannah Prout knew that his invitation would, in all probability, be declined but he nevertheless decided to offer. He called early at the house in the hope of catching his friend before he went out. Jocelyn Kidbrooke was less than welcoming but he agreed to speak to his visitor. They adjourned to the drawing room.

'Why did you come here?' asked Kidbrooke.

'If we talk in your home, you'll be reminded that you have a wife and children. I think that's an important factor.'

'Don't preach morality at me, Elkannah. You've enjoyed every vice in London so it ill befits you to set yourself up as an arbiter of other people's behaviour.'

'That's not what I'm doing,' said Prout.

'Then why does your voice have that sanctimonious ring to it?'

'I came to issue an invitation.'

'Ah, yes,' said Kidbrooke. 'It's the visit to Newmarket. When I saw Sir Willard last night, he warned me that you'd try to get me out of the city on the day of Sir Martin's funeral.'

'You've always liked racing.'

'I'm engaged in a much more important race of my own at the moment – so are Sir Willard and Henry. That's why none of us will stray one inch outside the capital.'

'I think you should reconsider that decision, Jocelyn.'

'Why?'

'Your presence at that funeral will cause Araminta pain.'

'Your absence will surprise her.'

'I've written to offer my condolences.'

'But what about the many blandishments you sent her in the past – the gifts, the invitations, the *billet-doux*? Won't she find it strange that a man who professes to love her will neglect her on a day when she needs every ounce of support she can get?'

'I do not see it that way.'

'I respect your right to do so, Elkannah. By the same token, you must respect my right to view the situation as I choose. In short,' said Kidbrooke, pointedly, 'this conversation is over.'

'So you *did* have a pact.'

'A pact?'

'To ignore my advice and attend the funeral,' said Prout, sharply. 'You, Henry and Sir Willard have lined up against me.'

'We've done nothing of the sort.'

'Yes, you have.'

'We simply agree with each other.'

'The three of you came to a formal agreement.'

'Henry and Sir Willard may have done so,' said Kidbrooke, 'but I was not party to it. I've argued from the start that it was a case of each man for himself. I've not consulted them for a second and I doubt if they consulted each other.'

'I got the strong impression from Henry that the three of you had a verbal contract and that he was going back on his earlier promise to me.'

'You were misled.'

'Do you give me your word?'

'I'll happily do so, Elkannah. I can't speak for the others but there's been no collusion on my part. I've not wavered in my view that Araminta is fair game in her bereavement.'

'I find that notion shameful.'

'Nobody is forcing you to accept it.'

'Henry and Sir Willard seem to have done so.'

THE PAINTED LADY 237

'Then each has acted of his own volition. Why have you suddenly decided to bark at my heels?' complained Kidbrooke. 'I had enough of that from Sir Willard. As soon as he saw me yesterday evening, he was yapping away like a dog after a fox.'

'What had you done to offend him?'

'I'd seized an advantage that he should have taken.'

'Advantage?'

'His brother-in-law, Cuthbert Foxwell, hired a gardener who had formerly been employed by Sir Martin Culthorpe. Having worked for Araminta's husband, the man had privileged information. I decided to avail myself of it by hiring the gardener myself. When I did so,' he recalled, 'Sir Willard didn't make the slightest protest.'

'Why was he so angry now?'

'He had just discovered the link between Araminta and the gardener. When the man worked for his brother-in-law, Sir Willard was quite unaware of that link.'

'How did he find out?'

'Henry's brother told him.'

'Christopher? Why should he get involved?'

'He seems to be poking his nose into anything and everything,' said Kidbrooke. 'It was he who set that unsightly constable on to me. I hope that Christopher Redmayne comes in person next time. I'll have the pleasure of telling him how I despise meddlers like him.'

Listening to the recital of events, Jonathan Bale did not realise that his friend had omitted some crucial details. Christopher had deliberately concealed the fact that he and his brother had visited a Molly House. Such places were anathema to Bale and he would have passed on the address of the establishment to a magistrate. All that he was told was that the missing portrait had been in the safe hands of the valet from the start.

'Why didn't Emile tell us that?' he asked.

'He wanted everyone to believe a theft had taken place.'

'In doing that, he was misleading an officer of the law. They may do things differently in France, Mr Redmayne, but we take a dim view of that sort of thing in England.'

'I did make that point to him, Jonathan.'

'I'd like to do so myself, sir. He wasted our time.'

'Let's not criticise him too harshly. His ruse did prevent the portrait from being stolen and I know for a fact that one thief did gain access to the house.'

'Do you know the man's name?'

'Unfortunately, I don't,' said Christopher, shielding his brother from arrest. 'On balance, I feel that Emile's action had a purpose.'

Christopher did not add that part of that purpose had been to fuel the valet's interest in Araminta to the point where he actually tried to become her. The constable would have considerable difficulty in understanding why any man should do that.

'Putting aside the portrait, sir,' said Bale, 'I'm more worried by what you've just told me about the gardener.'

'Abel Paskins has disappeared. It was Henry who found that out for us. Nobody at the house knew where Paskins had gone.'

'So your brother did not speak to Mr Kidbrooke.'

'He wasn't there yesterday.'

'What about today?'

'Henry has agreed to tackle him on our behalf.'

'Your brother is being unusually helpful,' noted Bale. 'In the past, he has always done his best to hamper any investigation.'

'I fancy that he's seen the light at last,' said Christopher with gentle sarcasm. 'Father would be delighted.'

Bale was sombre. 'I've been thinking about that key, sir.'

'What key?'

'The one that opened the gate to Sir Martin's garden,' said the other. 'Without that, the killer would not have been able to get in and lie in wait for his victim. He must have had a duplicate made.'

'So?'

'That points us firmly towards Abel Paskins, sir. While he was working there, he would have had the key in his possession from time to time. He could have taken it to a locksmith to be copied. If we could find that locksmith,' suggested Bale, 'we might get a description of the man who wanted the duplicate.'

'Locksmiths are making spare keys all the time, Jonathan. How would one of them remember that particular commission?'

'I'd show them a key to the garden gate. If someone made a duplicate recently, I think that he might remember it.'

'But we do not have one of those,' said Christopher.

'Get one, sir,' said Bale. 'You have a friend in the house.'

It was something that Christopher had forgotten. Eleanor Ryle had cared enough about helping the investigation to slip away from her mistress and visit Fetter Lane. Since they were in the study, Christopher had pen and paper to hand. He dashed off a letter to the maid then summoned Jacob.

'I want Nigel to deliver this immediately,' he said, handing over the missive. 'He knows the way to the house.'

'Very good, sir.'

'Tell him to await a reply.'

Before the servant could do so, the doorbell rang and he went off to answer the summons. The haughty voice of a woman was heard then Lady Lingoe was ushered into the study.

'Good morning, Mr Redmayne,' she said. 'Forgive this intrusion but I come on a matter that will brook no delay. It concerns Monsieur Villemot.'

'Then you'll not mind if Jonathan stays,' said Christopher, 'for he is helping me to prove Monsieur Villemot's innocence.'

After introducing Bale to his visitor, he offered her a seat. Lady Lingoe arranged herself on the couch and Christopher sat close to her. Cowed by her appearance and aristocratic mien,

Bale took the chair that was farthest away from her. He marvelled that his friend could be so at ease in the company of a high-born lady. Being in her presence only accentuated his feelings of social inferiority.

'Let me go straight to it,' said Lady Lingoe, ignoring the constable as if he were not there. 'I've just come from Newgate.'

'How is Monsieur Villemot?' asked Christopher.

'They would not let me see him.'

'Why not?'

'He tried to kill himself last night. He begged the prison sergeant not to allow me in. I regard myself as a friend of Jean-Paul,' she went on with unconcealed affection. 'Why did he have me turned away? The only explanation is that he's come to the end of his tether. He's set on taking his own life.'

'What happened last night, Lady Lingoe?'

'He attempted to hang himself. Can you think of anything more deplorable? A dear and gifted man like that is driven to suicide, and all because of a crime he did not commit. I was distressed beyond measure when I heard.'

Christopher was on his feet. 'I'm not surprised,' he said. 'I'll visit the prison myself and insist on seeing him.'

'That's what I was hoping you'd do, Mr Redmayne.'

'Thank you for coming.'

'Keep me informed of what transpires.'

'I will, Lady Lingoe.'

'And give him...' She smothered the words she was about to say. 'And please pass on my warmest regards.' She rose to her feet. 'You know where to find me, Mr Redmayne.'

'You're welcome to stay here with Jonathan.'

'No, I need the comfort of my own home. Goodbye, Mr Bale.'

'Goodbye,' he said, getting up awkwardly.

Christopher took her to the front door to see her off. When he came back into the study, he was carrying his hat.

'I'll go at once, Jonathan.'

'What about me, sir?'

'You have to stay here for a while.'

'Why?'

'Someone might bring you a key to that garden.'

The funeral of Sir Martin Culthorpe was due to take place that evening and a pall hung over the whole house. Servants went about their duties in a respectful silence and guests spoke in hushed voices. Since her mistress had asked to be left alone in her bedchamber, Eleanor Ryle was able to retire to her own little room. Letters were still arriving from friends and well-wishers but she had never expected that one message would be addressed to her. The butler delivered it in person. Delighted to have a private moment with Mr Rushton, she opened the letter in his presence and read it.

'What does it say, Eleanor?' he asked.

She looked up. 'I have to ask you a favour, Mr Rushton.'

Overcoming his aversion to the prison, Christopher entered Newgate and asked to see Jean-Paul Villemot. The prison sergeant was at first dubious about allowing the visit but a handful of coins helped him to make up his mind. Christopher was taken to the Frenchman's cell by one of the turnkeys. He knew immediately why the artist had refused to see Lady Lingoe. After his failed attempt at suicide, he had been stripped of most of his clothes and fettered to an iron ring in the wall of the cell. Embarrassed to be seen by Christopher, he would have felt utterly humiliated if Lady Lingoe had viewed him in that situation.

Crouching down low, the visitor spoke through the bars.

'How are you?' he asked.

'Not well.'

'What made you do it, Monsieur Villemot?'

'It was the only thing left to me.'

'That's not true,' said Christopher, 'and it's a terrible indictment against the rest of us that you should have reached this point. You must know that taking one's own life is a crime and a sin. It would leave a terrible stain on your reputation.'

Villemot groaned. 'What reputation?'

'The one you took such pains to build up over the years. Would you sacrifice that in a single moment of despair? You must have been brought up as a Roman Catholic. Were you never taught about the consequences of suicide?' asked Christopher. 'The Church would renounce you. By law, you'd be buried in unconsecrated ground.' Villemot started. 'Is that what you wanted?'

'No, Christopher.'

'Then why did you do it?'

'I could not put up with the shame,' said Villemot.

'So you decided to let your family and friends live with an even greater shame. That's what they would have had to do. The stigma would have stayed with them throughout their lives. People *care* for you, Monsieur Villemot,' he said with feeling. 'They love, respect and admire you for what you've become. Did you not stop to think of the pain you'd be inflicting on us all by doing what you tried to do?'

'I am sorry,' said Villemot, tears coursing down his face. 'I have spent the whole night praying for forgiveness.'

'Will you promise to do nothing like this again?'

'Yes, Christopher.'

'If I have anything to do with it,' said the other, 'you'll not have the time. We'll get you out of this place very soon.'

'Do you *mean* that?' pleaded the artist.

'I give you my word.'

Sympathy welled up inside him. Villemot looked even worse than on his previous visit. Unshaven, unkempt, caked with filth and visibly aged by his ordeal, Villemot was forlorn.

'You had another visitor,' Christopher told him.

'Hester?'

'Yes. She was not permitted to see you.'

'How could I let her?' said Villemot, rattling his fetters. 'What would she think of me if she saw me chained up like a wild animal?'

'I think she'd feel as I do – grateful that you were still alive. Lady Lingoe sent her warmest regards,' said Christopher. 'I'm sure that Emile would do the same.'

'Emile,' sighed the other. 'Poor little Emile – I forgot about him.'

'In your dejection, you forgot about a lot of people. The worst thing is that you forgot about yourself, Monsieur. You forgot who you are and what you are.'

'I'm a condemned man.'

'You've not even been brought to trial yet.'

'I've been charged. They tell me in here I will be convicted.'

'They're only baiting you,' said Christopher. '*You* know that you didn't commit that murder and so do we. All that we have to do is to work together and we'll have the evidence to get you released.'

'What evidence?'

'It's being gathered even as we speak, Monsieur Villemot. But I still need you to cooperate more with me.'

'There's nothing that I can do.'

'Yes there is. You can explain why you lied to us.'

'I tell you no lies.'

'You did,' said Christopher. 'When you commissioned me to design a new house, you told me it was for you and your wife.'

'That was true.'

'Yet you are not married.'

'Who told you that?'

'Emile.'

Villemot was hurt. 'Emile betrayed me?'

'No,' replied Christopher, careful to correct him. 'That's the last thing he'd do. Emile is fiercely loyal. What he said slipped out by mistake. He refused to give me any details. All I know –

all that I suspect, at least – is that you are not married. Is that true?'

'Yes,' admitted the other, head on his chest.

'Then why tell me that you were?'

'It is private.'

'I took you for an honest man, Monsieur Villemot.'

'And that is what I am,' retorted the other, looking up. 'The house will take time to build. When it is finished, I was hoping to move into it with my wife.'

'Monique?'

'That's her.'

'But you are not married to her at the moment?'

'No, Christopher.'

'Why not?'

'She already has a husband.'

'Oh, I see.'

'I do not think so,' said Villemot. 'Why do you think I leave my own country? Paris is a finer city than London – they would not have thrown me into prison there.'

'But you had to leave for some reason?' guessed Christopher. 'Was that reason connected with Monique?'

'Yes, it was.'

'But you still nurtured hopes of being together one day.'

'I did until last night – not even she could keep me alive then.'

'Monsieur Villemot,' said Christopher, 'this may seem like prying but, given the situation, I feel that I have to ask the question.'

'Ask me anything – I am not afraid.'

'You admitted that you went to Lady Culthorpe's house that day and that you went into the garden out of curiosity.'

'That is so.'

'I put it to you that you were not curious about the garden but about the lady who lived in the house. That's what took you through that gate. You were enchanted by her.'

After agonising for a full minute, Jean-Paul Villemot nodded.

'You see my dilemma here?' said Christopher. 'I am asked to believe that you love someone enough to want to marry her and have a house built for her – and yet you pursue someone else.'

'I did not pursue Lady Culthorpe,' snapped the other.

'I'm not making any moral judgement here, Monsieur Villemot. I can understand how you could be drawn to someone like her when you are able to spend so much time alone, and when your work allows you to gaze upon her so intently.'

'What are you trying to say to me?'

'That you are infatuated with Lady Culthorpe.'

'No!'

'Then what took you to her house that day?'

'She interested me.'

'I think it was much more than interest.'

'It was,' confessed Villemot, blurting out the words. 'It was like a passion. She is a very beautiful lady, so young, so perfect. I could not believe the coincidence.'

'Coincidence?'

'Araminta could almost be her twin.'

'Who?'

'Monique. She and Araminta, they look so alike.'

'And you were bewitched by the similarity between the two?'

'It was a miracle,' said Villemot, smiling for the first time. 'Every time I see Araminta, I am looking at my Monique. Every time I put the paint on the canvas, I am touching the woman I love. That is why it is the most important portrait that I paint in England. When I work on it, I'm able to be with Monique once again.'

Christopher understood for the first time what had impelled the artist to go to Araminta's house. Since she would no longer be sitting for the portrait, Villemot would be losing touch with her physical presence. He wanted to see her in her own home. He had followed her carriage and lingered outside the house. One mystery had been solved but another remained.

'You said you were in that garden for a couple of minutes,'

said Christopher. 'Where did you go *afterwards*?'

Villemot jerked backwards as if he had just been jabbed in the ribs by the point of a dagger. He sounded hurt and defensive.

'I cannot tell you,' he said.

Eleanor Ryle was starting to worry. Hours had passed and there had been no summons for her mistress. She hoped that Lady Culthorpe had been asleep, gathering her strength to meet the demands of the funeral, but she knew that was unlikely. Since the murder of her husband, Araminta had enjoyed very little sleep and much of her slumber had been filled with disturbing dreams. Deciding to check on her, Eleanor went swiftly upstairs and tapped on the door of her bedchamber. There was no response. She opened the door slightly and peeped through the gap, only to discover that the room was empty.

The maid went into the bedchamber and looked around in dismay. Her mistress had not stirred from the room before without calling for her. Eleanor was like a human walking stick, something to offer unquestioning support. Now, it seemed, she had been cast aside and that troubled her. She wondered where Lady Culthorpe could possibly be. There were family members staying at the house but they had respected the widow's request to be left on her own. It was highly improbable that she would have sought company.

Eleanor crossed to the window and looked out at the garden. Even under a leaden sky, it looked full of colour and blossom. A stray thought floated into her brain like a dry leaf blown by the wind. It produced an immediate reaction. Leaving the room, she went down the backstairs and out into the garden, following a path that twisted its way between trees, shrubs and flowerbeds. Eventually, she came to the shaded grotto where Sir Martin Culthorpe had been murdered. There, dressed in black, sitting on a bench, dwelling on memories that brought a faraway smile to her face, was Araminta Culthorpe.

'I wondered where you were, m'lady,' said Eleanor.

'What?' Araminta came out of her reverie. 'Oh, it's you.'

'Why did you come here?'

'I felt drawn back to this place, Eleanor.'

'But it has such unhappy memories for you, m'lady.'

'That's not what I found. It's an odd word to use perhaps, but I feel renewed. Being able to come here has dispelled some of my gloom. It was almost as if my husband beckoned me back to this spot. He wanted me to conquer any fears I have of this grotto, to remember the many happy moments he and I spent in this garden.'

'It's good that you can feel like that.'

'I have to, Eleanor, or there's no point in going on.'

'You must go on, m'lady.'

'I know – and I will. Sir Martin would expect it of me. I'll tend this garden with the same love that he showed.' She gave the maid a shrewd look. 'Do you have something to tell me?'

'No, no.'

'I can see it in your eyes. What's happened, Eleanor?'

'Nothing, m'lady.'

'Come on, I insist on knowing.'

'Wait until after the funeral,' said Eleanor. 'That's the only thing that matters now. Forget everything else.'

Araminta was persistent. 'Is it something to do with Monsieur Villemot?' The maid pursed her lips. 'Well – is it?'

'Yes, m'lady.'

'Go on.'

'Mr Redmayne – *Christopher* Redmayne – is more certain than ever that Mr Villemot was not the murderer. To prove it beyond doubt, he asked for some help from us.'

'What sort of help?'

'He wanted to borrow a key to the garden gate.'

Jonathan Bale did not enjoy the wait. Left alone in Christopher's house, he was restless and uncomfortable. When Jacob offered him refreshment, the constable was even more ill at ease. Having no servant of his own, he could not bring himself to allow someone else to fetch and carry for him, unless it was his wife. Nigel eventually rode back to Fetter Lane and handed over the key. Bale went off on his mission at once.

If Abel Paskins had indeed borrowed the key, he reasoned, the man would have wanted the duplicate made as quickly as possible. The gardener would therefore have chosen a locksmith nearby so that the key was not missing from the house in Westminster for long. Bale set off at a brisk pace and maintained it all the way. The first locksmith he found had never seen the key before but he gave the constable the name of a rival whose workshop was only streets away. Bale soon made the acquaintance of Elijah Sayers.

'What do you want?' asked Sayers, bluntly.

'I want you to look at this key.'

'I don't have the time.'

Bale was assertive. 'Make some time, Mr Sayers.'

'I'm too busy. If you want a duplicate, you'll have to wait at least a fortnight before I could take on more work. Find someone else.'

'I don't want a duplicate,' said Bale, 'I want information.'

After introducing himself, Bale explained why he was there. Elijah Sayers did not appear to be listening to him. He continued to use a file on a large key and did not even look at his visitor. Sayers was a short, wiry man in his fifties with a shock of grey hair sprouting on both sides of his balding head like a pair of supplementary ears. He wore a leather apron over his filthy working clothes. Filled with smoke from the little forge, the workshop was a long, low, narrow room that was never swept, with keys of all sizes hanging from the rafters. Locks were arranged haphazardly on a rough wooden table. The place was so filled with shadow that Bale wondered how the locksmith could see well enough to practise his trade.

Sayers glanced up, eyes gleaming in the half-dark. He thrust out a hand and took the key from Bale. After a brief examination, he handed it back and returned to his work.

'Do you recognise it?' said Bale.

'Yes.'

'How can you be so sure?'

'Do you recognise people you once arrested?'

'Of course.'

'It's the same with me and my keys, Mr Bale,' said the other, turning to spit into the forge. 'They're like humans to me – each one has a different face and character. I'd know that anywhere.'

'Why?'

'Because I made a tidy profit out of it.'

'Who brought it in?'

'A man in a hurry,' said Sayers. 'He wanted me to make another key while he waited. I told him I had other customers waiting for their locks and keys. He'd have to take his turn.'

'What was his reply?'

'He said it was urgent. The gentleman who'd sent him had to have a duplicate that day. Money was no object. He'd pay whatever was asked. I took him at his word.'

'You made the key?'

'Yes, I did – and I charged him four times what I would have done. He paid up without any argument then watched me do my work. Afterwards, he rushed off.'

'Did he give his name?'

'No, Mr Bale.'

'What about the gentleman who sent him?'

'Oh, he told me what he was called.'

'And what was that?'

'Mr Kidbrooke – Mr Jocelyn Kidbrooke.'

Chapter Eleven

Henry Redmayne was racked by indecision. As a rule, he made up his mind about his social calendar with remarkable speed but not in this case. Should he or should he not attend the funeral of Sir Martin Culthorpe? It was a dilemma that vexed him for hours on end. If he went, would his presence be noted and appreciated by Araminta or would it alarm her? If he stayed away, could his absence please or disappoint her? More to the point, would it simply hand an advantage to his rivals? Elkannah Prout might avoid the occasion but Jocelyn Kidbrooke would definitely be there and, Henry suspected, so would Sir Willard Grail. Both might attract favourable attention from Araminta and it worried him.

After lengthy cogitation and much soul-searching, he made a provisional decision to go to the funeral but that only pitched him headfirst into another frothing pool of uncertainty. What should he wear? Henry needed something appropriate yet individual, muted apparel that showed his respect for the deceased yet somehow caught the eye of the widow. He began to work his way through his wardrobe, trying on and discarding item after item. He was preening himself before the mirror in his bedchamber when someone rapped on his door.

'Who is it?' he called.

'Christopher,' replied his brother, opening the door to walk in. 'I was told that you were dressing.'

'Dressing and undressing,' said Henry, turning at a slight angle to admire the cut of his long waistcoat in the mirror. 'What I really need is a tailor to provide me with a new suit for the occasion.'

'What occasion?'

'Nothing that need concern you.'

'*What* occasion, Henry?'

'It does not matter.'

Christopher looked at the clothing scattered over the huge bed and draped over every available chair. Evidently, the occasion mattered a great deal to Henry. It was therefore easy to identify.

'You are surely not going to the funeral?' said Christopher with a blend of disapproval and disbelief. 'How could you even conceive of the idea, Henry? You are not wanted there.'

'I might be missed by Araminta.'

'Gratefully.'

'You don't know that, Christopher.'

'I know that she'd prefer the event to be a private affair, involving only family and close friends.'

'I see myself as Araminta's closest friend.'

'You'd only be intruding.'

'I want to help her through her bereavement.'

'I've told you before,' said his brother, 'that the best way to do that is to fade out of her sight. If you want to ingratiate yourself with Lady Culthorpe, assist me in solving the crime.'

Henry adjusted his wig in the mirror. 'I've already solved one crime for you,' he said with a touch of arrogance. 'I found the stolen portrait. That should endear me to Araminta.'

'There's no reason that she should ever hear about it – and I certainly wouldn't tell her about the way in which she is revered at the Molly House. If she knew that Emile had impersonated her in front of Samson Dinley and his like, she'd be deeply offended.'

'Do you mean that I get no credit for what I did?'

'You get an immense amount of credit from me, Henry.'

'That doesn't count. I want to impress Araminta.'

'Then I'll give you a chance to do so.'

Christopher told him about Villemot's failed attempt at suicide and his refusal to see Lady Hester Lingoe when she visited Newgate. Henry was interested to hear that the artist had been hounded out of France because of his love for a married woman, but he refused to believe that she could have matched Araminta for beauty.

'Araminta has no peer,' he insisted, 'and certainly no twin.'

'I'm only repeating what Monsieur Villemot said.'

'No Frenchwoman could compete with a true-born English lady.'

'You'll have to take up the issue with him,' said Christopher, 'and you can only manage that if we prove his innocence. What I need you to do for me is to find out exactly what happened to him after he left the garden of Lady Culthorpe's house.'

Henry was baffled. 'How could I possibly do that?'

'Because you know her much better than I do.'

'Who?'

'Lady Lingoe.'

'Is *that* where he went?'

'It must be,' said Christopher, 'though he won't admit it. A man like Monsieur Villemot would only hold back information in order to protect a woman. He has a sense of chivalry.'

'Why should he want to protect her?'

'That's what you must discover. The fact is that he was very excited when he returned to his studio that day – *why*?'

'I can think of one explanation,' said Henry with a sly grin. 'He was invited to take full advantage of Lord Lingoe's absence, then he was forced to listen to Hester, reading Juvenal to him in bed afterwards.'

'Make discreet enquiries.'

'Leave it to me.'

'How well do you know Lady Lingoe?'

'Not as well as I'd like, Christopher – though I've come to

admire her much more since I saw that portrait of her at the studio. If Hester wishes to be a naked huntress, I'd gladly be her quarry.'

'You are on a mission to save Monsieur Villemot's life,' said his brother, tartly, 'not to pursue your own questionable ends. If, as I believe, he did go to her house from Westminster, what sort of state was he in? That evidence could be significant. If Villemot *had* killed Sir Martin Culthorpe, he would probably have been nervous, distracted or triumphant. Only Lady Lingoe can tell us the truth.'

'I'll call on her later.'

'Go now, Henry.'

'But I've not chosen what to wear.'

'The fate of an imprisoned man is much more important than your choice of attire,' scolded Christopher. 'Think back to the time when *you* languished behind bars at Newgate. How would you have felt if I'd spent hours going through my wardrobe instead of doing all I could to secure your release?'

'A sound argument,' conceded Henry. 'Urgency is in request. I'll go to her house at once. It's a pity I'll not be able to dress the part,' he went on, surveying the wide array of clothing. 'If I'm calling on Hester, I should really do so in the toga of a Roman Emperor.'

After his visit to the locksmith, Jonathan Bale began the long walk back to Fetter Lane. He prided himself on having obtained a vital clue from Elijah Sayers and could not wait to pass it on. Lengthening his stride, he headed in the direction of the Strand and reflected on the way that his friendship with Christopher Redmayne had widened his sphere of activity and given him an insight into the higher levels of society. Those insights only served to confirm his prejudices and reinforce his republican leanings but he was nevertheless grateful to the young architect. One way or another, Christopher had provided him with an education.

Bale liked to believe that his friend had learned a great deal from him in return. Christopher had been taught how onerous and wide-ranging the duties of a constable were, and he had also seen how a family of four with a very modest income managed to get by. Bale was so preoccupied with this thoughts that he did not realise he was being followed. The man stayed well back. Wearing rough garb and with a hat pulled down over his forehead, he was a sturdy individual of middle height, around the same age as Bale. Over his shoulder, he carried a spade and looked as if he was going off to work in a garden.

There was too much traffic about at first and far too many pedestrians who might act as witnesses. The man therefore bided his time. When Bale eventually turned down a side street, his shadow saw his chance and began to gain on the constable. A horseman was approaching and there were a couple of people talking on a corner, but there was nobody to stop the attacker or to overpower him after the assault. It was the moment to strike.

Breaking into a run at the last moment, he took hold of the spade in both hands. Bale heard the footsteps and turned on his heel to see who was behind him. The man swung the flat of the blade at his head, intending to crack his skull open and knock him unconscious. Bale had a split-second to react. Pulling his head sharply back, he ducked instinctively and turned his face away from the oncoming spade. The implement caught him on the side of the head. It was only a glancing blow but it was enough to knock him from his feet and open up a gash on the side of his skull.

The man did not stop to assess his victim's injuries. His only concern was to get away from the scene of the crime as swiftly as possible. Running fast, he dived down the first lane he came to and raced on until he was certain that he was not being followed. When he saw that nobody was behind him, he joined the main road and sauntered along with the spade over his shoulder. A hundred yards behind him, Jonathan Bale lay motionless on the ground.

* * *

Lady Hester Lingoe took her visitor into the library and offered him a chair. She was dressed once more as a Roman priestess though there was nothing at all spiritual about her manner. Henry Redmayne was given no time to take stock of his surroundings.

'Why did your brother send you, Henry?' she asked.

'I came of my own accord.'

'You lost interest in me when I married so let's not pretend that this is anything more than a search for information.'

'You malign me,' said Henry with a grin of admiration. 'I never lost interest in you, Hester. I merely thought it proper to liberate you from my attentions when you took your marriage vows. In any case, my interest was soon revived when I saw that portrait of you at Villemot's studio.'

She smiled. 'Yes, I'm rather proud of that.'

'Did you enjoy sitting for it?'

'Immensely.'

'Villemot would have enjoyed working on the painting, that much is beyond doubt. Any man with the privilege of gazing upon your beauty day after day was bound to be enthralled by it.'

'Jean-Paul is an artist. He was not there to gloat.'

'I'm not for a moment suggesting that he was,' said Henry, wondering if every Roman priestess had worn quite so much powder on her face. 'All I mean is that, in those circumstances, an artist and his model are inevitably drawn close.'

'So?'

'You must have got to know him very well.'

'What are you implying?' she asked, sitting opposite him and subjecting him to a long, challenging stare. 'I hope you've not been sent to pry into my personal life.'

'Only insofar as it affects Villemot,' he said, his tone emollient. 'Since you twice went to Newgate to see him, it's reasonable to assume that you and he are more than passing acquaintances. I speculate no farther than that.'

'Thank you, Henry.'

'When he saw Villemot in prison today, Christopher found him in a miserable condition. He's overcome with shame at what he did and promises that he'll never try to take his own life again.'

'That's comforting to hear.'

'Villemot was also more honest about his past.'

'In what way?'

'Well, he admitted that he was not actually married – even though he's talked frequently of his wife and employed my brother to build a house for the two of them.' He paused for her to comment but she said nothing. 'It seems that he was compelled to leave France because of his romance with a married woman. This lady – Monique, I believe she's called – apparently bears some resemblance to Araminta Culthorpe, though it can only be of the faintest kind.' He stopped again but she maintained a watchful silence. 'Did you know all this?'

'Some of it,' she acknowledged.

'Is there anything you'd care to add, Hester?'

'Only that I'd be glad if you told me precisely why you're here.'

'Then let's abandon all the formalities,' he said, looking her in the eye. 'On the day that Sir Martin was killed in his garden, did Villemot come here?'

'Is that what Jean-Paul is claiming?'

'He refuses to answer the question. Christopher knows that the man was away from his studio for over two hours, but all that Villemot will confess is that he spent a short time at Araminta's house in Westminster. Where did he go afterwards?' pressed Henry. 'If we know that, it might help in his defence.'

'How?'

'We could then have a witness who saw him immediately after the time when the murder took place. Villemot is, by all accounts, a man of high emotion. Had he committed the crime,' said Henry, 'he would surely have been agitated as a result.'

'There are other causes for agitation.'

'So he did come here?'

'Yes,' she said, 'and that fact is proof of his innocence in my opinion. If Jean-Paul were a killer, he'd never have come near this house. He'd have fled the scene in a panic without knowing where he was going. He's not a phlegmatic Englishman, trained to hide his feelings. He expresses them freely. That's what made him such delightful company,' she added, dreamily. 'Jean-Paul is honest, impulsive and wonderfully spontaneous.'

'Some Englishmen can be spontaneous,' he insisted with a mischievous smile. 'We are not all dull and phlegmatic. I've been famed for my spontaneity.'

'Unfortunately, you are famed for other things as well. I won't embarrass you by saying what they are.'

'Happy is the man who can hear his faults and put them right.'

'I thought you wanted to talk about Jean-Paul.'

'I did, I did,' said Henry, quickly. 'Why did he not tell my brother that he came to you that day?'

'Because he's intensely loyal,' she replied, 'and that's another quality you lack. He wanted to guard my reputation. If it became common knowledge that a handsome Frenchman spent time under this roof in my husband's absence, people would draw some unkind conclusions. I'd be compromised.'

'Was he very agitated when he got here that day?'

'Yes, he was – agitated but also excited. Jean-Paul needed someone to talk to and I was the only person he could trust. He poured out his heart to me.'

Henry sat forward. 'What exactly did he say?'

Sarah Bale had been the wife of a parish constable for long enough to know that it was pointless to rebuke him for any injuries that he picked up in the course of his work. Bruises, cuts and abrasions were an accepted part of a job that involved keeping the peace. Bale never complained. Whenever he had been hurt, all that he wanted was for the wound to be treated so that he could go back to work again. His wife's sympathy was something he could take for granted.

'It's a bad one this time, Jonathan,' she said as she finished bandaging his head. 'What did he use to hit you?'

'I think it was a spade,' he replied, 'though it felt more like a giant anvil. He was a strong man.'

'Does it still hurt?'

'I can stand the pain, Sarah. It's the folly of it that stings me.'

'Whose folly?'

'Mine, of course,' he said. 'I never let someone creep up on me like that. If I'm being followed, I usually know at once. Not this time, I fear. My mind was on other things.'

'At least, you're still in one piece.'

She kissed him gently on the cheek then stood back to admire her handiwork. Encircling his head, the bandage hid the wound itself but it could not conceal the dark bruise that spread down the side of his face. He looked battered and faintly sinister. She could tell that the injury was still smarting but she knew that he would never admit it. Bale had a stoical attitude towards pain. It was something that had to be mastered so that it could be ignored.

When someone knocked on the front door, Bale tried to rise from his chair. Sarah pushed him back into it with a firm hand before going out of the kitchen. She soon returned with a visitor.

'There you are, Jonathan,' she said. 'I told you there was no need to struggle over to Mr Redmayne's house. He's here in person.'

'Whatever happened?' asked Christopher, looking at his friend in dismay. 'Are you all right?'

'Much better now that Sarah's seen to me,' said Bale. 'The main thing is that I found that locksmith. I know who wanted the key.'

'Forget the key, Jonathan. Your welfare comes first. When

you didn't come back to my house, I knew that something untoward must have occurred. Tell me all.'

Because his wife was there, Bale gave only a terse account of the attack, trying to make it sound less threatening than it had been. Christopher felt guilty for having sent his friend on an errand that had put him in such danger. Bale brushed aside his apologies.

'I got what I went there for, sir,' he said, taking the key out of his pocket. 'I showed this to a locksmith named Elijah Sayers.'

'Did he recognise it?'

'Straight away, Mr Redmayne.'

'That was lucky. There must be hundreds of similar keys.'

'They're all different to Mr Sayers and he remembers this one.' Bale handed it to Christopher. 'He described the man who brought it in and it sounds as if it might have been that gardener.'

'Abel Paskins.'

'Yes, sir,' said Bale. 'And I wouldn't be at all surprised to learn that it was the same Abel Paskins who tried to do some gardening on my head. He knew how to handle a spade.'

'You're lucky to be alive, Jonathan,' said his wife.

'It'll take more than a tap on the head to stop me, Sarah.'

She snorted. 'A tap! Is that what you call it?'

'That's all it felt like.'

'Nonsense! The kind man who brought you back home on that cart said that you were unconscious on the ground. When he first saw you, he thought you were dead.'

'Don't fret about that,' said Bale.

'Did the customer give his name?' said Christopher.

'No, Mr Redmayne, but he told the locksmith the name of the gentleman who wanted the duplicate made so quickly. I think you can guess who it was.'

'Jocelyn Kidbrooke, by any chance?'

'That's him, sir.'

'But you were told that Paskins no longer works for him.'

'If he committed a murder on Mr Kidbrooke's behalf, he'd have been well-paid for his work. He might not need to go on gardening, sir.' He put a hand gingerly to his head. 'I've a feeling that Paskins is still working for Mr Kidbrooke. We both need to be careful.'

'I'll take over from now on, Jonathan. You deserve a rest.'

'Not until we've caught the pair of them,' said Bale, struggling to his feet. 'I've a score to settle with Paskins.'

'And I've one to settle with Jocelyn Kidbrooke,' said Christopher. 'By plotting the murder of Sir Martin Culthorpe, he almost robbed me of a commission to build a new house here in Baynard's Castle Ward.'

'Which one do we arrest first, sir – Paskins or Mr Kidbrooke?'

'I think we'll start with Kidbrooke.'

'The truth of it is that I'm still dithering,' said Sir Willard Grail.

'You'll have to make a decision fairly soon,' warned Jocelyn Kidbrooke. 'The funeral will be in less than two hours.'

'I'm not sure that I wish to go.'

'Elkannah has been at you again.'

'He knew he'd be wasting his time.'

'Then why these last-minute doubts?'

'They're not really doubts, Jocelyn. I suppose that they are best described as faint rustlings at the back of my mind.'

'That's an affliction from which I've never suffered.'

'No conscience?'

'Not in this case, Sir Willard,' said the other, happily. 'It makes life so much easier when you don't have to consider the rights and wrongs of your actions. Morality can be such a nuisance.'

They were in the coffee house, seated in the corner so that they were not drawn into the general discussion at the common table. Sir Willard was in his customary flamboyant attire but Kidbrooke had dressed to attend the funeral. They made an incongruous pairing.

'When did Elkannah first stumble upon it?' said Kidbrooke.

'Upon what?'

'Morality.'

'Very recently,' said Sir Willard. 'He's gone through the best part of forty years without realising that such a thing existed. That's why his conversion has been so surprising.'

'Is it a conversion or a form of madness?'

'Both, I fancy.'

'What sane man would renounce his interest in Araminta?'

'And why did he break off his friendship with Henry simply because they had a disagreement? I'm *always* having disagreements with Henry Redmayne,' disclosed Sir Willard. 'He invites argument. It's one of his few virtues that he never bears grudges when I best him in debate. It's just as well because I do it so frequently.'

'Henry is a fool but an extremely likeable one.'

'How would you characterise Elkannah Prout?'

'Until recently,' said Kidbrooke, 'I'd have described him as one of the most amiable, wicked, depraved, heartless men in London. In short, inspiring company for thorough-going libertines like us. All that changed when Sir Martin was killed,' he went on. 'Elkannah had a sudden attack of religious principles and the vile disease warped his mind.'

'I hope that I don't catch it when I reach his age.'

'The only thing we are likely to catch is the French disease.'

Sir Willard laughed. 'That's why I choose my ladies with such care,' he said. 'Their purity is part of their charm.'

'As it is with Araminta, the princess of purity.'

'You never said a truer word, Jocelyn.'

Kidbrooke got up. 'I'll leave you to dither, Sir Willard,' he said. 'I have a funeral to attend. You'd be wise to go to it as well.'

'I'll think it over.'

They exchanged farewells. Kidbrooke left the coffee house but his friend remained to consider his own position. Sir Willard wondered if there was a positive gain in going to the funeral. He would have little chance of getting anywhere near Araminta. On the other hand, a list of mourners would eventually reach her and she might be touched by the fact that he was there. After several minutes of rumination, he decided to go to the church. Before doing that, he would need to change into something more suitable.

Getting up, he hurried towards the exit. The moment he stepped through the door, however, he found two figures barring his way. He recognised Christopher Redmayne as one of them.

'Good day to you, sir,' he said, brusquely. 'I've no time to speak to you now as I have an important appointment.'

'Our appointment is also important,' said Christopher. 'We've come to make an arrest in connection with the murder of Sir Martin Culthorpe.' He looked past him into the coffee house. 'I understand that Mr Kidbrooke may be here.'

Sir Willard was astounded. 'You're going to arrest Jocelyn?'

'Is he still inside?' asked Jonathan Bale.

'No, he left a short while ago.'

'Do you have any idea where we could find him?'

'Yes,' replied Sir Willard. 'At a funeral.'

Araminta Culthorpe looked out of the portrait with the steady gaze of a woman who was sublimely happy. Still unfinished, the painting had been reclaimed from the studio and now stood beside the dressing table in Araminta's bedchamber. After looking at the portrait, she let her gaze shift to the mirror and she saw a very different face from the one that graced the canvas. Whitened by grief and lined by anxiety, it was thrown into sharp relief by her widow's weeds.

Eleanor Ryle, also in black, hovered behind her mistress.

'How do you feel now, m'lady?' she asked, softly.

'I feel as if I'll never get through the service,' said Araminta, 'but I know that I must. I'll find the strength from somewhere.'

'Everyone is waiting downstairs.'

'There's plenty of time yet before we need leave.'

'I thought it might help to be with your family,' said Eleanor.

'I just want to be alone at the moment.'

'Do you want me to leave?'

'Please, Eleanor – and take the portrait with you.'

The maid was surprised. 'Take it away?'

'Yes,' said Araminta. 'It reminds me of Monsieur Villemot.'

Instead of sinking further into despair, Jean-Paul Villemot made an effort to control his feelings. He even dared to embrace a distant hope. In trying to commit suicide, he had shocked himself and he was deeply grateful that he had been stopped in time. He thought of all the people who would have been rocked by the news that he had ended his life at the end of a noose in a London prison. It would have been an appalling epitaph. The very notion now made him shudder.

When his visitor arrived, he was relieved to see Emile again, even if they were prevented from speaking their native language. The valet had brought food, wine, unlimited sympathy and news from the outside world. Knowing how fragile his master was, Emile did not upset him by mentioning that the portrait of Araminta Culthorpe was no longer at the studio. Nor did he reprove him for attempting to take his own life. He sensed that Villemot had already castigated himself mercilessly.

'How are you?' asked Emile.

'I'm a little better today.'

'Good.'

'I was at my lowest point a day or so ago. Now,' said Villemot with a brave smile, 'I know I have something to live for.'

'You do, you do.'

'How are you managing without me?'

'The studio, it is very empty.'

'What about Clemence?'

'She misses you – we both miss you.'

Emile reached through the bars to squeeze his master's hand.

It felt cold and damp. Yet there was a hint of spirit about Villemot and that was gratifying. He tried to offer encouragement.

'You will not be here long,' he said.

'I feel as if I've been here forever, Emile.'

'They will get you out. They are very clever.'

'Who?'

'Monsieur Redmayne and his brother, Henry,' said the other. 'They are good men. They will save you.'

Henry Redmayne disliked seeing Jonathan Bale at the best of times. When the constable's head was swathed in bandaging, and when the bruise made his face even more ugly, he was a daunting presence. Henry shot a look of dismay at his brother.

'Did you have to bring this walking gargoyle with you?'

'Jonathan has a right to be here,' said Christopher. 'He discovered a valuable clue for us. A duplicate key to the garden of Sir Martin's house was made on the instructions of a certain gentleman.'

'A friend of yours, Mr Redmayne,' said Bale, solemnly.

Henry was startled. 'A friend of mine?'

'Mr Jocelyn Kidbrooke.'

'Never!'

Christopher explained how the information had come to light and how Bale had been assaulted as a result. Henry was forced to congratulate the constable and he even offered a token of sympathy. The three of them were in the hall of the Bedford Street house. Dressed for the funeral, Henry was descended upon before he could leave. He was glad to see his brother but wished that he had come alone.

'What did Lady Lingoe say?' asked Christopher. Henry glanced uneasily at Bale. 'You can speak in front of Jonathan. I told him about my visit to Monsieur Villemot. He's aware that it was the resemblance between Lady Culthorpe and his beloved that took Villemot to Westminster on that fateful day.'

'Does he know that Villemot's beloved is already married?'

'Yes, Mr Redmayne,' said Bale. 'I'm sorry to hear that there are people in France – as well as here – who do not respect the institution of holy matrimony.'

'But Villemot *does* respect it,' said Henry, irritably. 'That's why he wishes to make this lady his wife. Unfortunately, Monique Chaval is married to a member of the French government, a vindictive man with the ear of the King. He's almost forty years older than his poor wife – even in France that must verge on indecency.'

'They were married in a church,' Bale reminded him.

'A Roman Catholic church,' rejoined Henry. 'I'm surprised that an unrepentant Puritan like you considers that to be a proper union. It's certainly a wretched one for his wife. Chaval bullies her, starves her of money and keeps her locked away in his mansion. It was only because he wanted to show her off to his friends that he decided to have her portrait painted.'

'Choosing Monsieur Villemot as the artist,' said Christopher.

'You can guess the rest. He fell in love with Monique and, when he heard how cruelly she was treated, he was determined to flee the country with her. Unfortunately,' said Henry, 'the plot was discovered and Villemot was lucky to escape with his life.'

'Yet he still nurses the ambition of marrying her.'

'He does – and with good reason. Old age and too much wine have taken their toll of Chaval. He's also been something of a roué.'

'What's that?' asked Bale.

'A French version of my brother,' explained Christopher.

'Oh, I see.'

'Chaval is in decline,' said Henry, ignoring the censorious look he collected from the constable. 'Villemot only has to wait until he passes away and he can claim his bride. According to Hester, the lady does look remarkably like Araminta.'

'Did he go to Lady Lingoe's house that day?' said Christopher.

'Yes, he did.'

'Then why didn't he admit it to me?'

'For the obvious reason,' said Henry. 'He didn't want you to make any unflattering assumptions about him and Hester. That's what I did and she took me to task over it. Hester assures me that their friendship is essentially Platonic, and since she has a bust of Plato in her hall, I'm inclined to believe her.'

'Something must have taken him there,' argued Christopher.

'It was fear.'

'Of what?'

'A vengeful husband, of course,' said Henry. 'Chaval knows that his wife is still coveted by Villemot because he was courageous enough to sneak back to France in order to see Monique. As a result, the love-struck artist received death threats from Chaval.'

'But he's perfectly safe in England.'

'That's what he hoped, Christopher.'

'Does he have cause to believe otherwise?'

'He thought that he did. Something happened at Sir Martin's house to give him a real fright. It made him ride off at once. Hester said that he was shaking all over when he got to her house.'

'What frightened him?' said Bale.

'Somebody was watching Villemot from behind a tree.'

'Did he know who it was, sir?'

'No, Mr Bale,' said Henry. 'Given the threats against his life, he was afraid that the man had been sent by Chaval. If he'd spoken to me, I could have put his mind at rest but I wasn't there at the time.'

'What could you have done, Henry?' said Christopher.

'I could have told him that the man was no assassin sent from France. He was an English gentleman whose sole interest in being there was Araminta.'

'How do you know?'

'Because of what Villemot told Hester,' said his brother.

'What scared him was that the man was peering through a telescope. As Villemot came out of the garden, he saw the telescope glinting among the trees. He felt that he was being hunted and he fled.'

'Who was the man with the telescope?'

'The person you're looking for, Christopher – Jocelyn Kidbrooke.'

Drizzle had started to fall out of an overcast sky, making a sad occasion even more sombre. The first mourners had already started to arrive at the church and others soon came in their wake. Sir Martin Culthorpe had been a popular man with many friends who wanted to pay their last respects to him. It was not long before a ring of coaches besieged the church. Interested bystanders lurked nearby so that they could watch the funeral cortege appear.

Jocelyn Kidbrooke had been among the early arrivals but he had not taken up his seat inside the church. Positioning himself where he had an excellent view of the whole scene, he ran his telescope across the sea of faces and picked out a number that he knew. It was a curious instrument and it had taken him time to master it but it gave him a distinct advantage over his rivals. In order to see Araminta, they had to get close to her but Kidbrooke could watch her at will from a distance. Where they would get only a mere glimpse of her, he was rewarded with continuous surveillance.

None of the others were there yet. Elkannah Prout had vowed to stay away from the funeral and Sir Willard Grail's attendance was by no means certain. Kidbrooke fancied that Henry Redmayne would be unable to stay away and that he would do his best to get near to Araminta at some point. Kidbrooke was not worried that any of his rivals would have an edge over him. With his telescope in his hands, he felt that his position was unassailable.

The telescope did not stay in his hands for long. It was

snatched away by Jonathan Bale. When its owner swung round to protest, he was staring into the face of Christopher Redmayne.

'Give me back my telescope!' demanded Kidbrooke.

'We need to use it as evidence,' said Christopher.

'Of what?'

'Your involvement in the murder of Sir Martin Culthorpe.'

'But I had nothing whatsoever to do with it!'

'You may not have stabbed him with that dagger, Mr Kidbrooke, but you paid the man who did. His name was Abel Paskins.'

'And unless I'm mistaken,' said Bale, whisking off his hat to reveal the bandaging, 'you also instructed Paskins to attack me when I came to Westminster earlier.'

'I haven't seen Paskins for days,' said Kidbrooke, 'and I certainly wouldn't pay him to commit a crime. He needed no incentive from me to do that. Abel Paskins was a deep-dyed villain. After he left my service, I learned that he'd stolen several things from my garden.'

'Offer these excuses to the magistrate, sir.'

'They're not excuses, Mr Bale.'

'On the day of the murder,' said Christopher, taking control, 'you were seen outside Sir Martin's house.'

Kidbrooke blanched. 'It was not me.'

'How many people own a telescope like this one?'

'Very few – it was highly expensive.'

'You were seen with it in Westminster. And do not claim that you dined with your wife that day,' Christopher added, 'because we have it on good authority that Mrs Kidbrooke was in Hampshire. You were expected to dine at Locket's with my brother, Henry, and some other friends, but you did not turn up. We know why.'

'You were keeping watch for Abel Paskins,' said Bale, grimly, 'while he was stabbing Sir Martin in the back.'

'You'll have to come with us, Mr Kidbrooke.'

Bale took the man's arm. 'You're under arrest, sir.'

'I can't leave now,' yelled Kidbrooke, trying in vain to shake his arm free. 'I haven't seen Araminta yet.'

'You disgust me,' said Christopher, hotly. 'How can you dare to come to her husband's funeral when you were the agent of Lady Culthorpe's distress? She'll hate you for what you did.'

'So will every decent human being,' said Bale.

'But I was not involved in the murder,' protested Kidbrooke. 'I'd swear that on the eyes of my children.'

'Do you admit that you were at the house on that day?'

Kidbrooke was shamefaced. 'Yes, Mr Bale.'

'Then your guilt is clear.'

'No,' said the other with passion. 'I'm only guilty of wanting to see Araminta so much that I lay in waiting near her house for hours. I went there to look at her, not because I had murderous designs on her husband. I worship her,' he went on, piteously. 'I wouldn't harm Araminta for the world. The last thing I'd even think of doing is to have Sir Martin killed. What could I hope to gain by such cruelty?'

The speech had such a ring of truth about it that Bale let go of his prisoner. Christopher had the same reaction. Much as he disliked the man and the Society of which he had been a sworn member, he had to accept that Jocelyn Kidbrooke's argument was a strong one. Inciting someone to murder Araminta's husband would not bring her any closer to him. She would retreat into mourning and be out of his reach. He remembered the gardener.

'We thought that you poached Abel Paskins so that he could tell you about Sir Martin's household,' he said. 'You knew that he'd once worked as a gardener there.'

'I did,' confessed Kidbrooke, 'and I pumped him for every detail I could. But I wanted to learn about Araminta and not her husband. I also recognised that Paskins was an exceptional gardener.'

'And a practised thief, by the sound of it.'

'I found that out to my cost.'

Bale was confused. 'If you didn't instruct Paskins to commit the murder,' he said, running a hand across his jaw, 'then who did?'

Elkannah Prout arrived on horseback and reined in the animal not far from the church. As he dismounted and tethered his horse, he found that Abel Paskins was waiting for him. The gardener stepped out from behind a tree and touched the brim of his hat in deference.

'Did you do as you were told?' said Prout.

'Yes, sir,' replied Paskins with a smirk. 'I hit him with a spade.'

'Good man.'

'That's one of them you don't have to worry about, Mr Prout.'

'Bale was only the assistant,' said the other. 'The person who troubles me is Christopher Redmayne. He's much more acute and he's the kind of gallant fool who never gives up.'

'I'll take care of him, sir.'

'It's the one sure way to stop him,' said Prout. 'It's a pity – I rather liked the fellow. But we can't have anyone finding out the truth. Christopher Redmayne is all yours.'

'How much will I earn?'

'The same as I paid you for Sir Martin's death.'

'I'd have killed him for the pleasure of it,' said Paskins with a curl of his lip. 'Sir Martin was a tyrant in the garden. Everybody thinks he was such a fine man but he could be vicious if you crossed him. He was always picking on me and making me look like a fool in front of the other gardeners. I loathed him.'

'I was grateful to be able to harness that loathing.'

'What happens next?'

Prout silenced him with a gesture. The funeral cortege was approaching and he craned his neck along with the other bystanders. First in line was the funeral cart, draped in black, pulled by black horses and containing the coffin that held the body of Sir Martin Culthorpe. Hats were doffed on both sides of the road. It was the carriage bearing the chief mourners that interested Prout. He could just see Araminta through the window as the vehicle rolled past and the sight made him sigh with a mingled sadness and joy. Grieving with her now, he hoped one day to be sharing her happiness.

'What happens next?' repeated Paskins.

'I want you to kill Christopher Redmayne.'

Christopher waited until the cortege had gone past and until the coffin had been carried into the church. Replacing his hat, he used the telescope to look along the line of people on the other side of the street. When a familiar face came into view, Christopher paused.

'That looks like Mr Prout,' he said.

'Impossible,' declared Jocelyn Kidbrooke, standing beside him. 'Elkannah went to Newmarket to watch the races. He swore that he would not come anywhere near the funeral.'

'Then he must have changed his mind.' He handed the telescope to its owner. 'I'm certain that's him.'

'Let me see.' Kidbrooke peered through the instrument. 'By thunder,' he exclaimed. 'It *is* Elkannah! And do you know who the man beside him is?'

'No,' said Christopher.

'It's Abel Paskins.'

'Paskins?' echoed Bale with interest. 'Where?'

It was his turn to look through the telescope. When he picked out the gardener, he studied him for a long time. His head began to pound at the memory of the fearsome blow it had received.

'Well?' asked Christopher. 'Is that the man who attacked you?'

'I don't know, sir – it could be.'

* * *

As befitted the solemn occasion, everything moved at a slow pace. Mourners arriving in the cortege entered the church sedately. Those who had gathered outside now began to file in. Elkannah Prout decided to follow them. He had seen Sir Willard Grail join the queue of mourners but Jocelyn Kidbrooke was nowhere to be seen. Prout surmised that his friend must already be in the church. Of Henry Redmayne, there was also no sign at all. It appeared that he had elected to stay away altogether.

Prout intended to sit at the rear of the nave where none of his friends could see him. As far as they were concerned, he was at the races in Newmarket. It was a ruse that had to be maintained. Prout shuffled on behind the others. Before he got anywhere near the church door, however, he saw Christopher Redmayne bearing down purposefully on him. The moment their eyes met, he knew that his villainy had been discovered. Prout had to get away at once. While everyone else was moving forward with an unhurried tread, he broke into a trot in the opposite direction.

Christopher went after him, his youth and superior fitness allowing him to make ground easily on the other man. Prout, however, had his accomplice. Abel Paskins was still standing near the horse.

'Stop him!' yelled Prout. 'This is Christopher Redmayne.'

'I'll handle him, sir,' said the gardener.

Pulling out his dagger, he brandished it at the oncoming figure, forcing him to slow down. Paskins advanced on Christopher, intent on using his weapon, but he was suddenly deprived of it. Jonathan Bale came up behind him, felled him with a blow to the neck then kicked the dagger out of his hand. Paskins rolled on the ground.

'Remember me?' said Bale, removing his hat. 'This is what you did when my back was turned. It's not turned now,' he went on, grabbing the man by the throat and lifting him to his feet. 'Let's see what you can do in a fair fight.'

Paskins roared with anger and threw a punch at him. Blocking it with ease, Bale plunged his fist hard into the man's midriff, knocking the breath out of him and making him squeal in pain. The gardener soon recovered and grappled with his opponent, getting in some sly punches to the ribs and trying to crack Bale's nose open with a jerk of his forehead. The constable had quelled too many tavern brawls to be caught by the manoeuvre. Pulling his head back, he took the blow on the chin before pushing Paskins away from him.

The gardener responded by aiming a kick at his groin but Bale was too quick for him. Moving adroitly sideways, he caught hold of the flailing foot and yanked Paskins off his feet. The man hit the ground with a thud. Before he could move, he had Bale on top of him, using his weight to subdue him and punching away with both fists. The gardener's face was soon running with blood and his strength was draining fast. Nothing he could do could get his opponent off him. Fired by the need for vengeance, Bale pounded on remorselessly until resistance finally stopped.

Elkannah Prout had watched it all with horror. Seeing that his accomplice had been overpowered, he mounted his horse and tried to ride off. Christopher stood in his way. He remembered how Bale had unsaddled Villemot when the artist had tried to ride off from Lady Lingoe's house. Whisking off his hat, the architect waved it wildly in the horse's face. It reared up on its hind legs and flung its rider backwards. Prout was badly dazed by the fall. When he had caught the reins and calmed the horse, Christopher tethered the animal before moving to stand over Prout.

'You should have gone to Newmarket.'

'I had to be here,' insisted Prout. 'Araminta is mine.'

'You'll never get anywhere near her again,' said Christopher, hauling him up. 'Unless she decides to attend your execution, that is.'

It was several days before Araminta Culthorpe felt able to see them. In the aftermath of the funeral, she had shunned company of any kind and spent most of the time alone in her bedchamber or the garden. She had not even allowed Eleanor

Ryle to stay with her for long. As the full facts about the murder began to emerge, however, she saw how indebted she was to the efforts of Christopher Redmayne and others. When she felt strong enough, she invited him to visit her at the house in Westminster. Henry was overjoyed when the invitation was extended to him.

The two brothers met her in the drawing room with its generous proportions and exquisite furniture. Rising from the table where she had been writing letters of thanks, Araminta did her best not to look so forlorn. When her visitors sat side by side on the couch, she took a chair opposite them.

'I thought you had nothing whatsoever in common,' she said, looking from one to the other, 'but I see now that I was mistaken. You've both shown your mettle and I'm deeply grateful. So, I am sure, is Monsieur Villemot.'

'We believed strongly in his innocence,' said Christopher.

'I never doubted it for an instant,' added Henry.

'Fortunately,' she recalled, 'someone else thought that he'd been wrongly accused – my maid. Eleanor is a wonderful companion. I never thought that she would help to solve a murder as well.'

'Her assistance was invaluable,' said Christopher. 'She's a young woman with initiative, Lady Culthorpe. But she's not the only person who deserves plaudits here,' he went on. 'Thanks to my brother, Lady Lingoe was able to provide some useful information and the real hero was a parish constable, Jonathan Bale.'

'Yes, I heard about the way that he was assaulted.'

'He was able to turn the tables on his attacker.'

'He was able to arrest Abel,' said Henry, disappointed that his weak pun did not even earn a smile from Araminta. He felt a twinge of guilt at his earlier stalking of her. 'May I take this opportunity to apologise for sending you those unwelcome verses?'

'I prefer to forget that they ever existed, Mr Redmayne.'

'Then they did not, Lady Culthorpe. They were figments of my imagination.' He clapped his hands. 'Whoosh – they've gone forever!'

'I'm grateful – and I owe you thanks for another reason. You were considerate enough to stay away from the funeral.'

'It never occurred to me to go,' said Henry, saying nothing about his last-minute decision to stay away. 'I wish that others had shown the concern for you that I did.'

She turned to Christopher. 'Have you seen Monsieur Villemot?'

'Many times,' he replied.

'Does he still wish to have a house built here?'

'Work started again the day that he came out of Newgate.'

'I'm so glad that we've not frightened him away.'

'You could frighten nobody away,' said Henry, beaming at her.

'It's I who've been frightened away, Mr Redmayne,' she told him, meeting his gaze. 'I'll be quitting London for a while to live on my late husband's country estate. You might pass on that information to your friends. Their attentions can cease forthwith.'

Henry was suitably reprimanded. Now that he was in the same room as the woman he had idolised, he saw how cold, ruthless and unwelcome his pursuit of her had been. He had been a willing member of a Society with base intentions and uncompromising methods and he was chastened, all the more so since the founder of the Society had been driven to commit a murder by his obsession. He left his brother to continue the conversation.

'Monsieur Villemot is wondering about the portrait,' said Christopher, tentatively. 'He still regards it as his finest work.'

Araminta gave a pale smile. 'I'm flattered to hear that.'

'In due course, he'd like to finish it.'

'I daresay that he does, Mr Redmayne.'

'May I tell him that that will be possible? In view of what's happened, that portrait has taken on great significance for him. It brought him untold and undeserved suffering,' Christopher reminded her. 'If he were allowed to complete it, those unhappy memories of Newgate might be obliterated.'

'One day, perhaps,' she said, thoughtfully. 'One day.'

It was too soon for her to make the decision. Christopher did not press her on the matter. When she had expressed her thanks to them again, he signalled to his brother that it was time to leave and they bade farewell. Before they were shown out, Araminta exchanged a handshake with each of them. Henry was thrilled that he had actually touched her. When he came out of the house with Christopher, his right hand was tingling with pleasure.

'She *likes* me,' he said, joyfully. 'Araminta likes me.'

'Lady Culthorpe likes what she saw of you today,' said his brother. 'She viewed you as a person who took great pains to prove Monsieur Villemot's innocence. Had she known that you'd tried to steal her portrait from the studio, however, and heard what underhand methods you employed to do so, she'd never have let you cross her threshold. Be grateful that we were able to display the better side of Henry Redmayne for once.'

'I thought I did that when I wrote those poems.'

'They've helped to drive her out of London.'

'I was not her only correspondent,' said Henry. 'Jocelyn and Sir Willard showered her with letters and gifts, and Elkannah sent her a copy of Shakespeare's sonnets. Poetry is the proper expression of true love. That's why I addressed Araminta in heightened language.'

'Heightened language that concealed the lowest desires.'

'I confess it straight, Christopher. When I saw her today, I felt thoroughly ashamed that I'd been a member of that dreadful Society. It was Elkannah Prout who drew me into it.'

'He was determined to win by any means,' said Christopher, 'even if he had to suborn someone to commit a murder. Unlike the rest of you, he was prepared to be patient.'

'Yes,' said Henry, sadly. 'We were like eager schoolboys, chasing their first kiss from some rosy-cheeked girl. The moment that Sir Martin was killed, we thought more of our foul ambitions than we did of Araminta's distress. While we pushed forward, Elkannah drew back and affected indifference. Since Araminta had chosen an older man as a husband, he hoped that his age and his forbearance would in time recommend him.'

'He was a cunning man. When he had that key made, he told Paskins to give the name of Jocelyn Kidbrooke to the locksmith. That misled us. His most clever trick,' said Christopher, 'was to dine with you and your friends at the very time when he knew that Sir Martin would be murdered. That lifted any suspicion from him.'

'Elkannah has always been a devious rogue. Well,' said Henry, 'he was a lawyer. What else can one expect? I should have known that he'd find out that Sir Martin had dismissed a gardener who nursed a grievance against him. He engaged Paskins as his killer, taking him away from Jocelyn.' He laughed. 'One poacher was outdone by another. Jocelyn Kidbrooke only wanted information from Paskins. Elkannah wanted someone with an urge to kill Sir Martin.'

They had walked to the rear of the house to collect their horses from the stables. When they saw the large, iron garden gate, they stopped to look at it. Christopher thought of the artist.

'If that gate had been open,' he said, indicating it, 'I can see that it must have been a strong temptation to Monsieur Villemot. He'd been to the house before to choose the dress from Lady Culthorpe's wardrobe that he wanted her to wear in the portrait. He knew that her bedchamber overlooked the garden. What took him in there was the vague hope of a glimpse of her at the window.'

'I'd have done the same in his place, Christopher. This is where Araminta lives. It would have been like stepping into the

Garden of Eden. I might even have been rewarded with a sighting of her.'

'Monsieur Villemot was rewarded with a spell in Newgate. He also tore the sleeve of his coat on a briar. His visit to that garden was a disaster for him.'

'The wonder is that he still wishes to remain in England.'

'He likes it here.'

'After the way he was treated?'

'He's unable to return to France,' said Christopher, 'until he can finally claim Monique as his wife. Paris is still full of her husband's family and friends so they could never live there.'

'Instead, you've designed them a French house in England.'

'By the time it's built, he may well have a beautiful wife with whom to share it.'

'What will he do until then?' said Henry.

'Oh, he has plenty to keep him occupied in the meantime. There are gorgeous young women all over the city who want to sit for a portrait by Jean-Paul Villemot. Now that he's been exonerated, he's more popular than ever. He'll be just like Henry Redmayne in that Molly House.'

'*Me?*'

'Yes,' said Christopher. 'Surrounded by painted ladies.'